CW00517984

UNRAVELED
DARK SOVEREIGN
BOOK THREE

BELLA J.

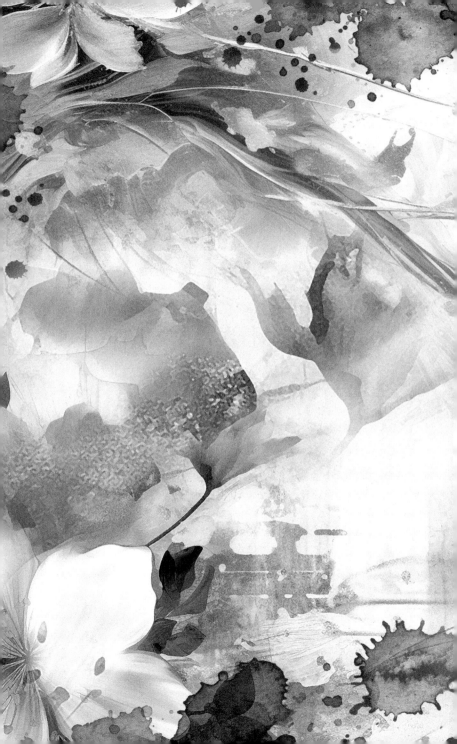

DARK
SOVEREIGN

UNRAVELED

international bestselling author

BELLA J.

Copyright ©2022 by Bella J
All rights reserved. This book or any portion thereof may not be
reproduced or used in any manner whatsoever without the express
written permission of the publisher except for the use of brief quotations
in a book review. This is a work of fiction. Any resemblance to actual
living or dead person, businesses, events, or locales is purely
coincidental.

FOREWORD

Unraveled is part three of the Dark Sovereign series, and should be read after Alexius (Book 1), and His Wife (Book 2)

Unraveled is a DARK mafia romance that contain scenes that might offend sensitive readers.

What to expect:
Dub-con
Child neglect
Violence
Sexual situations that can make some readers feel uncomfortable

Unraveled concludes Alexius and Leandra's story.

CHAPTER 1
LEANDRA

My heart is racing so fast, I'm sure it'll tear out of my chest any moment. Adrenaline floods my system, and my rapid breaths are spurts of vaporized moisture as hot air collides with the winter chill. My bottom lip trembles from the cold, and I clutch my coat tighter against my chest, trying to run through inches of snow, icy tentacles slashing my naked legs. There was no time to pull on pants when I woke up to the sound of my bedroom door being unlocked. I slipped on a pair of boots and grabbed the first coat I could get my hands on when I realized someone had opened the door for me.

Mirabella. I know it was her. She promised she'd find a way to get me out of here.

It's pitch black around me. I choose not to run down the driveway or any cobbled walkway. Too many lights would make it easier for me to be seen, so I dart through the trees, branches hidden beneath the snow crunching under my boots.

A chill licks the back of my neck, and I stop, holding my breath while glancing around, listening for even the faintest sound.

Footsteps. I can hear footsteps in the distance, and it's closing in on me fast.

"Shit." I change direction, running as fast as my feet can carry me, dodging tree branches as I look over my shoulder.

I catch a glimpse of movement behind me, and I know it's him. I can feel it—the energy that has my heart racing even faster, the vein in my neck pulsing in a panicked rhythm.

"I know you're out here, Leandra."

It is him.

I slip in behind a tree and press my back flush against it, holding my breath and pulling my shoulders in, trying to make myself invisible. It's dark, and the moon isn't full tonight. Hopefully, the shadows will hide me well.

"You can run all you want. You know I'll eventually catch you."

I inhale quietly, listening, trying to calculate what my next move should be. Do I stay put? Do I run?

"Tell me, stray. How did you get out?"

I press my lips together.

"Did someone unlock the door for you?"

His footsteps crunch across the snow.

"Did that someone manage to distract Maximo so he

would leave his post and give you the perfect opportunity to slip out?"

How did Mirabella do that? How did she get her brother out of the hall? Maximo knows how Mirabella feels about me being locked up. He knows she wants to help me get out; she's tried many times but failed. So how did she do it this time?

"I can practically hear your thoughts going in overdrive, Leandra." There's amusement in his voice, and a shiver runs down my spine as I listen to him getting closer. "Did you really think it would be so easy for you to get out? That every security detail I had in place around you would all fail at the same damn time and give you the opportunity to run from me?"

Oh, God.

He *tsks*. "Surely you know me better than that. Look at the lengths I went to to make sure you can't leave me."

I flatten my palm on my belly, my breathing coming out in short, fiery bursts.

"Are you connecting the dots yet?"

It was him. He unlocked my bedroom door. He *wanted* me to run. Why? So he could hunt me down like I'm prey?

"You are, aren't you?"

This is all a game. He started this because he craves the thrill of the chase, a predator who needs to sink his teeth into something he hasn't tasted for a while.

Me.

There's a sudden rush of excitement in my chest—heated desire rising inside me like the tide. I can't help it.

I can't control it. No matter what he's done, what I feel for him can't be switched off. It's still there, and it's fucking with my head because now I no longer know if I want to escape...or if I want him to catch me.

God, I'm a mess, a pathetic heap of womanhood who still desires a man who lies and deceives as easily as he cuts through his meat at the dinner table. Effortlessly.

The sudden silence has me holding my breath, listening. His footsteps are gone. Silent. I can't hear anything other than my heartbeat pulsing between my ears.

There's that touch of awareness licking the back of my neck again. It's him. He sees me. I can feel his heated gaze burning my skin.

I don't think. I don't analyze my odds of escaping.

I run.

Snow falls from the waiting branches, some landing on my collar and slipping inside my jacket. I gasp from the ice against my heated flesh but don't stop running. I can't. I don't want to. Yet I don't want to escape either. Not anymore. I want him to catch me, but also, I don't. It's a thrill I've never felt before—a charge of energy that runs rampant through my bones and down my core. It fuels me to run faster, to make sure I'm a prey worth hunting.

I weave through the trees and out into the open where snow hardly touches the well-manicured lawns of the estate. For a moment, I'm disoriented as I look in every direction, unsure where to go. The stars are visible here, glinting against the black night.

A strong arm grabs my waist, and I yelp as I'm pulled down to the ground, my knees scraping against the grass.

"Let me go!" I thrash against his hold, but it's a futile attempt, and he easily clamps my arms above my head, his weight pinning me down.

Sapphire eyes burn with fiery excitement, specks of snow clinging to his dark hair creating a stark contrast against the backdrop of the night sky.

He flexes his hips, grinding his hard length against my thigh, his stare slipping to the nape of my neck. "You can't get away from me, stray."

"You planned this," I grit out between clenched teeth.

"Of course I did." He leans down, brushing his wet lips across my jaw. "You and I both know this is the shit we live for. The adrenaline. The rush. The fucking hunt that lets us unravel."

My body quivers beneath him, and he moves, settling between my legs.

"I knew you'd run," he rasps, tracing the tip of his tongue down my neck to the hollow below my throat. "I knew you'd let me chase you."

"You're a sick bastard."

"Yet your body wants me anyway." He grips my wrists in one hand and reaches down, unzipping his pants and pulling out his cock, dragging the velvet tip against my inner thigh before yanking my nightdress up my waist.

"Don't," I warn, but there's zero conviction in my

tone—and he hears it, his only response a sly grin that carries promises of sin.

"I'm serious, Alexius. Don't you fucking touch me." I try to break free from his grip, writhing beneath him, when he pulls my panties to the side and slips a finger inside me, the sensation causing me to arch my back and moan loudly.

"There she is." He smirks, gazing down at me. "My filthy little slut whose cunt is always wet for her bastard husband's cock."

"Fuck you."

"In a minute."

Arrogant asshole.

His thumb finds my clit, and my pussy clenches around his finger. "You can run to the ends of the Earth, and I'll still find you." He leans down, brushing his lips along mine as he pushes a second finger into me, and my eyes roll closed. "Your body wants me, stray. And you're wasting your time trying to fight it."

"I can still try."

"Oh, I'm counting on it. Fighting me makes your pussy taste so much sweeter." He adds pressure on my clit, drawing circles, moving his fingers inside me, forcing my body into submission. "God, you're beautiful like this. Ready and craving my cock."

"Are you going to talk me to death or fuck me?" I challenge, bucking my hips, taking his fingers deeper.

A low growl vibrates up his throat, and he pulls his fingers out of me, leaving my pussy empty and needy, before driving into me with a sharp, hard thrust. I cry out, arching my back, the pressure between my legs both a punishment and pleasure.

"Am I giving you what you want, stray?" He's breathless and fucking me hard with short, quick thrusts, hitting me deeply every time. "Is that greedy little pussy of yours happy now that I'm inside you?"

"Not even a little." It's a lie. But this is a game. One he started.

The grin on his face is cocky and sexy at the same time, his breathing growing louder and thicker, his pace rushed and relentless as he fucks me into the cold grass. He lets go of my wrists, but I keep my arms above my head as he folds his fingers around my throat, squeezing. "Say it."

"Say what?"

"My name."

"Fuck you," I bite out, and he lets out a breathy laugh, tightening his grip and restricting air from reaching my lungs. I gasp and claw at his hand, trying to pull it away, but he only fucks me harder, his fingers biting into my jugular.

"Say. It."

"No." The veins in my neck thicken under the pressure of his grip, but he doesn't let go, and I don't obey.

"Say my fucking name."

I suck my bottom lip into my mouth.

"Jesus. I swear to God, woman, if you pass out, I won't stop fucking you."

The taste of blood bursts onto my tongue, and a frenzy takes over. Madness clamps down and takes possession of me, and it's so fucking freeing. To not have to control myself anymore. To not be the one who makes the decision to succumb because my body leaves me no choice. The fire between us leaves us no choice.

Alexius lets go of my throat, hooks his arm underneath my knee, and jerks my leg up so he can bury himself deeper inside me. It hurts like this, deep and raw, but that's how I crave it. That's how I need it, and he knows that. He knows me and my body like I'm an instrument he's mastered. Every touch, every kiss, every plunge of his cock is exactly how I need it to be.

His hand is on my throat again but snakes around to the back of my neck, his fingers fisting my hair as he forces me upward, our lips colliding in a heated kiss. A desperate one. A fusion of mouths selfishly wanting to devour the other. He tastes like whiskey and mint and something that's uniquely him. It's a taste I've come to love and crave, a taste that haunts my dreams and rules my nightmares. A taste that leaves me breathless for him...and only him.

Pleasure builds in my core, and it spreads down my legs and up my spine. "I have to come."

"You know the rules," he growls into my mouth.

"Please let me come."

"Say my name first. Fucking scream it." He fucks me faster. His rhythm is uncontrolled, his thrusts impossibly deep—a brutal display of unrestrained lust—and I can no longer stop it, my body quivering and pussy clenching his cock as an orgasm tears through me.

Abruptly, he tightens his grip in my hair, and my

scalp stings, but no pain in the world can stop me from shattering. "Say it, goddamn you, woman!"

Pleasure sinks its teeth into me, ravishing me, consuming me to a point where I'm sure it would break me in half.

Alexius curses, then buries his face in the crook of my neck, his back arching as he comes inside me. I feel every throb, his hot cum spilling into me with every jerk of his cock.

Why did I even try to deny it? Why did I try to fight him? It's useless. I know that now. This man can be the evil hiding behind everything that's wrong in this world, and I'd still want him. I'd still love him. Because somewhere between marrying him and him tricking me into becoming pregnant, we became one. And now I realize that nothing can change that. Nothing can split us back in two.

Nothing.

I close my eyes, and loll my head to the side, spent and exhausted. I don't want to fight it anymore. It hurts too much trying. So, I surrender with only one name on my lips. "Alexius."

Then...I wake up.

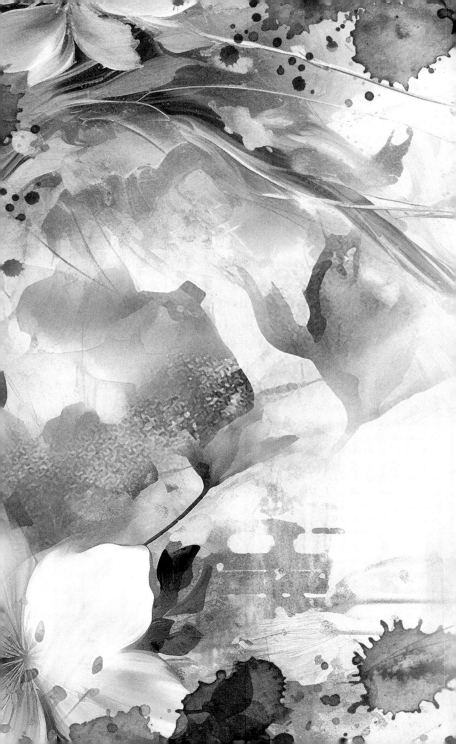

CHAPTER 2
ALEXIUS

"This is bullshit." Venom drips from Mira's words, and rage roils behind her eyes as she glowers at me like I'm the spawn of Satan. She's practically drilling holes into my forehead with a glare that could cut through bone.

"She's a fucking person, Alexius. Not a goddamn animal you can keep in a cage."

I lean forward with my palms on my desk, pinching my eyes shut, praying to God for the patience I need with this woman. "This is none of your business, Mirabella."

"The hell it isn't. Leandra is my best friend, and you're keeping her locked in a room and you can't even tell me why."

I'm surprised Leandra hasn't told her about the birth control switch. They've been talking through a locked door almost every day, discussing what a jerk I am. Mira has asked so many times what the hell was going on, but none of this has anything to do with her, so I don't owe her any type of explanation or reason. If Leandra wants to tell her what happened, that's up to her.

"This is insane, Alexius. Can't you see how fucked-up this is?" Mira's green irises burn with a wave of anger I can understand, but it does nothing to persuade me to change my mind.

Nicoli appears by the door, and I simply lift a brow at him. Mira's back is turned toward my brother.

I let out a breath. "I'm trying my best not to lose patience with you, Mira. But this is your last warning. My relationship with Leandra is none of your business. It is not your place to question or challenge the decisions I make when it comes to my wife. So, for the last damn time, stay out of it."

"I don't know about you, Alexius, but I can't exactly walk around this place singing goddamn Christmas carols when I know you're keeping your wife locked in a room for God knows what."

"Stay out of it, Mira," I warn.

"Goddammit, Alexius. The least you can do is let her leave her fucking room. This place is a goddamn prison on its own. Even if she wants to leave, you and I both know she won't be able to put a foot out the front door without you knowing."

"I'll handle this situation as I see fit."

"You're handling it like a fucking psychopath."

My angered glare levels her. "Disrespect me like that again, and I'll—"

"Lock me in my room, too? Treat me like a petulant child as well?"

"If you act like one, yes."

Mira's eyes are frozen on mine, disdain simmering in their depths. "You're scared of losing her. I get that. But nothing—and I mean nothing—justifies this, Alexius."

I take a second to simmer down, trying to keep myself from saying something I'll regret. Mirabella has been and always will be an important person in my life. A sister I never had. But the situation between my wife and me is complicated, to say the least, and as much as I love Mira, I will not allow her to interfere.

I cross my arms and lean back against the edge of my desk. "For the last time. Stay the fuck out of my goddamn business."

Mira's cheeks turn a fiery red, her savage fury beaming from her glowing cheeks. There's no mistaking it. She hates me. But at this point, I don't give a shit.

Her heels dig into the carpet on my office floor as she approaches, pausing mere inches from me, lifting her chin with defiance I've seen her showcase so many times before. "I always knew you were an asshole. Cruel. Even cold-hearted at times. But I never thought of you as an unjust man, Alexius. And what you're doing to Leandra, the future mother of your twins, it's unjustified and downright despicable." Her eyes narrow as she leans closer. "Your father would be disappointed."

"Mirabella! That's enough." Nicoli's voice crashes through the room, and she visibly gasps, unaware of his presence until now.

Her face is instantly pale, and I'm sure her shoulders slump the tiniest bit. It never ceases to amaze me the effect my twin brother has on her. It's everywhere, in her eyes, on her cheeks, her lips, her frame. She is no less bound to him as I am to my wife, yet Nicoli refuses to acknowledge it. *Dumbass.*

With a visible breath, she steels herself, her jaw set as she turns to face him. "You're okay with him keeping her locked up? You condone his actions?"

"That's not important. What's important is that I know my place in this family." Nicoli steps inside, his hands tucked into his pants pockets. "But it seems like you've forgotten yours."

She flinches, pain scattered in her eyes' radiance. But her shoulders remain squared, her will iron-cast. "Maybe I have," she says. "But at least I haven't forgotten how to be a decent fucking human being."

Rage erupts and slices through the tension as she storms out with angered footsteps, the loud slam of the door an echo of her fury. Understandable. But inconsequential.

Nicoli simply stares at me, dark strands hanging down his face. It doesn't take twin telepathy to know my brother isn't exactly thrilled with me either. But as he said, he knows his place.

"She's upset." I state the obvious, pouring us a drink.

"Upset? She's practically frothing at the mouth." Nicoli takes a seat on the couch, loosening his tie, and I hand him his drink. His brows furrow as he studies me. "I'll always support you, brother. No matter what."

"I feel a but coming."

"No but. Just a question."

I sit down across from him, and his strained expression doesn't go unnoticed. I sigh. "If you have something on your mind, just say it."

"Do you know what you're doing?"

"The truth?" I tap my finger on the armrest.

"Yeah."

I lean back. "When it comes to Leandra, I don't have a fucking clue. But what I do know is there's not a chance in hell she's walking out of here. Especially now that she's carrying my children."

"I agree."

I frown. "You do?"

"Yeah. I don't necessarily agree with your actions to keep her from leaving, but," he shrugs, "I know that if it were me, I wouldn't let her walk out my door either."

"This isn't how I intended all of this to play out," I say, swirling the glass and watching the amber liquid ripple against the crystal.

"You're kidding, right?" He lights a cigarette, a plume of smoke drifting toward the ceiling. "You didn't think fucking with her birth control and her finding out about it would end with her wanting your balls on a poker?"

"She wasn't supposed to find out."

"Of course not. But she did. Problem is, you made a big mistake turn into a giant-sized dick that's been fucking you in the ass ever since you locked her bedroom door." He points upward at the second floor, the cigarette caught between two fingers. "And now you need to figure out a way to unfuck yourself."

"Jesus Christ." I roll my eyes, pulling my palm down my face. "You're such an asshole."

"I don't disagree. But at least I'm a smart asshole. You're just an asshole. Seriously, though," he puts out his cigarette, "what are you going to do?"

Whiskey laps onto my tongue, and I swallow, relishing how it burns as it travels down my throat. "I know what I'm not going to do." I peer at him. "I'm not losing her."

"What if you already have?"

"I haven't." My reply is curt. It's a thought I refuse to dwell on or acknowledge in any way. Losing Leandra is not an option. Not now. Not ever. "I'll figure it out," is the only answer I give him, and he nods.

"I have no doubt that you will." For a moment, his expression becomes solid. "Whatever you need from me, you've got it, brother. I will always support you, no matter what."

I take a deep breath, my chest widening beneath my white dress shirt. Knowing I have his support gives me a sense of relief. "Thank you, Nicoli."

There's a long silence, and memories of Leandra and our trip to Rome play like a movie inside my head. Our days under the Italian sky now feel like a single moment in time that was just ours. Minutes, hours, days we didn't share with the Dark Sovereign or the Del Rossa family. It was just me and her and this insane connection that never stopped pulsing like it was a living entity of its own. And now look where we are. Leandra is pregnant with my twins because I fucked with her birth control to keep her from leaving me once our agreement ended. And now I have her locked in her room, taking every precaution to ensure she stays right here. Even the kitchen staff is escorted by security when delivering her meals to her room. I tried doing it once and ended up with a ruined suit because she thought the spinach cannelloni would pair well with Armani.

"You really love her...don't you?" Nicoli studies me, and my guess is his question is only partially rhetorical.

I slam back the whiskey, placing the glass down before shifting in my seat, looking him in the eye as the truth teeters on the tip of my tongue. Fuck this. If I can't allow myself just a sliver of vulnerability toward my own twin brother, then I'm fucked whether I speak the truth or not.

I stand, buttoning my suit jacket. "I don't just love her. That woman owns me, brother. And it's fucking with my head because, for the first time in my goddamn life, I know what it feels like to fear losing someone." I pull a hand through my hair. "Considering that we just buried our father not too long ago, that says a lot."

Nicoli's expression remains solid, and I half expect him to take a piss at me. But instead, I see understanding in his eyes and feel a kinship stretching between us. He knows exactly what I'm talking about...because it's his own fear as well.

He licks his lips as he gets on his feet. "As I said, I support you, and I'll always have your back. Just," he clears his throat, "take it easy with Mirabella. She might have grown up with us in this house, but she's nothing like us."

I nod, and Nicoli shrugs off the weight of our conversation by slapping his hands together, his face curling in lines of mischief. "You ready to put Uncle Roberto out on his ass?"

"God, yes."

"I suspect you gifting Mother a luxury cruise getaway for the next few weeks is not coincidental."

I smirk. "Of course not."

"You do know she's coming back? You're just delaying the inevitable, telling her that her brother is no longer part of this family."

"I'm aware. But I suspect Mother won't be returning after her cruise." I open the door. "She's going to the vineyard in Tuscany, and I don't think she's coming back."

"What gives you that idea?" Nicoli walks out, and I close the door behind us and start down the hall.

"I don't know. Call it a gut feeling. There was something about how she said goodbye, walking through the entire house and talking to herself in Italian. It felt...final."

"Maybe it's better that way," he says as we stalk across the foyer. "She's had enough of all the Dark Sovereign shit. She needs to spend her last years in peace."

I nod in agreement as I pull the gold key from my pocket, slipping it into the lock and opening the large pocket door. The overhead track runs smoothly as the mahogany disappears into the wall cavity.

The familiar honeyed scent of beeswax greets us, and Nicoli and I walk over to the oval table.

"I have to be honest," Nicoli starts. "It still feels weird in here without Dad."

"It does," I agree, sauntering over to the magnolia-colored curtains, glancing out over the courtyard. The sky is gray, and snow falls gently, its glittery surface draping everything it touches in a blanket of white. It looks peaceful outside. Tranquil. Meanwhile, there will be a war raging inside this room once my uncle decides to grace us with his presence.

"Fucker is late as always," Nicoli complains, taking his seat next to my chair.

"So are our brothers."

"I'm here." Caelian saunters in and slips on his suit jacket. "Is Isaia joining us today?"

"Who the fuck knows?" I say, reaching for the tape recorder in my pocket and placing it on the table.

Nicoli raises a brow in question.

I smirk. "I thought it a good idea to remind our uncle just how fucked he really is."

"Nice touch."

"Good morning, gentlemen." Uncle Roberto stands by the door, the buttons of his suit straining across his fat belly. The sight of him grates down my spine, and I'm pretty sure that if I didn't know today would be his last day here, I'd leap across the table and choke his last breath out of him.

"Roberto." I straighten and square my shoulders, my eyes not leaving him. "You're late."

"I'm not in a hurry to meet with the man who killed my son."

"I'm assuming you're referring to Rome, your only son? The coward who abandoned his own family?"

Roberto's eyes narrow. "You know I'm not talking about Rome."

"Oh. You mean Jimmy?" I shoot him a taunting smirk. "He's not your son. But I can see why you'd think that since you're both arrogant pricks."

"What did you do with his body?"

I scoff. Asshole would do anything to find Jimmy's body. Not because he wants to lay his supposed son's body to rest, bury him and get closure. No. He wants proof that I killed Jimmy so he can paint me the villain, gather an army, and come at my throat. But that is not going to happen, and he knows it. There's not a chance in hell he'll ever find Jimmy, or at least what's left of him. All he has is a shitty piece of paper scribbled with words that means nothing if there isn't a body. Micah's letter saying I killed Jimmy isn't worth a fuck.

I settle my stance, keeping my glare locked on my uncle. There's no need to say a goddamn word because he can read everything I want to say to him on my goddamn face. Go to hell.

He notices the tape recorder, and his top lip curls upward at the corners. "Tell me, Alexius, what is it that you expect to happen here today?"

"Not much. Just you getting what you deserve."

"And what's that?"

Caelian snorts. "A whole lot of nothing."

Roberto simply glowers in his direction for no longer than a second before settling his attention on me. The smoke billows from the tip of his cigar, the smell of burning tobacco becoming more potent with his every exhale. "Seventeen years, is it?"

"Is what?" I ask.

"How long you've waited to get rid of me and take away everything that's mine."

"What's yours?" I grit out. "You're fucking joking, right? None of this is yours." I swipe my hand through the air. "All of this is what my father built."

"With my father's money."

"That doesn't say much about you, does it, now, Uncle? The fact that your father would rather give his money away than see you piss it all away."

"You've always been a little shit."

"And you've always been a snake."

"Well," he smirks like the arrogant fuck he is, "I do tend to lay low, striking only when threatened."

"I'm past the point of threatening, Roberto. This family will no longer fund your pathetic existence."

"Pathetic?" he snaps, letting out a taunting laugh. "Oh, dear boy, you have no idea."

I step closer, my patience hanging by a thread. "The Savelli family is no longer part of the Dark Sovereign. From this day on, these five seats will only be filled with men of the Del Rossa family."

"You're one short," he taunts, but I simply shrug it off.

"My wife is pregnant. I'm sure I'll have an heir to fill Riccardo's seat one day. Where is he, by the way?" I pretend to search over his shoulder. "Did your brother not have the balls to witness your shameful exit?"

"On the contrary," Roberto takes a long drag from his cigar, the smoke trickling from the corner of his mouth, "my brother is bringing a guest."

"Really? And who might that be?"

Isaia appears by the door, swiping at his shoulders, getting rid of the snow clinging to the leather of his jacket. "You'll never guess who I found on my way in."

I cut my glare in his direction, surprised my little brother decided to show up. But there's a prickle of warning trickling along my skin, especially since Roberto's smug grin is planted on his ugly motherfucking face.

"Who is it?" I walk up to Isaia when he steps to the side, allowing our guest to enter. For a second, I don't recognize him, his familiar face taking two heartbeats to trigger my memory. And when it does, my instincts erupt.

"Rome," I mutter.

He smiles, dark brown eyes gleaming. "Hello, cousin. It's been a while."

"What are you doing here?"

"I would say that's pretty obvious, is it not?" His gaze cuts to Nicoli, then back to me. "I'm here to take my father's place. I am his heir, after all."

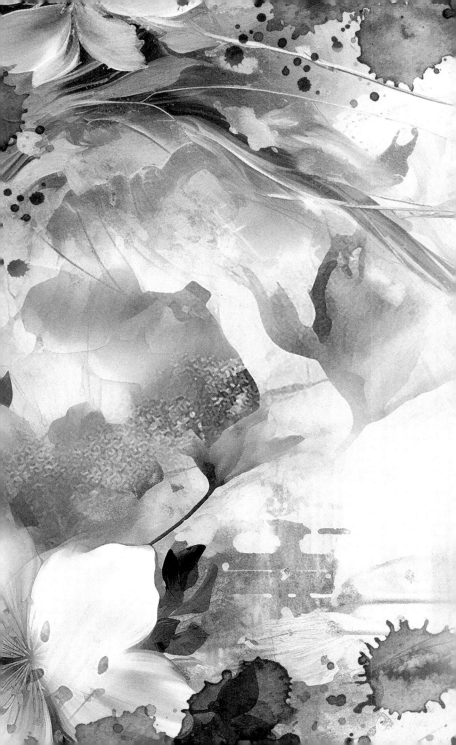

CHAPTER 3
LEANDRA

I'm flat on my ass, leaning my back against the door, listening to Mira speak on the other side. She's been flinging the f-bomb left and right for the last ten minutes, going on about Alexius and what an asshole he is and how angry she is at Nicoli for not defending her.

But me? I'm just sitting on the floor, lost in my thoughts, wondering—hoping this is all just one terrifying nightmare and that I'll wake up in bed next to Alexius, feeling his arm draped over my side, his palm clutching my breast. I want this all to be nothing but a bad dream and to realize that the man I love didn't betray me. He didn't lie to me. He didn't deceive or manipulate me.

But he did... and my heart hasn't stopped aching since he locked this door. It's as if someone has torn a hole inside my stomach, a gaping, oozing, grotesque wound that weakens me with every passing second.

I'm such a fool.

All those times he refilled my birth control, it never once crossed my mind that his display of trust and responsibility was a masked deception as he plotted to shackle me to him for the rest of my life.

"Fucker won't budge," Mira spits out. "He's hellbent on keeping you in this room. I don't get why neither of you can tell me what the fuck is going on."

I tilt my head back against the wooden door, craning my neck and staring at the ceiling. "It's between Alexius and me, Mira."

"Listen, this isn't me being nosy. This is me hoping that a man I love as a brother isn't a complete psychopath. I've already seen him shoot a fucking guy in the head without blinking. And now he has his wife, who he's supposedly in love with, locked in a room? My mind is fried."

I sigh, my chest heavy with an ache I can't put into words. I know how much Mira cares for the Del Rossa brothers. I've seen how she looks at Alexius—it's the same way she looks at Maximo. With love. Affection. Respect. Call me insane or delusional, but I just can't tell her what he did, no matter how despicable and unforgivable it is. I can't take away from her the only family she's ever known. It's my burden to carry, and it would be selfish of me to load it onto her. Plus, it's my own damn fault for trusting him after he showed me his true colors so early on in our relationship—or, rather, agreement. I should have known better. So, the shame is on me for loving a man who prefers power over love. And that's exactly what this is. Getting me pregnant so I wouldn't leave, so he could have a hold on me, that's power. It's what he wants, what he craves. To make everyone bend to his will.

"Leandra?" Mira's voice is soft. Gentle. Almost pleading.

"Yeah?"

There's a slight pause before she speaks. "Stop fighting him."

"What?"

"I don't know what he did or what happened. But I know fighting him will only make things hard for you and the babies."

"Mira, I'm not just going to sit back while he keeps me hostage in this damn room," I blurt.

"I get that. I do. I'd be pissed at him, too, if I were you. I mean, I am pissed at him for doing this, but..." There's a long pause, and I lean my head to the side, listening. "You're pregnant with his babies, Leandra. And the truth is, you'll never be rid of him. Whether you're here or somewhere else, he's the father of those twins, and nothing you can do will change that. I know him...*well*, I thought I did. But what I do know is there's not a chance in hell he'll let you walk away with his children."

My skin crawls with a sudden chill. "What are you saying?"

"I'm saying he's not going to let you take his children, and if you continue to fight him and not agree to stay, you'll end up having to make the most difficult decision of your life."

I close my eyes. "Which is?"

"Your freedom...or your children."

Mira goes silent, and I lean my head to the side. She's right. I know she is. In the end, no matter what road I choose to take, it will all lead to me being forced to choose, a decision I never thought I'd be in a position to make.

"Oh, God. Speak of the devil," Mira says, and I hear her move on the other side of the door.

I sit up straight. "Is he coming?"

"Yup."

I'm on my feet, turning to face the door and taking a few steps back like I'm expecting a beast to break through the wood.

"Alexius," I hear Mira say. "Finally come to your senses?"

"Leave, Mira," he replies, and I eye the lock as he slips in the key. My heartbeat echoes between my ears and my palms are sweaty as I continue to move back. I'm not scared of him. Even after what he's done, I know he won't hurt me, or he would have done it already. Instead, I'm scared of what I feel for him, fearing the pain of having my heart hacked open with a serrated blade every time I see him. His face. His eyes. His lips. His presence. It's all a reminder of how much I fucking love the man who betrayed me so unapologetically.

My hand is on my belly when the door opens, and our eyes meet. God, he's so beautiful, it makes my heart ache. No amount of anger I feel can change that. Shadows fall over his face, but it does nothing to tame the iridescence that gleams from irises I've lost myself in so many times before. His tall frame is wrapped in a pristine suit, broad shoulders carved from power, and a stare that makes everything else disappear. Everything I promised I would say to him is gone. Every last word, every curse, every demand, vanished.

For one reckless moment, I forget about what he's done, remembering the moans that not so long ago filled this room, my cries of ecstasy proof of how much I loved everything he did to me. How much I loved him.

How much I still love him.

The connection between us hasn't weakened even the tiniest bit. It's still there. Strong. Potent. Undeniable.

And then I remember...

He clears his throat. "I've arranged for a doctor to come to the house to monitor the pregnancy, make sure you and the babies are okay. I'm having one of the spare bedrooms set up with all the necessary equipment so the doctor can continue to make house calls."

I lift my chin. "You can't keep me locked up in here forever."

"Continue to want to run from me, and I will."

I bite the inside of my cheek and watch as he closes the door, locks it, and slips the key into his jacket pocket. "How are you feeling?"

"Hurt. Betrayed. Sick to my stomach. Pick one."

"I'm talking about you and the pregnancy."

"Oh, you mean our babies? The two lives growing inside me, something I had no say in?"

"Leandra," he breathes out, rubbing his palm across the back of his neck. "I didn't come here to fight."

"Did you come here to let me go, then?"

The way he glowers at me from under thick lashes answers my question with a resounding 'no.'

"Didn't think so." I cross my arms. "You can't keep me locked up forever."

His blue eyes flash with determination. "And I can't let you go either."

"Then what the hell are we supposed to do?"

"It's easy. Accept that you're my wife, that you're having my children, and that there is nothing in this entire goddamn world that will change that. Ever."

I scoff. "Nothing about what you just said is easy. It's not *easy* to accept the fact that you've been manipulated and deceived by the man you love."

He steps forward, and I take a step back. I don't trust small distances between us. It makes it too easy for the constant pull between us to take over. Even through anger and hurt, my body still yearns for him. My blood still sings for him. I hate it. No matter how hard I try to make it stop, it doesn't wane, not even a little.

No matter how hard I try to stay strong, it's impossible to steel myself against the emotions he so easily evokes in me, especially when those intense azure irises pin me with such intensity I can hardly breathe.

His shoulders straighten as he slips his hands in his pants pockets. "I won't lose you, Leandra. I don't care what I need to do to ensure that."

"Stop." I clench my jaw as tears threaten to show weakness in my armor. I don't want him to see anything other than anger when he looks at me.

He moves closer, and I instinctively look away, afraid the walls will crumble.

"Look at me."

"No." My chest constricts.

"Leandra. Look. At me."

"I can't." A tear escapes as I turn my back toward him. "I can't look at you because it hurts too much."

I close my eyes for a second, and he's behind me, his presence wrapping tightly around my shoulders, squeezing the oxygen from my lungs. My skin burns for his touch. My lips yearn for his kiss. And my soul weeps to be rid of the hurt so I can do the one thing that feels more natural to me than breathing...lose myself in his arms.

He leans down, brushes his cheek against my hair, then inhales deeply. "God, I miss you, stray."

A whimper escapes me, my heart screaming as my insides coil up. There is no battle as cruel and gruesome as the fight that rages between one's head and heart. Two pieces of yourself wanting nothing more than to destroy each other. And no matter which part wins, the other will die. Either way, you will lose a piece of yourself.

"It's been too long since I've had you."

"It's been days."

"Hours feel like eons."

I cry when he wraps an arm around my waist, pulling me against him, and I swear to God I want to die. Smelling him, feeling him, loving him—it's killing me. It's tearing me apart, pulling me in two different directions, and I'm afraid I'll never be whole again.

"Stop fighting me, Leandra." His hand slowly travels down my hip, fingers teasing along my pants' waistband, his touch disarming me so easily. "Stop denying me what I crave."

"Never." A tear laps down my face. "You hurt me."

"You're fucking hurting me now." He rolls his hips, and I let out a breath feeling the stiff length of his cock pressing against my lower back. "You feel that? I've been this hard for you for fucking days."

"There are ways to get rid of that by yourself."

"You think I haven't tried?"

His hand slips inside my pants, and I suck in a breath, leaning back against him, the warmth of his body instantly fogging my mind. I'm hyperaware of every hard curve of his body, every ripped muscle under his shirt, and it's fucking with my self-control.

"No matter how many times I make myself come, I can't stop wanting your cunt." His hand dips lower and drags a finger through my slit, groaning into my hair as he inhales deep. "Jesus, stray. I want inside this pussy of yours."

"I hate you," I say, as if the lie would make up for the involuntary action of bending my knees slightly, parting my thighs so he can touch more of me.

"No, you don't. Feel how wet you are for me." His finger sinks deeper, and I arch my back against him. "You want me inside you, don't you, stray?"

"What I want is irrelevant. What I need is to get the fuck away from you."

His fingertip brushes over my clit, and I bite my lip,

stifling a moan. "Then run," he murmurs against my ear. "See what happens when I catch you."

Flames lick my skin, and my need to burn incinerates my will to fight him. My body is ash in his palms, and our connection is in control. It always has been.

I fist my hands at my sides, the pressure of his finger on my clit causing my legs to weaken. "Alexius, stop."

"Give me what I want, Leandra." He grinds his cock against my ass. "Give me what I crave, and let me have you."

I move my hips, pressing my ass harder against him, and I shiver when I hear him groan.

"Keep doing that, and I swear to God, I won't wait for your permission to fuck you."

"Alexius," I whimper.

"Say it, Leandra. Just fucking say it." His finger slips inside me. "Let me. Fuck you."

I'm two breaths away from giving in. My determination to fight him is nothing but fragments of something that would never be strong enough to stop me from wanting him, from loving him.

"You know as well as I do it's pointless fighting *us*." His breath is warm seduction skidding along my ear. "Your cunt is soaked. So fucking ready for me."

His words, his dirty mouth, have always been my drug, my heroin, an addiction that will destroy me.

"Mom, please stop. Can't you see it's killing you?"

"I'm already dead. I died the day you took your father from me."

"Please stop. Your addiction will destroy you."

"I don't care."

I do. I care.

I fucking care.

"Alexius, stop." I grab his hand between my legs, but he slips a second finger into me, the ache intensifying threefold.

"I love you, stray, and you love me. You can't deny it."

I have no idea where I get the strength, but I tear myself from his arms and pivot and look at him with intent. "I do love you. It's loving you that's making everything so much worse. It would be easier if I could just hate you."

He reaches out, but I step out of his reach. "Stop, please."

"Never. I will never fucking stop." Blue eyes flash with something dark.

"Don't you get it? This isn't something you can fix." There's no controlling my tears anymore.

"There is nothing to fix," he snarls. "Don't you get that? This is your fear controlling you."

"My fear?"

"Yes. You're afraid of what we have, afraid to accept who you really are."

"And who am I, Alexius? Huh? Who the fuck am I? Oh, wait, this is the part where you tell me I'm your wife, right? That's your answer to everything. 'You're my wife. You belong to me,'" I taunt.

"No!" He storms up close to me, his irises a burning inferno, their intensity causing me to hold my breath. "That woman who has the courage to acknowledge her desires and take what she wants, demanding what she needs while on her fucking knees in front of me, that's you. The real you."

"You don't know me."

"The fuck I don't. You're scared because when you're with me, you have the courage to acknowledge the side of you that you've spent years convincing yourself is wrong and distorted. You find your confidence in my arms, stray. With me, you're free, and it scares the living shit out of you. And that's why you've been trying to find ways to make me your villain, so you can blame me rather than *be* you. The real Leandra Del Rossa."

He cups my cheeks, gripping tightly, bringing his lips inches from mine, and I'm certain if he lets go, I'll collapse. "You are mine, and I am yours. There is nothing that can change that. I don't care if you villainize me for the rest of your goddamn life, I will not let you go."

Tears lap down my cheeks and onto his fingers. "What you did," I choke on a breath, "I'm not your toy, Alexius. My life isn't yours to play with."

"I did it because I didn't want to lose you."

"You had no right."

"That's not the way I see it."

"Then you're seeing it wrong," I sob.

A growl tears from his throat as he jerks away, pulling a hand through his hair, his expression hard lines of frustration. "The way I see it, I'm a husband who loves his wife and is willing to do anything to keep her."

"Even if it means breaking my heart?"

"Broken hearts mend." His nostrils flare, his eyes a raging storm of chaos. "We can get past this."

I shake my head, sucking my bottom lip into my mouth and tasting heartache in my tears. "No, Alexius. We can't."

"Don't say that," he snaps. "Don't fucking say that."

"It's the truth." I fall back against the cabinet as my legs grow numb, my eyes downcast as I clutch my belly, taking in one labored breath after the other, trying not to suffocate. "But it doesn't matter."

"What are you saying?"

"I'm saying nothing matters. How I feel doesn't matter because I already know how this will play out. I know you'll never let me walk away with our babies." I glance up at him. "You'll make me choose. My freedom, or them. And I will choose them. I will always choose my babies. But I will never forgive you. Never."

His eyes flash with hurt, and I can see the pain in their blue depths. It's right there, mirroring my own, and cuts so damn deep I'm convinced I'll bleed dry.

I sniff and wipe at my cheek, scoffing. "How is that for irony? You wanted me to stay, and now I am. Yet...you lost me anyway."

Our gazes remain locked, the silence excruciating.

It's the strangest thing. Even through the impossibility of forgiveness, there's still this flicker inside me that's determined to stay lit, fighting not to be smothered by Alexius' betrayal. There's a part of me still hoping that maybe...*just maybe*...

Maybe what? I'll forgive him? We'll go back to being

Alexius and Leandra? Back to lovers unraveling within each other's arms?

No.

Never.

That can never be again.

I swallow hard, trying to keep more tears from falling when he steps close, so damn close the pain in my chest intensifies threefold. This time he doesn't reach for me, he doesn't touch me, and I can't be sure if my eyes are tearing up because I want him to.

His eyes cut from mine to my lips and back up again, and I see nothing but pure resolve stir within blue. "Your fight won't outlast what we share, stray. What we have can burn cities to the fucking ground."

"What we had is gone."

"Liar," he bites out. "Even now, you feel it. Beneath all that hurt, all that anger, you still feel it. It's too fucking strong. And as God is my witness, Leandra, I will remind you just how strong it really is. Every. Goddamn. Day." He drags his teeth across his bottom lip. "I swear it."

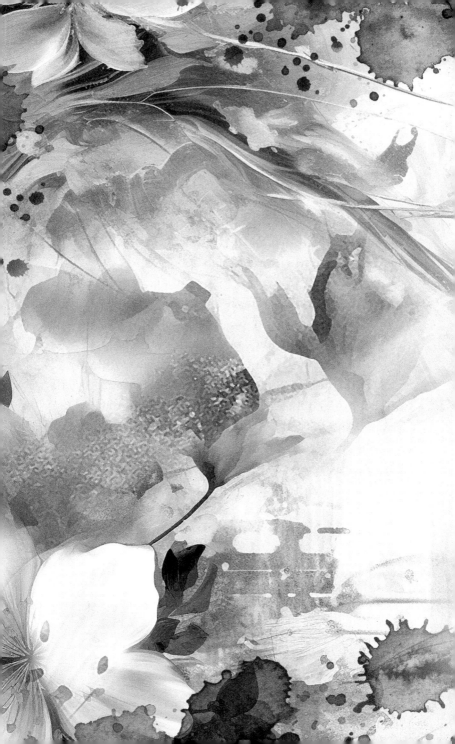

CHAPTER 4
ALEXIUS

I've never been more convinced that I'm half human, half devil—or some sort of fucking unholy beast because...*by God*...Leandra has never looked more exquisite than she does right now. That red-hot rebellion that blazes in her eyes, the wild anger fused with a soul-deep misery caused by a war raging inside her as she fights her feelings for me—it's fucking beautiful. The fiery passion. The blistering desire.

The spark of attraction surges between us no matter how fucked-up things are. It's still there, and it's stronger than ever. I know it. She knows it. It's a ticking time bomb, and I can't wait for it to explode.

The more she fights me, the more I want her. The more she denies me, the harder my dick gets. And the more she hates me, the more I want to bury myself so deep inside her she'll never be able to forget how much she fucking wants me.

I cross my arms as I study her and drink her in,

allowing myself to appreciate the sight. Her raven hair shines in the soft light trickling past the curtains, splashing over her delicate features with a golden glow. The tear stains on her cheeks highlight the contour of her face. It's like her tears magnify her allure, and I can't stop myself from reaching out and touching her cheek. She lets me. She doesn't retreat or fight me, her skin soft and hot against my fingertips. My gaze drops to her belly, and the thought of a piece of me growing inside her drives me fucking wild with a possession that makes my dick throb. "God. I want you so damn much, stray. My body aches for you."

"Alexius—"

"Have you touched yourself, thinking about me?"

"Stop."

"I've been palming my dick every morning thinking about you, jerking off like a goddamn teenager in the shower. But instead of coming inside you, I have to watch my cum run down the drain."

Her cheeks flush, and I acknowledge the small victory with a slight uptick at the corner of my lips, knowing how much she loves my filthy mouth.

"I know you're angry with me. But you can't tell me you haven't thought about me once, thinking about what it feels like to have my cock slip inside you so easily because your body remembers me. Your body knows who it belongs to, and your pussy aches to be stretched while I fuck goddamn stars into that pretty little head of yours."

"Jesus, Alexius."

She tries to turn away, but I grab her chin and force

her to look me in the eye. "Tell me you're not aching for me, stray."

She's sucking her lower lip into her mouth as if afraid her words might escape. But she doesn't have to say it. I can see it in the flush on her cheeks.

A tear laps onto my thumb, and I place it in my mouth, sucking it off and tasting her sadness. "Bittersweet," I say and step closer, touching her chin with my thumb and forefinger, forcing her to look up at me. "You think it's my deception causing your tears, but it's not. It's your love for me that makes your soul weep." I lean down, watching as she shuts her eyes and lets out a pained whimper when I kiss her cheek, lapping up a tear with my lips. "To you, your tears mean sadness. To me... it's hope."

"I hate you," she whispers, and I smile, pressing my mouth against her forehead.

"You don't. Not even a little."

"You have no idea how I feel. How much you fucking hurt me."

"I do," I whisper, dragging my lips down to her temple, breathing in deep and appreciating her sweet scent. "I know I hurt you. I lost your trust. But I won't apologize for doing what I needed to ensure you never walk away from me." I step up close, and her body shivers against mine. She makes no attempt to step back, and I snake an arm around her waist, gently placing my hand on the small of her back. "You cannot expect a man to regret the decisions he's made when he made them out of love."

"It's not love. It's control. That's what you want, and you feel powerless without it."

"That's true." I trace my lips down the shell of her ear, and I can almost hear her heartbeat quicken. "So imagine how it feels for a man like me when a woman makes the power and wealth acquired through generations seem insignificant."

Her shoulders tremble, and she leans her head to the side, making me wonder if it's an attempt to distance herself from me or an offering for me to take what I want.

She lets out a labored breath and moves her arms in between us, but the way she pushes against my chest is nothing but a halfhearted attempt. "You can justify your actions as much as you want. There is no reason in this entire goddamn world that can make what you did okay," she whispers, and all I want to do is devour her mouth and swallow her words because they mean nothing compared to the desire that thickens around us with every passing second.

"Oh, but there is one reason," I say, brushing my lips down the side of her neck, "and it's the only reason I need to warrant every action I've taken, and every action I'll take in the future to ensure you stay mine, and mine alone."

She turns her face back toward me, denying me to taste her delicate skin any further. "And what is that?"

My eyes search hers, the air around us palpable with a passionate mix of hate, pain, longing, and an all-consuming lust. "Love," I reply softly. "My love for you is all the reason I'll ever need, stray."

Her eyes start to glimmer with unshed tears as she takes a step back, my arm falling away from her waist. "You don't know the meaning of love."

"Just because my love doesn't fit the mold of what you think love should be? I told you, Leandra, I warned you that my love would be a burden you'd have to carry for the rest of your life. Well, here it is." I spread my arms wide. "The fucking burden of my love."

"Deception. Lies. That's the burden I have to carry for loving you?" She swipes at her wet cheeks, newfound defiance ignited in amber hues. "God, you're a selfish asshole."

"And you're afraid of what we share."

"What?" She recoils.

"Admit it. You've been afraid of this connection between us since the first time I fucked you in that boutique. If not for the placebos, you would have found a way to sabotage our relationship sooner or later because when you're with me, you have no choice but to be who you truly are. The true Leandra Del Rossa, and not some stereotypical poor girl society has programmed you to be. And you can't accept that. You can't accept who you really are."

"You don't fucking know me," she snaps, her cheeks red as anger starts to simmer.

"I know every little part of you, inside and out." My cock stirs. "No one knows you as I do, and no one else will have the privilege. I'll make sure of it."

"By keeping me locked in here?"

"No. As a matter of fact," I take the key and unlock

the door, opening it and standing to the side, "you can leave your room whenever you want. I won't keep you locked up in here anymore."

Her eyes narrow with distrust. "You're letting me leave?"

"Your room, yes. But you'll stay on the estate at all times."

"So, I'm still a prisoner?"

"If you choose to see it that way."

"Then how the fuck do you see it?"

I shrug. "Protection."

"From what?"

My eyes meet hers. "From making the wrong decision."

I half expect her to challenge me, to snap back with some wise-ass remark or well-aimed sarcasm. I can almost see the words forming on the tip of her tongue. But she chooses silence, her eyes studying me as if she's trying to see inside my head. I wouldn't be surprised if she could because this woman has managed to infiltrate the deepest parts of my being, occupying every corner of my soul, controlling my thoughts and haunting my dreams while I sleep without her next to me. It's the worst part of hell I've ever experienced.

There's suspicion in her eyes as she watches me. "What's going on?"

"There's no hidden agenda here, Leandra," I say, trying to set her at ease. "I realize that having you locked up is unnecessary when this estate is heavily guarded at all times."

"In other words, I'm still a prisoner. I just got awarded a bigger cell with outside courtyard privileges."

"See it as you will. But for now, this is how it will be." My gaze falls to her belly and drags back up to meet her eyes. "You belong here with me. All three of you. And until you see that, until you realize that no matter what happens, your place is at my side and in my bed, you'll be guarded at all times."

"Like your captive," she snaps.

"Like the one thing I can't stand to lose."

Her lips part, her throat bobbing as she swallows. Even in an oversized turtleneck and black tights, her hair in a messy bun and no make-up, she's still fucking stunning.

I smile. "I saw it the day I walked into your apartment, determined to make you accept my offer."

She reaches behind her ear, sinking her nail into the scarred flesh. "What did you see?"

I step out the door and into the hall, glancing back at her. "What a beautiful mess you are, and the disaster we'll be."

It takes everything I have to walk away from her, to not slam the door and lock us in so I can prove to her what we have is stronger than the betrayal she clings to. All it would take is a slick slide of my dick inside that sweet pussy of hers, and she'd be reminded who owns her, who loves her, who gives her the ecstasy she needs. With every step farther away from her bedroom, I'm fighting the urge to turn around. It's been too long since I've had her, tasted her, felt her. All I can fucking think about is watching her face as I sink into her, witnessing the pleasure on every crevice of her beautiful face while I make her come.

Fuck.

As if I don't have enough shit to deal with, I have my goddamn cousin's unexpected arrival to deal with. Rome Savelli. The prodigal son returns.

I round the corner into the dining room and find Caelian leaning back on the couch, staring at the whiskey in his glass. He looks up when he hears me, then glances at the antique grandfather clock. "When two brothers need a drink at eleven a.m., that means shit is quite close to hitting the fan."

"I won't argue that." I pour myself a drink, slam it all back, swallowing before pouring a second glass, deciding to nurse this one rather than gulp it down.

"So, Rome is back," Caelian says, taking a sip of his drink and pulling his lips in a thin line as he swallows. "I have to admit. I didn't think he'd ever come back."

"Neither did I. He took the first opportunity he got to leave this family, his father, only to come back now."

"Why did he leave in the first place?"

I walk over to the fireplace, staring into the flames. "He was there with Roberto when I overheard our uncle say how he wants to kill Dad, wipe out the Del Rossa bloodline. "

Caelian shifts to the edge of the seat. "Roberto wanted him in on it."

"I suppose so. Rome would have been the heir to this empire if Roberto succeeded in killing Dad. It only makes sense that Roberto would want him in on family business as soon as possible."

"Is that why Rome left?"

I turn to face him. "I've always suspected it. But I don't know for sure. Who knows what went on behind closed doors in the Savelli house? All I know is Roberto had to pull a huge motherfucking unicorn out of his ass to get Rome to come back."

"It doesn't make sense," Caelian mumbles, staring out in front of him as he shakes his head.

"It doesn't matter whether it makes sense or not. He's here, and he's taken Roberto's place in the Dark Sovereign."

"You're not going to fight it?" Caelian stands, placing a hand in his gray suit pants pocket. "You're going to accept it? Just like that?"

I pull a hand through my hair. "What would you have me do? It's his right to take his father's place. I had what I needed to get rid of Roberto, but I have nothing on Rome."

"Do we really need something?" Caelian challenges. "The Dark Sovereign is ours, and we can do whatever the fuck we want."

"That's not how it works, and you know that."

He gulps down the last of his drink and slams the glass on the table, visibly on edge. "We don't have any alliances to placate. We can do whatever the fuck we want because all this," he holds his arms out wide, "is ours."

"We might not have alliances, Caelian, but we have a

reputation to uphold. If we cause civil unrest between our two families, we'll lose the trust of our business partners. We can't bend the rules simply because it suits us."

"That seat is Isaia's. You know that as well as I do. He deserves to be in that room with us, Alexius."

I throw my head back and groan, knowing all too well what this is really about. "Listen, if Isaia has something to say about the new turn of events, he can come say it to my face and not bitch to you about it."

"On the contrary," Caelian says, crossing his arms, "Isaia didn't say shit. He left after the meeting this morning without saying a single fucking word. He's too proud to make a scene even though Rome's unexpected arrival robbed him of something we promised to give him."

"Do you think I'm happy about this?" I shoot back. "Do you think I wanted Rome to waltz in here and fuck up our plans? No. But he did, and now we need to regroup. Figure out where we go from here."

Caelian throws his hands in the air, his frustration rippling from his tense shoulders, cursing as he starts to pace. "We're going to lose him, Alexius."

"Who? Isaia?"

"Yeah." Caelian stills, his face nothing but hard lines. "Things are already tense between the two of you. He buried his girlfriend—"

"Melanie was not his girlfriend." I roll my eyes.

"It doesn't matter what she was. The point is she was something to him. He lost her. He lost Leandra."

"He never had Leandra," I growl, instant anger bursting through my veins, clawing at every muscle. "You can't lose something you never had, and he sure as fuck didn't have my wife."

Caelian holds up his hands, sighing. "Wrong choice of words. But what I'm saying is Isaia needs this. He needs to be a part of this with us. He's been an outsider long enough, and if we don't do something to include him, we're going to lose him, and I don't want to see that happen."

Caelian's eyes resemble my dad's—gentle green hues peeking from behind hazel swirls. When he's angry or annoyed, it's more brown than green. Mother always joked about his eyes being the transition color, from Nicoli's and my blue eyes to Isaia's dark brown. Isaia has our grandfather's eyes. He has our grandfather's silent and aloof personality too. No one can figure him out. Well, my wife seems to be the one who's come the closest to uncovering that my little brother does, in fact, have a beating heart hidden inside his chest.

I take off my jacket and toss it onto the couch, loosening my tie. "What do you want me to do, Caelian? It's not like I invited Rome to join this fucking shitstorm just to complicate the matter even further. Roberto found a fucking loophole, one we could never have predicted because our cousin coming home seemed highly un-fucking-likely. Now all we can do is stay one step ahead of him. The man already wants my head on a stake ever since I told him about the recording of him plotting to murder our father. And after Micah's anonymous letter to him about Jimmy, the man wants blood."

"You know how this is going to end, right?" Caelian's eyes narrow as he studies me. "In the end, it's going to be you or Roberto, one killing the other. That's the only way this war with our uncle will stop. But think about it, Alexius." He inches closer, and his jaw tics. "If Roberto lays a motherfucking finger on you, Nicoli, Isaia, me, we'll hunt him down and tear his spine out. But if you kill him, Rome won't let you get away with it. So, no matter what we do, a civil war is inevitable."

CHAPTER 5
LEANDRA

I t's a miracle I'm still standing. It doesn't matter how angry I am at Alexius or how much my heart bleeds, all it takes is a simple touch, and he disarms me in a way that leaves me without breath.

It's madness. I should hate him. Be immune to his touch, his presence, the words that drip from his lips like honey. But instead, I'm standing here using every ounce of strength I have to fight this insane connection that keeps drawing me to him. It's like there's this invisible line we're both linked to, and the harder I try to get more distance, the closer it pulls us together.

I wish I knew how to hate him. It would be so much easier. But the truth is I don't. I don't hate him. Not even a little. The anger is there. It's in my blood, surging and raging every time I think about what he did. It's just not strong enough to smother what I feel for him.

God. I think I'm borderline insane because from the

moment he walked in, all I wanted was for him to just fucking take me as unapologetically as he always did. I wanted his touch to take away the uncertainty. I wanted him to kiss away the pain and fuck me until his betrayal no longer resonates through my heart. Why can't it just be that simple?

"Jesus, Leandra," I mutter, pulling my fingers through my hair, feeling pretty damn pathetic. What kind of woman am I for still wanting him after what he did?

The open door gives me a misleading sense of freedom. I'm not naive. I know I'm still trapped. My cage just got bigger.

Mira's face pops into view, and I jolt, slapping my palm on my chest. "Mira. My God. You scared me."

"I see he's not keeping you locked up anymore."

"Don't let the open door fool you." I grab a coat from the closet and pull on a pair of boots. "He won't let me off the estate."

"Where are you going?"

I wrap a black scarf around my neck. "I've been locked in this room for days. Right now, I want fresh air."

"But it's snowing outside. You'll freeze to death."

"I'll be fine. I just want to go outside for a while."

"Leandra."

I'm almost at the door when she raises her voice.

"Leandra, stop."

I still. "What, Mira?"

"I know you're angry. I know you must hate him right now."

I turn to face her. "I don't hate him. And that's the problem." I slip on a pair of gloves. "It would be so much easier if I could hate him."

Her expression softens, but her eyes flash with concern. "I need you to promise me something."

"I can't promise I won't leave when I get the chance."

"No. Not that." She shakes her head and steps up, taking my gloved hands in hers. "Promise me that no matter how angry he makes you, how much you think you hate him—"

"I don't hate him, Mira."

"Just promise me, okay?" she presses. "Promise me that whatever happens, you won't lose sight of what really matters. And that's the little lives you're carrying inside you. What you want, what Alexius wants is no longer relevant. What's best for these babies is what matters the most."

I've met all kinds of people working as a waitress. But I've never encountered someone whose heart is as pure as Mirabella's. There's a kindness in her that's almost too good for this world. And it amazes me how she grew up in the Del Rossa world, yet her compassion remains untainted by it all.

I squeeze her hand before pulling her in for a hug. "I promise."

"Good." She brushes her palms across my shoulders before leaning back and smiling. "Now go dance in the snow, or whatever it is you want to do out there. I'll have some hot cocoa waiting for you once you're done freezing your ass off."

Her smile is infectious, and I find myself smiling, too, even though my world has imploded, and it seems like things are only going to get worse.

"Oh, and Leandra," she turns to face me, her eyes narrowed, "in God's name, please don't do anything stupid."

"Like what?"

"I dunno. Like, try to leave?"

I roll my eyes. "I'm not that stupid."

"Says the one who fell for Alexius Del Rossa."

"Not funny," I scold.

"It's a little funny." She winks before her heels echo across the lacquered floors. I swear, if it weren't for Mira, I would have gone mad a long time ago.

The halls smell like freshly polished wood. Lavender. It's a scent I've grown to love since living here. It reminds me of him. This is his home, after all. Who the fuck am I kidding? Everything reminds me of him. The smell, the colors, the windows, the floors, the goddamn oxygen in this place reminds me of him and how he consumes me.

The house is quiet. Still. To me, it's a relief since the last thing I need right now is to run into one of his brothers and pretend that everything in my life is okay when it's all just falling apart. When I enter the foyer, seeing the tall Christmas tree, the lights lit and presents heaped beneath it, everything crashes back like a tidal wave—the memory of thinking I finally have the world, only to have it ripped away.

My fists clench, and my chest aches. Anger rises, and I'm so close to breaking and losing control over my emotions. Every flicker of the Christmas lights edges me to the point where I want to do something drastic. I want to scream. I want to break everything I can get my hands on, shatter the windows, and destroy the walls. I want to burn shit down and light the entire world on fire around me. I want to hurt him like he hurt me, see his regret tear him apart in the same way his betrayal ruined me. I need a sense of power, even if it's only short-lived. But that's impossible. I could destroy the world, and Alexius would still own me. That's the worst part. I'm helpless when it comes to the love I feel for him. It's toxic, but it's undeniable.

I rush out the front door as fast as my feet can carry me. The icy tentacles of winter whip against my cheeks, and I pull my scarf tighter, slipping my hands in my coat pockets. Leaning my head back, I close my eyes and inhale deeply, the cold air burning my lungs. The air is clean, fresh, and carries renewed strength to every muscle as I exhale some of the tension that's been infecting me in that goddamn room.

Translucent and shimmering snowflakes float mid-air, carried by the calm breeze. The garden is draped in a blanket of white, the scenery serene as I stroll, kicking snow with my boots. I know I'm not free. Far from it. But I try to imagine I am. That everything is right in my world, even if just for a few moments, so I can fully appreciate the beautiful sight winter has laid at our doorstep.

"And here I thought I was the only one eager to exchange a cozy fireplace for winter's pinch."

I pivot, the gravel of the walkway crunching beneath my boots, and I face a man I've never seen before, his dark eyes so intense, I can feel myself shrink under his watchful eye.

"I'm sorry. Who are you?" I ask.

"Rome Savelli." He holds out his hand, crowding me with his six-foot-four frame and broad shoulders. "Alexius' cousin. You are?" Dark brown eyes narrow as I place my gloved palm in his.

"Leandra. Alexius'...um," I let go of his hand, trace a finger down my temple, and smile absentmindedly. "I'm not quite sure what I am to your cousin at the moment."

"Ah." His face flashes with recognition. "You're his wife. The one he's been keeping locked up."

I choke on air. "Excuse me?"

He shrugs and gestures to the house. "Not much is kept secret around here. So, tell me, did he let you out, or did you escape?"

"I...um—"

"If it's the latter, I'll have no choice but to help you get away from here. God knows I've been trying to escape this place for years."

I purse my lips, somewhat amused. "Based on the whispers I've heard, you managed to escape a long time ago. So why did you come back now?"

He cocks his head and grins, his dark chestnut hair neatly cut. "I guess one could say I've learned that no matter how far you run, you'll never be free of this place or this family." He slants a brow. "A lesson you'll learn soon enough, it seems."

"It's quite bold of you to assume I want to escape."

A sly grin tugs at his lips. "Why else would you be out here in the cold rather than inside, where it's comfortable and warm?"

"Maybe I'm just enjoying the fresh air."

"Or maybe you'd rather brave the icy weather than the chilly atmosphere in there." He indicates the house, and I frown at him.

"You might not resemble your cousin much, but the two of you are equally outspoken."

"I can see why he likes you."

"Likes me?" I scoff. "We're married. I'd hope he does a little more than just like me." I have no idea why I said that, given the current state of our relationship.

"Maybe he likes you a little too much, hence the reason his head of security is currently standing over there keeping an eye on you." He nods his chin in the direction over my shoulder, and I turn to see Maximo watching us. Rome inches closer, slanting a brow as he stares down at me. "I'd love to know what it is you did that pissed off my cousin to such a degree he'd resort to locking you in your room."

Rome's assumption of me being in the wrong and earning my punishment is not only offensive, but it demands a response. I step closer, confident enough to keep his melted chocolate gaze. "I find it worrying that everyone around here knew Alexius locked me up in my room, even you who only just arrived, and yet no one bats an eyelash. Everyone just accepted it." I lean my head to the side as I study his unmoving expression. "It's quite disturbing, don't you think?"

"Not compared to what else goes on in these halls." The corners of his eyes crinkle, and I'm not quite sure what to make of Alexius' cousin. Another enigma, just like my husband. Either it's a blood-related thing, or it's something in this place's water, turning these men into mystery riddled magnets.

He snickers then pulls the collar of his coat higher up his neck. I catch a glimpse of a partly hidden tattoo as it disappears beneath the wool fabric, but I can't make out what it is. "Well, it was nice to finally meet you, Leandra. I hope to see more of you around here." He smirks. "That's if you don't get yourself locked up again."

My skin heats, but the mischief tugging at his lips has me more amused than angered. "Hopefully, we'll run into each other before you decide to run away again."

He sucks his bottom lip into his mouth, the corners curled upward. "I like you," he remarks before turning and walking toward the house.

"Asshole," I mumble as I watch him leave.

"I heard that."

My cheeks flush.

"Next time, use your inside voice."

"Next time, I'll just say it to your face."

He waves at me over his shoulder. "Looking forward to it."

I shake my head and watch him disappear into the house. For some reason, I'm smiling. My brief chat with

Rome was weird, yet somehow it was the most normal conversation I've had in a while.

I've heard other members of this family talk about Rome. Alexius referred to him as a coward for leaving his responsibilities behind. Now he's back. But something tells me Rome isn't back to spread Christmas cheer.

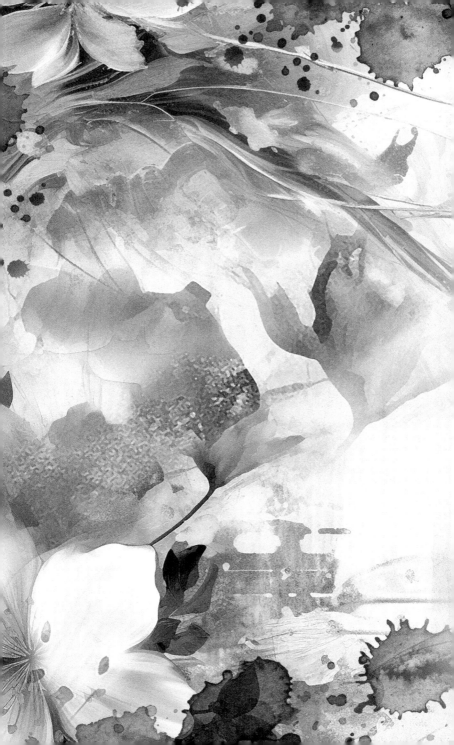

CHAPTER 6
ALEXIUS

I watch them through my office window. He's standing too close. He's touching her hand. His gaze lingers on her lips for too long. His expression is far too entertained while keeping the company of another man's wife.

My wife.

Jealousy is bitter and caustic as it burns my throat with every swallow. Possessiveness gnaws at me with sharpened teeth, tearing at my flesh and hitting bone. My fists are clenched claws that want to rip his fucking throat out. I should go out there and fuck her while he watches, bend her over, make her scream and mark her like a goddamn animal. I'm two seconds away from doing just that when he turns and walks away, and I can finally take a breath, only to have the oxygen torn from my lungs by a single goddamn sight.

Her smile.

She's smiling as she watches him walk away. Why the

fuck is she smiling? What did he say to her? What did they talk about? Jesus Christ.

I pull my palm down my face, biting my lower lip, chewing the side of my tongue as possessiveness poisons me, eating me alive.

Leandra's smiles are mine. No one else's. They're woven into my bones and blood, yet lately, all I've done is make her cry. And up until this moment, I was okay with that, wanting her tears, craving her sorrow because it meant she still felt something, and something is better than nothing. But now that I'm reminded of how fucking beautiful she is when she smiles, how her dark, almond-shaped eyes light up when happiness fills her, I thirst for her smile and her laughter. Her joy is my paradise in this fucked-up world, and I just watched another man get a piece of it.

God, I need her so damn much. It's a hunger that burns my veins and consumes my thoughts. I want her touch, her kiss, her desire. I need her passion, her lust, her body against mine. I need to feel her heartbeat, see her smile, and hear her laughter, her moans, her cries of ecstasy.

Yet, here I am, watching her smile because of another man.

Another man I'm going to...

"Alexius, here you are."

A growl rips from my throat, and I reach for my gun behind my back, spinning around and launching at Rome, slamming his back into the wall, his breath exploding from his mouth.

"What the fuck?"

I force my arm against his chest, pressing my elbow on the pulsing vein in his neck as I attempt to stop air from reaching his lungs. I press the muzzle of my gun against his jaw. "Stay the fuck away from her," I seethe.

"Oh, right." His eyes widen with recognition, dark irises lit with a gleam of malice. "You saw that, huh?"

"Stay. The fuck. Away from my wife."

"We were just talking."

"I don't give a fuck," I spit out, squeezing my gun harder to his jaw wanting nothing more than to paint my walls with blood and brain matter. "I don't care that you're family, Rome. If you so much as look at her the wrong way, I will gut you."

"Funny," he moans as I add more pressure to his throat. "I don't see Isaia walking around with his intestines hanging out, and from what I've heard, he's more than looked at her the wrong way."

I narrow my eyes, and he smirks. "Rumors spread fast, cousin. Surely you know by now these halls can't keep secrets."

"My office sure as fuck can," I hiss, dragging my gun up the side of his face, pressing it against his temple. "And if you choose to play games that involve my wife, I'll wash your blood off my carpet for a week with a goddamn smile on my face."

Nicoli walks in and raises his brows. "Why am I not surprised? Alexius, put your gun away. Let's grab a bottle of bourbon and settle this like men."

Rome snickers, and I snarl, pressing my gun harder

against his head. "This is your first and last warning. Stay away from Leandra."

"Seriously?" Nicoli cocks a brow at Rome. "Leandra? Listen, cousin." He crosses his arms and steps closer. "I can try to stop my twin from kicking your ass for coming home and screwing up all our plans. What I can't do is find a cure for being dumb as fuck."

"I simply introduced myself."

"One does not simply introduce yourself to my brother's wife," Nicoli says. "You see her, turn around, walk away, and pray to God that Alexius didn't see you breathe in her direction."

"Jesus," Rome mutters. "I never would have guessed some woman would have Alexius by the balls."

"She's not just some woman." As I step back, I let go of him with a jerk, aiming my gun at his forehead. "She's my wife, and she's pregnant."

"Pregnant?" Rome's eyebrows almost touch his hairline as he straightens his coat collar. "She's having your child?"

"Twins," I reply, deadpan.

"Well, that's great, cousin." He holds his arms wide, glancing between Nicoli and me. "You're going to be a dad. Hopefully you'll do a better job than our fathers. Although, locking up the mother of your children isn't quite what I'd call a good start."

"You should learn to shut your mouth when you don't know what the fuck you're talking about."

"As I said," he straightens his collar, "these halls talk."

I scoff, my fists burning to mess up his smug fucking

face. "You know, you have some nerve coming back after you left like a fucking coward."

"I had my reasons."

"You didn't want to get your hands dirty for this family like the rest of us. Yet here you are, back to come to your father's aid—the man who tried so fucking hard to wipe out my family but never succeeded because the worst mistake he ever made was underestimating us."

"No one is more aware of my father's shortcomings than I am."

"If that were true, you wouldn't be here helping him."

Rome inches closer even though I'm still holding the gun with my finger on the trigger. "It doesn't matter what my father did or did not do in the past. Being part of the Dark Sovereign is still my fucking birthright."

"A right you gave up the day you decided to be a fucking coward and ran away with your tail between your legs."

"You think you know everything, but you don't," he seethes.

"You showed me all I needed to know when you turned your back on this family."

"Girls!" Nicoli calls out. "You're both fucking pretty. Now, can we stop bickering like little bitches in heat?" I take my eyes off Rome for a second to see Nicoli take a seat on the couch, light a cigarette, and then lean back. "We can stand around insulting each other until the cows come home. It won't solve a single fucking thing."

"Right now, I don't want to solve shit." I bring my face inches from Rome's. "All I want is to hear you say you understand Leandra is off-limits. My wife will not be a part of this game you plan on playing. Not today. Not tomorrow. Not ever. Understood?"

Seconds tick by as we keep each other's glare. Part of me hopes he'll challenge me, give me a reason to slit his throat. But I'm secretly disappointed when he nods and says, "Understood."

"Good."

"Great." Nicoli claps his hands, cigarette hanging from his lips. "Now, let's have a drink and celebrate the fact that we've delayed bloodshed by another day."

"I think I've had enough of cowards for one day," I sneer, pressure building in my head as I keep a threatening eye on Rome for a few more seconds before stomping out of my office, slamming the door behind me. My cousin unnerves me, and the more I look at him, the clearer I see the smile on Leandra's face. It's an innocent act that sharpens the edge of my anger, eliciting the deadliest impulses in me. I've never been so close to madness as I am now. Longing for her, craving her like she's the heroin my veins need, is lethal when combined with the venom of my jealousy. My obsessive instincts are heightened, sharp, and deadlier than ever now that I don't have her.

I could kill a man with my bare hands for something as simple as breathing in a way I don't fucking like. Maybe this is what it means to truly be evil, having no control over your mind and your actions, no longer fighting the darkest parts of you, because what's the point? What's the point of trying to be a better man when the person who owns your heart no longer wants it? All that's left is this soul crushing rage while I go about my day being a miserable bastard.

Even my footsteps are angered, and I can hardly breathe, loosening my tie with a violent jerk and popping the button of my collar. I want to destroy something so badly, my every muscle is on the verge of exploding.

Fuck! I slam my fist into the wall, growling. My teeth are clenched, and my blood pumps violently and hard, swooshing in my ears. I've never felt like this before. My mind, my thoughts, my body possessed by the thought of her. She's this delusion that lives inside my head because she sure as fuck ain't in my bed anymore.

I punch my fist against the wall, followed by another, the plaster cracking under my rage, and I let out a roar of agony. All I see is her face, those sultry heart-shaped lips, long lashes that fan her cheeks as her eyes roll closed every time I slide my cock into her. Those soft, sensual noises she makes as I rock her body, it fucking haunts me. The feel of her nails clawing at the skin of my back, her heels digging into the flesh of my ass while her thighs trap me between her legs, forcing me deeper, not letting go. My wife consumes me. She weakens me. And not being able to touch her, kiss her, have her in every way possible has me dying a slow, painful death, my insides breaking more and more each day.

I lean my head against the wall, my mind sinking into darkness while I drown in my love for her. *God.* Why can't she just come to her senses? She knows as well as I do we're meant to be together. I saw it in her eyes. She knows she's mine.

"Alexius?"

My heart stutters and stops. I freeze, practically gasping for breath, struggling against the whirlpool of anger, frustration, and the worst torment I've ever felt in my life.

"Are you okay?" Leandra's voice is a sheet of silk around my throat, and I can practically taste her as her scent surrounds me. It's not her perfume, or soap, or shampoo I smell. It's a scent that's uniquely her. An exquisite fusion of love, affection, lust, and a flurry of indecent intentions.

I glance up, and the thread snaps as my gaze meets hers. I surge forward, grab her waist, and yank her against me, spinning around and pulling her into the first room closest to us.

"Alexius, what are you—"

The door slams shut, and I push her back against it. Without thinking twice, I crash my lips against hers, kissing her as if the antidote to my suffering is on her velvet tongue. I press my body against hers, slide my tongue in her mouth, and groan as I finally taste her after being without it for what feels like a goddamn eternity.

My one hand is on her waist while the other grips her jaw tightly, ensuring she can't move her lips away from mine. She tastes like poison and sunshine, a blend of death and salvation. And the best part? She's kissing me back, and it's heated, carnal, like she knows exactly what I need because it's what she needs, too.

It doesn't occur to me that this is a moment lost within a whirlpool of chaos. I'm out of control and don't give a fuck about a single second we've spent apart. I don't care that our reality has us separated.

"Stop," she breathes against my lips.

"Don't," I warn. "Don't say a fucking word." I take her mouth hard, sweeping my tongue deep, kissing her like I'm fucking dying inside, like she's the cure to every pain I've ever suffered in my entire goddamn life.

"Alexius, stop." But her lips are a complete contradiction to her words as she opens wide, giving my tongue access to every corner of her mouth. Her hands press against my chest, but I grab her wrists and pin them above her head with a violent jerk, the sound of her gasp rippling down my spine. Her breasts push up as her back curves, and the second I have both her hands secured in my palm, I reach down and cup her tit, my lips sucking and teeth nipping at her nipple through the fabric of her top.

"Oh, God." The sound of her sweet moans tears a low growl from my chest, my cock hard and aching to fuck. "We can't do this."

"We can." My lips are on hers again, and I snake my hand around her hip, clutching her ass, pushing her hard against my raging cock. "We can do this every second of every goddamn day."

"Alexius," her voice is a strained whisper, "please...stop."

"Don't say it."

"Please."

"Fuck!" I roar, grip her hips, and swivel her around, forcing her front against the wall, pushing my body hard against her, the curve of her ass giving my dick the friction I need. "You've made me wait too long, stray."

"Not long enough."

I nip at her ear and roll my hips. "You feel that? You have no idea how I ache to be inside you. I'm fucking suffering, and I can't take it anymore."

"You deserve it," she sneers over her shoulder, rubbing her ass against my hard cock. "You deserve to suffer."

I sweep her hair over her shoulder and drag the tip of my tongue up the side of her neck. "I'm done, stray. Done playing this game with you. It's time I make you realize that no matter what, you're mine."

"And how do you plan on doing that?" she murmurs, and I brush my lips up the shell of her ear.

"By using this body of yours until you can't walk," I tell her. "By leaving bruises on your skin, teeth marks on your flesh, and fuck that sweet little cunt of yours until there's no question who your body belongs to."

"I hate you," she spits out.

"Then I'm afraid you're going to hate me even more after what I'm about to do."

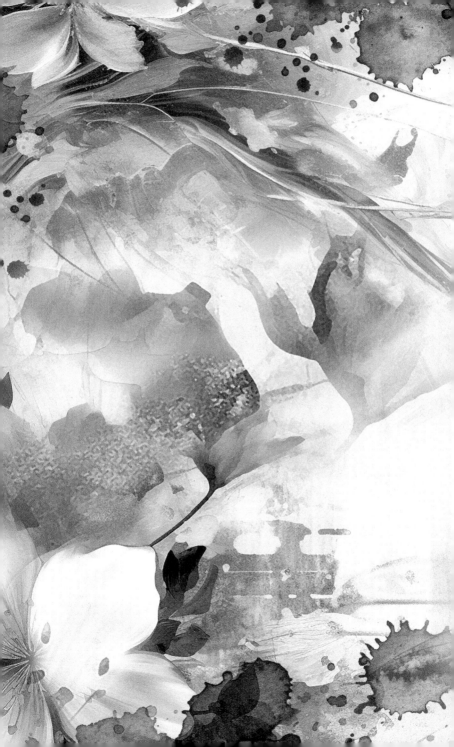

CHAPTER 7
LEANDRA

I've never known pain like this. My heart pounds with shards of glass burrowed deep within, his touch a reminder of how deep it cuts. But the flames—it's scalding, incinerating the last ounce of defiance I have. The agony is relentless, each breath unbearable while I feel him along my every curve.

I can't escape it. I can't run from him. He has me trapped, and I don't have the strength to fight him. I don't want to fight him. I want to surrender, give in, and forget that I have a heart that's been bleeding for days.

If I had one wish, just one, it would be to have the strength to forgive him, because the thought of not being able to is killing me slowly, sucking the life out of me like a parasite.

I lick my lips, my palms flush against the cold wall, my heart beating wildly making it impossible to take a breath. "We've done a lot of shit, Alexius. But would you go so far and take me against my will?"

He lets out a low snicker, his breath skidding along my ear. "Don't fool yourself, stray. I can fuck you now, I can fuck you tomorrow, I can fuck you every goddamn day for the rest of your life, and it will never be against your will. You know why?" He reaches around my shoulder, taking my throat between his fingers, applying pressure. "Because you want it just as much as I do. No matter how hurt you think you are, your cunt constantly aches for me. And I don't need to slip my hand between your legs to know you're wet. I can fucking smell it, and it's driving me insane."

I whimper, my eyes rolling closed. "You're an asshole."

"Is that all I am?"

"You're an arrogant prick too."

"What else?" he rasps, grinding his hard cock against my ass, burying his nose in the crook of my neck, inhaling deep, moaning like my scent is a drug to him.

I bite my lip. "Control freak."

"Keep it coming, stray."

"Bastard. Sick fucker."

"You can go on for days, call me whatever you want, I don't give a shit. As long as you spread your legs and let me bury myself inside you, you can call me all the names in the book. I don't fucking care."

"Jesus!" I cry out, teetering at the edge of madness.

His lips curl against my shoulder. "I'll be Jesus too."

"God, Alexius. Stop." *Don't stop.* I slam my palm against the wall, and he tightens his grip on my throat, pulling my head back. His touch is hot, burning as if branding my skin.

He yanks my shirt, tearing the fabric down my shoulder, and I gasp. "Nothing will change if we fuck, Leandra. I'll still be the husband you wish you could hate, and you'll be the wife I'll never give up."

"Go to hell."

"In a bit. I just need to make you come first." He winds his arm around my waist, his hand dipping between my legs, cupping my sex hard. A moan rolls from my tongue, and I squeeze my body harder against him.

"I hate you," I breathe out.

"Let's see how much you'll hate me with my cock inside you." He drags the tip of his tongue along my naked skin, and I shiver. The way he moans tells me he feels it; he feels the way my body trembles for him. I hate it. I hate that he has so much power over me, but what I hate most is the fact that he knows it.

I clench my jaw. "I hate you so damn much," I whisper, then hold my breath as his hand slides inside my pants. My legs tremble as he drags a finger through my slit, and he growls against my ear.

"Your body can never lie to me."

"Yeah. Only one of us is capable of bullshitting the other."

"Touché."

"Now, let me go."

"Never," he rasps in my ear. "You belong to me."

"But my heart doesn't."

He reaches down, and I moan as he slides a single finger inside me. "Here's the cold, hard truth, stray. Your heart hurts, and your pain wants you to run from me. But your body won't ever stop wanting to betray your heart. What we have burns so fucking bright, not even the sun compares."

"What do you want from me?"

"Right now." He leans closer, and I can smell his cologne, the whiskey on his breath. "Right now, I want you to let me fuck you until you see fucking stars. And once I've made you come, and I'm done staring at your creamed pussy, I want you to tell me how much you love me. That you'll stop fighting what you feel for me. Then I'm going to watch your tits get larger." He reaches down and cups my breast, squeezing before dragging his hand to my stomach, flattening his palm. "I'm going to watch your belly grow and feel my babies move inside you, knowing they are the best parts of both of us."

His hand dips between my legs, his finger circling my clit. "But right now, I just want to fuck you and make you come. I don't think that's too much to ask."

"That's your problem, isn't it? You don't realize just how much you ask of the people around you."

"Right now I'm just asking you to give in. To surrender and let your body have what it wants." His lips are on my earlobe. "My cock."

He thrusts against my ass, his dick hard and throbbing with a promise for pleasure. When he moves again, my feet lift off the ground, and I reach back, clawing at his neck, nails scratching and fingers digging.

There are so many voices inside my head, screaming at me. I've never felt this torn in my entire fucking life. How am I supposed to stay strong, stay standing when every ounce of my being is dying to be with him?

I'm so tired of fighting. The constant battle between my head and heart is exhausting. It's fucking killing me.

Just once.

I want to surrender...just once.

My control snaps, and desire takes over. Alexius' arm winds around my midsection, and he pulls me up, forcing me to bend my knees as he carries me with my back against his chest.

I refuse to allow my head the power to form a single coherent thought. I don't want to think about anything other than the anticipation of ecstasy. I don't want reality to seep through and give me even a sliver of control. I want to let go and fall.

With one arm, he swipes the desk clean, papers and pens, books and files flying and scattering to the ground. He sets me down on the mahogany wood, his fingers hooking in my pants' waistband, yanking my underwear down with it, jerking it off and tossing it to the side.

We're all hot breaths and manic lust, his cold hands pressing against my thighs, spreading me open, diving his tongue into my heated sex. My back is flush against the desk, and my hands weave through his soft hair as he licks from my opening to my clit, teasing and flicking the sensitive nub with his tongue, driving me crazy.

"God, I've been craving your taste, stray," he rasps,

causing the sweetest vibrations against my sensitive flesh. "You taste so good."

My body hums and blood sings while my insides burn. It's always like this with him. So out of control. So powerful. So goddamn right.

I rock my hips, thrusting into his mouth, needing more. Needing him to push me over the edge.

Alexius groans, reaches underneath my ass, and keeps me in place as he sucks my clit. There's no more resistance left in me. At least not now. He's won this battle, and I let him consume and devour me. I'd let him slaughter me if he wanted to.

Pressure starts deep inside my core, and I tighten my grip in his hair.

"Don't come." His voice is a low growl of demand, and he lifts his face from between my legs, my arousal glistening on his lips, and my breaths become more labored as I watch him pull out his cock—the sight of his thick girth and pre-cum coated dick reminding me of how it feels to be fucked by him. My husband. The man who owns me body, heart, and soul.

There's no time to think. No time to speak. We're both consumed, frenzied, completely possessed, needing our fix as addicts do.

Slipping his arms underneath my legs, he curls his hands over my hips and yanks me closer to the edge. Closer to him.

"Oh, God," I moan, the velvet tip of his dick nudging at my entrance.

"Say it."

I press down with my hips, taking the head inside me.

"Fuck!" he growls, slamming a palm on the table, the thud exploding around us. "Jesus Christ. Say it, Leandra! Say you want me to fuck you."

Again, I buck and move, taking him deeper, his thick length stretching me, sliding against my inner walls. I need more. I need him to fuck me, but I can't speak. I can't form the words. All I can do is push down hard, taking all of him with one thrust.

"Fuck!" His fingers dig into my hips, and with a feral growl, he starts to fuck me. Hard. Deep. Relentless. He keeps driving into me, hitting my deepest part, stretching me with divine pressure that builds stronger with every thrust.

"This is what you want." He jerks my legs up and over his shoulders, wrapping an arm around my thighs to squeeze me tighter against him, wanting his dick deeper inside me. "You want me to fuck you. You want me to use you. You like being my filthy little slut, don't you?"

I moan.

"Don't you?" He slaps my thigh, and it's a searing pain that collides with the pleasure, forcing me to scream.

"Yes! Fuck, yes."

"Yes, what?"

"Yes, I like being your filthy slut."

My muscles tremble, our bodies a frenzied blur of lust and desire. And we are so lost...so fucking lost. There's no way we'll ever find our way back from one another. This is us. This is what makes us feel alive. The intensity, the loss of control. Without it, we're nothing.

I throw my arms back, reaching for the edge of the desk, gripping it tightly as the pressure builds, my back arching as I writhe.

"You feel that?" He slams into me, the pressure inside me a fusion of pain and euphoria. "How my cock fills your pussy so damn perfectly."

"Hmm-mm."

"Now, imagine a life without this. Imagine a world where I don't get to fuck you." He pulls out and sinks back in. "That's hell, Leandra. Us being apart is hell." Alexius' breaths are labored, his voice strained. "This is what makes us feel alive."

My hips buck, the back of my thighs flush against his abs. "I have to come. Can I come?"

"Yes, baby girl. Come for me."

My scream is lost, muted by the wild beat of my heart echoing in my ears as I shatter, falling apart as he fucks me so hard the wood scrapes against my back even through the fabric of my shirt.

The orgasm doesn't stir. It doesn't flow from every corner. It detonates, tearing me into pieces of ecstasy, a rapture that rids my head of thought and my heart of pain. With every thrust, and every time he hits my center, the pleasure intensifies, my legs trembling and muscles quivering.

"You have no idea how exquisite you are when you come." Abruptly, he grabs my legs, hooking his arms around my knees, driving into me deeper, harder, never letting up. It's unrelenting, savage fuckery, and I wouldn't want it any other way.

My body keeps shaking, and I swear Alexius is deeper inside me than he's ever been. I can feel his cock swell, and for a moment—a single fucking moment of dangling outside our reality—I want him to come inside me. I need him to come inside me just like he has so many times before. Like he did when he secretly planted his seed inside me.

He growls, his body rigid, and he throws his head back, sweat beading at his temples. Alexius Del Rossa is larger than life. Regal. Powerful. A man whose authority winds around your throat, demanding respect. How did I ever think I could fight him? Think I wouldn't fall for him, lose myself for him? It comes naturally for everyone around him to be drawn to him.

He slams into me, and then I feel it—the way his cock jerks as he empties himself in me, his cum hot and thick, filling my pussy and coating my thighs.

My walls clench around him, my pussy throbbing from the aftershock of a climax that crashed against every bone. It still hasn't dissipated. It's still there, lingering in my loins, tightened around every muscle.

Alexius lets go of my knees and falls on top of me, his breaths coming in rapid waves.

I keep my hands on the edge of the table, staring up at the ceiling as reality starts to creep in from every corner. As the adrenaline wanes, the pain returns, easing back to the place that makes it impossible to ignore.

My heart.

"You lied to me," I whisper. "And it hurts. God, it hurts so much."

Alexius shoots up, his face tight with concern. "Leandra—"

"Make it stop. Please," I beg, my heartache as uncontrollable as the tears streaming down the sides of my face. "Make it fucking stop!" I sob, and he pushes himself off me.

I flinch when his cock slips out, and I turn onto my side, clutching my belly and bending my knees, feeling like a pathetic mess—a woman with no fucking pride. If I had any, I wouldn't have given in so easily to the man who changed the course of my life without blinking.

I'm a wreck because of him, and there is no way I can fix myself. Nowhere I can run to get away from him and the constant reminder of how fucking weak I am, unable to stop myself from wanting him, yet unable to forgive him.

My mind is broken, and my body no longer feels like it's mine. I have two babies growing inside me, and a man who's staked his claim. I lost...me.

"Leandra?" Alexius places his hand on my thigh, and I swear to God it runs flames across my skin.

I can't take it anymore. I can't handle the pain.

I jerk up and slap his hand away. "Don't touch me." Tears lap into my mouth. "Don't you fucking touch me." I hit his arm this time. And then his shoulder.

I hit him again. And again. Faster. Harder. His chest. His stomach. His face. I can't stop. I keep hitting him, wanting him to hurt, too, because I'm hurting, and it's not fair for him to be in control while I continue to break.

It's not fair.

My hands turn into fists, and I want to break him. I want to break him the way he broke me. "I hate you!" I scream. "I fucking hate you, you motherfucker!" I hit him with everything I've got, aiming for his face, his chest, every part of him I can get to.

And he lets me.

He doesn't stop me.

He lets me hit him over and over again, simply pulling his face away every time I aim for his jaw.

"I hate you! I hate you! You son of a bitch!" My mind is caught in a fit of hysteria. I don't think about anything other than hurting him or feel anything other than my own pain. "You don't deserve to be a husband. You don't deserve to be a father," I scream, and finally, he grabs my wrists and jerks me close, squeezing my hands between his chest and mine.

"You think you're the only one hurting? You think you know what real torture is?" He brings his face so close to mine, the heat of his breath warms the tears on my cheeks. "Real torture is knowing what I did, I did out of fear of losing you because I love you, yet I'm being punished for it."

"What you did was fucked up."

"That's what love is, isn't it? That's what it does. It spawns fear, the kind of fear that debilitates the strongest of men." He yanks me even closer, his expression nothing but hard lines and stone. "It makes us do stupid shit because the possibility of being hated is much easier to live with than the idea of not being loved."

"There is nothing you can say that can make this right."

"You think I don't know that? You think I wanted to hurt you?"

"It doesn't matter whether you wanted to or not. What matters is you did hurt me."

"And I hate the fact that I did."

"Yet, you refuse to apologize."

"I can't apologize for doing something I don't regret."

"Jesus Christ," I mutter and try to jerk free, so I can slide off the table, but he steps in between my legs, pushing himself against me.

"That's the worst part of all this, Leandra. The fact that I hurt you, but I don't regret doing what I did. Maybe if you saw regret in my eyes every time you looked at me, you'd find it in your heart to forgive me. But I don't regret it. I don't regret wanting to make sure I don't lose you. Don't you get that?" He narrows his eyes, tilting his head to the side. "I would much rather have you here hating me than have you out there feeling nothing for me."

"Well, then," I jerk my hands free from his grip, "mission accomplished."

Hurt flashes in his eyes, and it's the first damn sign of him being human after all. But I can't acknowledge his pain while I struggle to keep from drowning in mine.

I brush past him and grab my pants, slipping them on without daring to look in his direction. I stuff my panties in my pocket before looking around, not recognizing the furniture. "Whose office is this?"

Alexius rounds the desk and picks up the broken lamp from the floor. "My father's."

A lump forms in my throat, and I gather the courage to look at him, catching a glimpse of his grief for a moment, but decide to leave before he manages to reel me in again.

I reach the door when he says, "Stay away from him."

"Who?" I glance at him.

"My cousin. Rome." He lifts his chin. "Stay away from him."

"Or what?"

He straightens his shirt, the mask of a cruel and powerful man slipped back in place. "I'll kill him."

I challenge him with a single glare, and he lifts a dark brow.

"Don't test me, Leandra. I think we've both established to what lengths I'm willing to go when it comes to you."

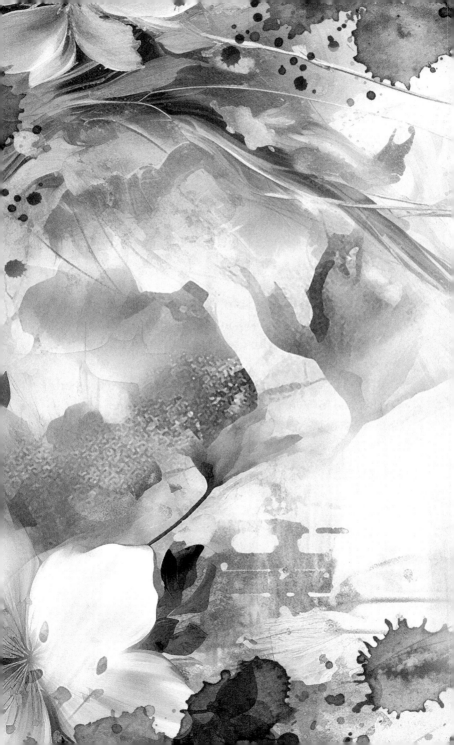

CHAPTER 8
ALEXIUS

The lamp shatters, and the lightbulb explodes off the walls.

"Fuck!" I grab the decanter and fling it across the room, joining the lamp on the floor in a dramatic wreck of glass and crystal. If Nicoli were here, he'd be whining over the spilled whiskey. It's probably a good thing—the alcohol seeping into the lacquered floors rather than my veins. I can hardly control myself sober; imagine what a fuck-up I'd be drunk. Everything went from total bliss to complete shit at the speed of light. One minute we were in Italy making love under the moon and prowling the halls of Mito, and the next, it's goddamn World War Three.

"Welcome to married life," is probably what my late grandfather would say. *"Good today, a royal fuck-up tomorrow."*

I pull my fingers through my hair, my muscles tense and strung tight. One would never guess I just had sex with my wife on my father's desk. Her butt-print is still sitting fresh on the pristinely polished mahogany. For days, all I could think about was fucking her, every filthy fantasy playing off inside my head every damn minute. But spilling my load inside her did nothing to satiate me. Nothing.

Instead, I feel worse than I did before. The way she looks at me with those pretty doe eyes, it's like she's no longer staring at her husband but rather the man who screwed up her life. God, I hate that I have to hurt her to keep her.

"Jesus," I mutter and fall back on the couch, rubbing my temples to block out the migraine threatening to drill a hole in my head from all this emotional fucking whiplash. How quickly happiness can turn into a total shit-show. It's like our trip to Italy never happened, our romance nothing but a fleeting moment in time.

There's a mess of broken glass and strewn papers on the floor. Good thing my mom's not here, or she'd have a fucking stroke if she saw my dad's office looking like this.

I wish he were here. Actually, I don't. He'd be so pissed off with me, I wouldn't be able to get a word in while he'd curse me in Italian, telling me how badly I fucked up.

The air in the room is still. Quiet. It still smells like the incense my mother would burn here—cinnamon, supposedly known for its ability to stimulate power toward wealth, prosperity, and business success. To four young boys, it meant pancakes.

It feels like yesterday when he summoned me here

while reading his newspaper. He was an old soul. No matter how many times Nicoli and I tried to get him to use electronics to catch up on world events, he preferred to hold the paper between his fingers.

He pulled the rug from under my ass that day by demanding I marry. I couldn't believe it when he gave me that ultimatum—get married and inherit the family legacy, or don't get married and watch my uncle take what's rightfully mine.

We sat here that day, arguing. I had to listen to him explain why taking a wife was vital to my role as head of this family and leader of the Dark Sovereign while he had to hear me argue that it was all bullshit. I didn't want to get married. I liked my life the way it was. Simple and uncomplicated. Taking a wife, having a pretty face at my side wasn't important to me. To me, that wasn't power or influence. It was just another responsibility piled on top of a thousand others.

But my father disagreed, and I can hear his words now as clearly as I did then.

"A pretty wife is not just a fuck toy, Alexius. She's not just a womb that carries an heir. A man's power is communicated and reflected off his wife's image."

Looking back, it seems he was right, but I was too stubborn to see it—too arrogant to admit that my father knew better. I can almost see him smirking at me now with that *I-told-you-so* look on his face.

Everything has changed since I married Leandra. It started as a mutually beneficial agreement supposed to be temporary, but now it's more. And as a man who didn't want to get married, I crossed a big, bold fucking line to ensure I stay married. She's made my life better in ways I never thought possible. Falling for her was not part of the plan. But when is it ever? People don't plan to fall in love. They just do. So here I am, a man who didn't want to get married in the first place. A man who had no desire to fall in love, especially not with the poor girl who waited tables at a dumpster diner. Yet that's precisely what happened. I fell in love with my wife, who now means more to me than anything else in the world.

Now I know what my mother meant when she said, *'Love is not the butterflies you feel when you're with someone. It's the brokenness you experience when you're apart.'*

That brokenness has been carving at my chest ever since Leandra demanded the distance that now festers between us. And I have no idea how to close the gap.

My phone rings in my pocket, and I sigh, closing my eyes, wishing the world would just go fuck itself. Can a man not take ten goddamn minutes to suffocate in misery without being interrupted?

Reluctantly, I pull out my phone. "Maximo."

"Where are you?"

I inspect my father's wrecked office, pausing at the desk I just fucked my wife on. "Aren't you supposed to know where I am at all times?"

"Oh, I know you're in your father's office. I was just being polite by asking."

"Did I not tell you to keep your eyes on my wife?"

"You did. How the fuck do you think I know where you are?"

I frown. "But if you're with her now, how do you know I'm still in my father's office?"

"Look out the window."

I get up and place my hand in my pocket when I look up at the second floor and find Maximo waving at me from the hallway window, looking like an idiot.

"Omnipresent fucker," I mutter with a grin.

"It's what you pay me for. Just doing my job."

I cock a brow. "You have that tone."

"What tone?"

"That tone that suggests you're going to tell me something that pisses me off." I turn my back on him and lean against the windowsill. "What is it?"

"It's about the other matter you asked me to keep a close eye on."

Warning prickles my skin. "What about it?"

"There's been a new development that might require us to call in a few favors."

"Jesus Christ," I curse, pinching my nose. "It's like someone opened the universe's asshole that keeps flinging shit my way."

"Want me to take care of it?"

I sigh, closing my eyes. "I'll go, but I want you with me. Get another set of eyes on Leandra and meet me out front. You can clue me in on what you know on our way there."

"Got it."

"Maximo?"

"Yeah?"

I rub the back of my neck. "Is she okay?"

There's a slight pause. "I don't think so."

"Fuck," I mutter, closing my eyes, my chest crushed under the weight of my wife's heartache. "I'll, ah...see you in ten."

I hang up and loosen my shoulders, rolling my neck from side to side, when Nicoli appears by the door, staring questioningly at the broken glass on the floor. "Bad day?"

"No. This is me on a good day."

"Ah. Sarcasm. That's my talent, brother. Not yours."

"Then what's my talent?"

"To fuck shit up, of course." He shoots me a cocky grin.

"Even though I'd love to stay and participate in some meaningless banter," I straighten and grab my coat, "I have shit to take care of."

Nicoli strolls in, shoulders squared and tie loosened. "Is there a problem I'm not aware of?"

"Yeah. But I'll go deal with it."

"Is it Rome?"

I shake my head. "No. This is something different entirely." I scoff. "It's not like I don't have enough shit to deal with."

Nicoli shrugs. "That's the thing about shit. It rarely comes in bits and pieces."

"Oh, my fucking God." I blink, unamused.

"Yeah." He winces. "Not my best joke."

"Listen," I turn to face him, "keep an eye out around here while I'm gone."

"You sure I can't help?"

"I got this." I slip on my coat as I stomp out the door, righting my tie and squaring my shoulders. I'm just hoping that whatever new development there is to this potential problem is something Maximo and I can get sorted out as quickly and as discreetly as possible. For this thing to blow wide open is the last thing we need.

It's the last thing Leandra needs.

CHAPTER 9
LEANDRA

I can still feel him everywhere as I rush to my room. When he had me locked up, all I wanted to do was get out. Now, all I want to do is go back in, stay there and hide. How ironic. Maybe that's his plan. Get me to lock myself up, so he's not the bad guy.

God, he's so infuriating, and everything he does is calculated and planned, manipulating everyone around him to move in a sequence he determines without anyone even realizing it.

Dictator. Asshole.

Or maybe I'm just full of shit and paranoid as fuck because my husband bred me like I'm some goddamn animal, got me pregnant and locked me in my room. It's so insane. I'm still having trouble wrapping my head around it. Only the occasional nausea and tender breasts manage to nail down the reality of it.

Now, the ache between my legs reminds me just how

fucked up everything is. My husband deceived and lied to me, yet I can't resist being branded by his touch, my twisted desire outwitting my broken heart. The lines have become so blurred that I no longer know where the lines are. I don't even know if there have ever been any lines when it comes to Alexius and me. I don't think so. Maybe that's why all this happened. We were doomed from the start because people can't just pretend that there are no limits, no lines that need to be drawn. You can't just unravel and expect there to be no consequences.

This is our consequence. It's both obsession and misery.

I wipe my tears with my sleeve while trying to keep the torn fabric of my shirt in place above my shoulder. Alexius didn't think twice before tearing at my clothes, and I didn't think twice about not stopping him.

I should have stopped him.

Should have. Could have. Didn't.

I'm such a fool. One touch, and he broke through my armor. One kiss, and I was done for. All the anger and pain in the world can course through my veins, and it would still not be strong enough to fight the pull between us. He was right when he said what we share can burn cities. But I'm afraid it'll destroy us first. Alexius is a powerful, enigmatic, confident man, which makes him a dangerous one, too—especially to me, a woman with his name engraved into her broken heart. A woman who, after all he's done, still feels connected to him in a way that seems almost supernatural. Surreal. I don't just love him. I breathe him as if I exist solely for him.

It's killing me.

I storm into my bedroom, slamming the door shut behind me. I know Maximo is out there in the hall. He's been following me, guarding me, and he's not being discreet about it, either. He doesn't care what I think or what others think. All he cares about is doing what Alexius tells him to do, just like everyone else around here.

I'm a sobbing mess when I reach the shower and turn on the faucet. I don't wait for the water to warm up before slipping underneath it, soaking my clothes. The cold water is like a thousand needles piercing my skin, but I need it, hoping it will drown out everything I'm feeling.

Heartache.

Regret.

Shame.

I should have fought harder. I should have resisted and not given in to the longing that's been tearing me open from the inside out. I should have been stronger, proving that he can't control me like he does everyone else around here. He doesn't have the right to. The last thing I want is to give him more power than he already has. But I gave him the confidence he needs to continue his display of control over me by giving in to my need for him. It doesn't matter what he's done. He's still the man my body yearns for, even if he is the husband who broke my heart.

Water soaks me, running from my scalp to the ends of my hair, and I imagine him sitting in his dad's leather chair with a smug grin on his face, smoking a cigar and drinking his expensive whiskey, gloating over his captive wife who couldn't resist him and his cock. It's a sickening thought. He admitted not regretting what he's done, bluntly saying he'd do it again. There's no remorse when I stare into his iridescent eyes, no apology in the way he looks at me. And letting him fuck me just proved to him that he could do to me whatever the hell he wants, and I'll still spread my legs for him. No matter how broken I am, I'd still be his filthy little slut.

Self-loathing slithers through the cracks, a dark cloud forcing all the oxygen from my lungs, a storm making it hard to breathe. I'm supposed to be stronger than this. I'm going to be a mother in a few months. How will I teach my children to be responsible and make good choices when I can't do it myself? The thought terrifies me. It spreads ice through my bones, squeezing my stomach, tearing at my insides with the teeth of barbed wire. It leaves me gasping for air, the bitter taste of fear on my tongue.

The water starts to warm, my wet clothes clinging to my body like the humiliation sticks to my soul. The ache between my legs reminds me of how weak and stupid I am. I made a fool of myself, and no matter how scalding the water is, it doesn't rinse off the shame.

I'm that girl again. The one who walked into this house for the first time, insecure, lost, and alone. The woman who felt scared and intimidated by a man who would become her husband. A stranger. A man who would ultimately take her heart and make it his and own her in every way.

All I've ever wanted was to know peace—to wake up every morning as blissfully happy as I was when I fell asleep. I might be the stray he picked up off the streets who somehow managed to survive a dark childhood. But I'm still just a girl who dreams of love and a happy ending. And I was so sure I had found that with Alexius, but I was wrong. So wrong.

I fall to my knees, water cascading down my face as I sob into my palms. Steam builds up around me, and I'm left to drown in my pain. I just want it to stop. I want to stop hurting. I want to stop feeling like I'm mourning. Like I got someone taken away from me. Someone who holds my soul in the palms of his hands.

Someone who says he loves me, yet his actions speak otherwise.

Someone who says he can't bear to lose me, yet everything he does pushes me away.

Someone who can mend and break my heart at the same time.

Someone I love so much, it's happiness and agony all at once.

Alexius.

I clutch my stomach, my cries hacking out of my chest. Every bone is being broken repeatedly, and I can't stop it. I'm being cracked wide open, bleeding fucking tears, and it only worsens with each passing second.

"Please make it stop!" I scream, crippled with agony, water pelting down. I can't breathe. There's too much pain weighing on my chest. "Please stop!"

"Leandra!"

"Make it stop!"

Arms wrap around me, and I choke on a breath when I'm clutched tightly. "What the hell is going on?"

I open my eyes and look up into soft, familiar brown eyes. "Isaia," I cry.

"Jesus Christ, Leandra." He wipes wet hair from my face, rocking me back and forth. "What did he do, huh? What the fuck did my brother do?"

New sobs erupt as if my wounds are torn open and clawed at. "Help me," I plead, folding myself into him. "Make it stop, please."

"I got you." He cups my cheek, tightening his hold around me. "It's okay, baby girl. I got you."

"I don't want to hurt anymore."

"Just breathe." He rests his chin on my head. "Deep breaths."

"I love him so much, Isaia."

"I know you do."

"And I don't know how to make it stop."

"Motherfucker doesn't deserve you," he mutters, his gaze following the trail his finger leaves on my cheek. "You're too good for my brother."

I bury my face in his chest, his shirt soaked, both of us flat on our asses in the running shower. It's comforting having his arms around me, but somehow it only makes me cry more. It's as if his being here, holding me, consoling me, is permitting me to be sad—giving me approval so I can acknowledge that I'm broken and allowed to weep.

I have no idea how long we sit there or when I stopped crying, but my entire life feels surreal as Isaia picks me up, helping me out of the shower. Everything is hazy. It's as if my mind decided to shut down, silencing my thoughts. Paralyzing me.

"Here. You need to dry yourself off before you freeze." Isaia holds out a towel, but I don't have the strength to take it. I'm exhausted, like I just lived a thousand lifetimes in an hour.

"Okay," he sighs. "Let me help you." He reaches for the hem of my shirt, his eyes searching mine for permission. I nod because I have no choice but to accept his help. I'm useless on my own, a complete fucking mess, and I'd probably stand here freezing to death without knowing it's happening.

Isaia moves closer, easing my wet shirt up my waist, and I lift my arms so he can ease it off and over my head. He throws my shirt in the hamper, and I don't care that I'm standing half naked in front of him. I'm too numb to care.

Keeping his steady eyes fixed on me, he takes the towel and starts drying my hair, squeezing water from the ends, gently fluffing moisture from the strands, rivulets of water running down my back. His white shirt clings to his chest, every roped muscle showing through the wet fabric, puddles of water gathering around his feet.

"I'm sorry," I whisper, and he stills.

"Don't."

"I really am."

"I don't know what my brother's done, but I already know you have nothing to be sorry about."

"I should be stronger than this, but I'm not."

"Leandra," he tips my chin up so I look him in the eye, "keep quiet and let me take care of you."

I purse my lips tightly, suppressing a fresh waterfall of tears. He knows how much I need this—how much I need to let go of the strength I've been grasping on to so I can keep myself from falling. I want to let go. And right now...he's here to catch me.

He moves to stand behind me, and I close my eyes as he eases the towel down my back. I shiver as the cold starts to slither across my skin, and Isaia places the soft towel over my shoulders. I take it between my fingers, pulling it tighter around me.

"You trust me, right?"

I glance halfway over my shoulder, nodding as I suck my bottom lip into my mouth.

He crouches and reaches beneath the towel, his touch calm and light, fingers brushing against my waist. Slowly, he slips my pants down and steadies me as I step out of them, water dripping from the fabric. Nothing about this makes me feel uncomfortable. All I feel is comfort. There's a sense of solace with him here, and for a moment I don't want him to ever leave. Somehow, the pain seems...less now that he's here.

I hang my head down as he straightens behind me,

and I clasp the towel tighter in front of my chest. I'm sure I have my tears and emotions under control...until he wraps his arms around my waist, hugging me against him so tight, his kindness overwhelms me.

The walls break, and I sink into him, letting go of all the strength I've tried to hold on to, and I fall. I'm breaking while Isaia holds on to all the pieces. It's liberating and freeing to let go, knowing someone is keeping me from hitting the ground. I'm not alone, and the relief is almost too much.

"You're always there," I say through tears, remembering how he walked me down the aisle. "You're always there when I'm alone."

"I care for you, and I always will." His arms tighten around me, and he rests his forehead against the top of mine. "I'll always be there for you, Leandra. No matter what."

"Thank you," I whisper, appreciating what he means to me more than words could express.

Abruptly, he sweeps me into his arms and carries me into the bedroom, placing me on the bed. I roll over on my side, clutching a pillow, and I swear I can smell Alexius on the silk—a fusion of wild spice cologne and sex. He's everywhere—on my sheets, my skin, my heart... inside me. Alexius is inside me. His babies are growing inside me. Twins.

Does Isaia know? He hasn't been around at all lately. I don't know what Alexius has told him.

The bed dips beside me, and Isaia gathers me in his arms, pulling me up so he can cradle me against his chest as he leans against the headboard. His being here soothes the storm raging inside me for too long, leaving me exhausted, so I close my eyes as calm sweeps over me.

"Sleep, baby girl," he whispers, placing a chaste kiss on my head. "I'm not going anywhere."

For the first time in so long...I sleep.

CHAPTER 10
LEANDRA

"Motherfucker!"

I'm jerked awake with Isaia getting hauled off the bed, Alexius cursing and swearing, yanking Isaia around. I sit up in time to see him launch Isaia across the floor, headfirst into the wall.

"Alexius!" I scramble to my feet, but I can't get near him as he grabs Isaia by the throat, his knuckles turning white as he squeezes, Isaia gasping for breath. "Alexius, stop!"

Maximo rushes in, and Alexius shoots him a deadly glare. "You, get the fuck out, now. This is between my brother and me."

A second passes before Maximo does the one thing he does so fucking well. Obey Alexius' every demand.

He leaves the room and closes the bedroom door behind him, my heart about to break out of my chest.

Alexius snarls in Isaia's face, shaking him violently.

"I'm going to kill you," he snarls. "You fucking jealous prick."

"Then what the fuck are you waiting for? Do it. Fucking pussy," Isaia challenges, and I'm nothing short of terrified, ice penetrating my lungs.

"You've always been a little shit stirrer, haven't you, little brother? Always loving to rock the boat and fuck over the apple cart. What, does it make your dick hard acting like an entitled cocksucker?"

"I'd rather be an entitled cocksucker than a lousy fucking husband."

"Motherfucker!" There's a sickening crack of bone as Alexius hits Isaia across the face, blood bursting from Isaia's mouth. The rage on Alexius' face is terrifying. His eyes are wild and feral, his lips pulled back from his teeth as he lets out a beastly growl like he's about to rip out Isaia's jugular. I'm suddenly frozen. Shocked. I can barely take a breath watching Alexius consumed with a fury so heated, it blurs the air around him.

"You fucking piece of shit!" He rears back, and his fist flies out again, crashing against Isaia's jaw, blood splattering against the cream-colored walls like fresh red paint.

"Stop this, please! Both of you," I cry, and Isaia sees an opening, landing a punch into Alexius' midsection, causing him to hunch over. Horrified, I suck in a breath, but the air doesn't reach my lungs. It's stuck in my throat, my heart bashing against my rib cage.

Alexius staggers back, and Isaia lunges at him, grabs him by the collar, and swings him around, slamming his back against the wall, and I swear the earth fucking quakes from the blow.

Isaia leans into his brother, jerking at his collar. "You're so fucking blind, man. Selfish prick. You can't see what's right in front you."

"What? That my brother fucked my wife?"

"Nothing happened!" Isaia snaps.

"Like fuck it didn't. You expect me to believe that after I find you in bed with my wife while she's wearing a motherfucking towel?"

"Yes. That's exactly what I expect you to believe because it's the goddamn truth!"

"Go fuck yourself." Alexius manages to push back, and I watch in horror as they grapple with one another, trying to tear each other apart like rabid animals frothing at the mouth.

Red-hot tears spill down my cheeks. "Alexius, he's telling the truth, I swear."

"You expect me to believe that?"

"Yes! Nothing happened."

"He won't believe you," Isaia grits out. "He's been searching for a reason to kick my ass."

"What do you expect? You're in love with my wife, you son of a bitch!" Alexius strikes his fist into Isaia's gut. Spit and blood bursts from Isaia's mouth as he topples over, and Alexius lands his knee on Isaia's chest, swings his arm, and a nauseating sound ruptures the air as he hits Isaia again, his knuckles stained with his brother's blood.

"Would both of you just stop!" I cry, but I'm being

ignored like I'm not even there, Alexius' eyes blazing like he has the wrath of hell burning behind them.

There is so much blood, thick and violent, spurting from Isaia's mouth and nose, his chin, neck, and chest covered in crimson.

"I've fucking had it with you." Alexius' voice is hard and guttural, a menacing chant of brutal cruelty. "I tried, Isaia. I fucking tried. But you just couldn't keep your filthy motherfucking hands off my wife."

"He didn't touch me!" I yell, but Alexius doesn't even look in my direction. It's like I'm invisible to him, his vision nothing but tainted red with hate and violence, all aimed at his little brother.

Everything is happening so fast, my mind is spinning, and my heart is pounding with panicked speed. But I'm paralyzed. I can't move. I can't think. I'm fucking terrified by the scene in front of me. Terrified of him. I've never seen Alexius like this before. Enraged and possessed, anger swirling thickly in his eyes, his face contorted in hard lines of rage.

More blood spurts from Isaia's mouth, and Alexius snarls, pushing his knees harder against Isaia's chest.

Isaia chokes and coughs, trying to get his brother to move. "Nothing...happened other than you fucking up...again."

Oh, God, Isaia. Shut the fuck up!

"Me?" Alexius wraps a hand around Isaia's throat, his large hand encompassing Isaia's neck. "You have some nerve, you arrogant fuck! But that's your problem, isn't it?

Thinking you can do whatever the fuck you want because life owes you a goddamn favor." He tightens his grip. "Or is it the fact that I won't share her that's completely fucked with your head?"

"Go fuck yourself!" Isaia grabs at his brother's hand, trying to get him to let go, but Alexius simply tightens his hold, Isaia's mouth gaped open and cheeks reddening from the struggle for air.

Oh, my God, Alexius is going to kill him.

"You walk around with your grim fucking face, hating everyone and everything, always trying to find ways to piss everyone off. Well, brother, you fucking pissed me off. You happy now? Is this what you wanted? Me losing my shit and beating the crap out of you?"

"Alexius, please," I crawl back onto the bed on all fours, afraid to get too close. "Please stop this."

He's too angry, a maddened God who can't see anything other than chaos.

Abruptly, he lets go of Isaia's throat, and Isaia gasps and coughs, gagging as he gulps down air while Alexius pulls him to his feet.

"I tried to give you the benefit of the doubt. I tried talking to you, warned you to stay away from her, but you wouldn't fucking listen. You just couldn't help yourself, could you? You just had to have what's mine."

With my hand in front of my mouth, I watch as he shoves Isaia against the dresser, hitting his back against the edge, a pained shriek tearing past Isaia's lips.

"Alexius, don't." I sniff, leaning back, ice slamming

into my chest when he looks at me with a glare that cuts straight through my heart.

"Did you let him fuck you?"

"Is that what you think of me? That I'm some whore who would fuck around while I'm pregnant with your babies?" I yell out the last few words. "Do you really think that low of me?"

"You've been hellbent on fighting me, waiting for a chance to fucking leave."

"Because you lied to me!" I shout. "You tricked me, made a goddamn fool of me, and you expect me to, what? Forgive you? Pretend that everything's okay, and act like our lives couldn't be more fucking perfect?"

"I expect you to love me, for better or worse. Remember that?"

"Are you seriously reminding me of our wedding vows? What about 'to love and to cherish?' Do you even know what that means? To cherish someone?" I sit up on my knees. "It means to protect and care for, to hold dear and that you recognize that person's worth. So, tell me how your lies and you manipulating me show that you recognize my worth. That you hold me dear."

His anger burns red on his cheeks as he leans closer, shoving his finger at his chest. "I did it because I love you. How many times do I have to tell you that?"

I scoff. "Probably a million times more because it's all bullshit."

Alexius pulls his lips in a thin line, his blue eyes turbulent with a violent storm as he leans close. "Did He. Fucking. Touch you?"

"No." My nostrils flare. "Nothing happened. I was in the shower crying over you. Having a fucking mental breakdown because of you. And all your brother did was help me. He comforted me, and I fell asleep. That's it."

"She's telling the truth, man," Isaia growls, spitting out a mouthful of blood.

Panic and fear coat my tongue with a rancid taste, a black cloud wrapping around the three of us with an ominous grip.

Alexius is a wall of menace, his shoulders widened and chest expanding. There's blood on his shirt, his knuckles covered in red. Right now, he's an animal—untamed and unpredictable. It scares the shit out of me, but there's something about the feral look in his eyes. How his authority melts the air around us. How his sheer dominance fills my breath and steals my will. It wakes something in me—something I have no right feeling. Not now. Not like this. It's insane.

Alexius bites his bottom lip and shifts his death glare between Isaia and me.

God, please let this be over. But the way his eyes darken, his frame growing larger, says it's far from over.

There's blood on Isaia's face, one eye already starting to swell. But he stands his ground, his stance wide and threatening. Challenging.

"I want to kill you, brother. I really do," Alexius threatens.

"Then fucking do it, you pussy."

"Isaia, no," I warn, knowing the last thing he needs to do right now is challenge his brother.

Alexius bares his teeth. "I'm not fucking stupid. Ending your life won't be worth the shit it'll pile on my goddamn doorstep. And kicking your ass until you're blind won't do a thing other than fuel this sick obsession you have with my wife because that's who you are. An arrogant, stubborn pussy." Alexius leans his head to the side. "There's only one way you'll realize that she's not yours, and that's if I show you who she belongs to."

My heart stops, and everything goes cold as I watch Alexius rushing toward me. I yelp when he grabs a fist full of my hair, pain searing my scalp.

"Alexius, what are you doing?"

"Talking to him didn't help. Kicking his ass won't help, either. The only thing that'll help is if I show him."

"Alexius, stop!"

His touch is hard and unforgiving as he pulls me to my feet, yanking the towel from my body, leaving me in my underwear while my breaths come out in short bursts. He doesn't give me a second to try to figure out what the hell is happening when he jerks me around, forcing me to bend forward, pushing my face into the mattress.

"Alexius, stop." Isaia's voice is a low rumble. "This has gone too far."

"Maybe if you see me fuck her, it'll sink into that thick skull of yours that she is not yours!"

"Alexius," I plead breathlessly, a cold shudder spreading up my spine when I hear the sound of his zipper.

"My brother watched me play with your cunt. Now he can watch me fuck you, too." He drags his cock along my ass, and I swallow when heat spreads between my thighs, my sudden arousal slick and warm.

He's hard. He likes this.

So do you.

No, I don't.

An ache spreads from my pussy up to my core.

Fuck. Yes, I do.

"What do you think, brother?" Alexius says behind me. "You think you'll be able to move the fuck on and leave my goddamn wife alone if you see her body break for me?"

Isaia readies to launch himself toward us when Alexius pulls out his gun, aiming it at Isaia, bringing him to a sudden halt, the metal glinting with murderous intent.

"What the fuck are you doing?" I scream at Alexius.

"What am I doing? I'm two seconds away from putting a bullet in my little brother's head."

"God, stop this!" I cry.

"I'm afraid God ain't here, stray." He keeps his gun aimed at Isaia, whose glare is shooting holes through Alexius' face.

I'm paralyzed with fear, but buried beneath it, something stirs. A faint flicker. A warmth slowly heating to burn. Is it...desire? Wicked wantonness corrupting me?

No. No. No.

He lets go of my neck, and I don't move when he slides a finger through my slit. I don't attempt to scramble away, and I have no fucking idea why. What I'm feeling is so hard to explain. My logical side says I should *want* to get away from him. I should *want* to run. But I don't. Right now, I don't want anything more than to stay, to let him use me to prove his fucking point to his brother. I'm his filthy little slut, as he has reminded me so many times before. And I love it. I love whoring my body to him. Surrendering. Letting him do whatever the fuck he wants to do to me because, in the end, I'll love it. I always do.

My hips buck, and my arousal coats his finger.

"Look at that," he says, and I can practically hear the smile on his face, "you want this, don't you, stray? You want me to show my little brother who you belong to."

"I know!" Isaia spits out. "I know she's yours. For fuck's sake, Alexius. Why do you think she was in the shower crying her heart out? Because of you!" There's nothing but venom dripping from Isaia's tongue. "She loves you."

"But that's not the problem here, is it? It's you!" Alexius' voice slams against the ceiling. "You are the fucking problem, the fact that you would fuck my wife if given half the goddamn chance. Your juvenile infatuation with her has gone too far, and it ends today."

He drags the head of his cock through my pussy before nudging at my entrance. Euphoria explodes and smothers the fear, waking something sinful and wicked in my veins. His thick cock stretches me as he slowly opens my walls by sinking in deeper, and I swallow a moan. It's punishing and exquisite at the same time. My head is a mess. I'm consumed and fucking horrified. But there's no denying the thrill and adrenaline rushing through me, my arousal coating my inner thighs, slicking up Alexius' cock. Every muscle in my body is pulled taut, welcoming the blunt pressure—anticipating, wanting, craving—yet my stomach crawls with how fucked up this is.

"Alexius, you better kill me before I kill you," Isaia spits out.

"I love how you assume she doesn't want this," Alexius taunts, slipping farther inside me while still aiming his gun at Isaia. "As you can see, I'm not holding her down anymore. She's on her knees, bent in front of me, because she wants to be."

I'd beg him to stop, but something's changed. My fight is gone, replaced with a thirst for what would be the most wicked display of ownership, and my body is all for it.

"Her pussy is wet, brother. Her cunt isn't resisting me. It's throbbing, sucking me in deeper." His palm comes down hard on my ass, the searing pain causing me to moan. "Tell him, stray. Tell him I'm not doing anything you don't want."

I look at Isaia, and the moment our eyes meet, he sees it. He sees the need, the wicked desire, the fucked-up lust that I'm trying so hard to fight, but it's just too strong.

"Say it," Isaia demands, his dark eyes a deadly war. "If you don't say it, I will kill him. I swear it."

"I want this." My voice shakes, and my body trembles because of what I just said, admitting how screwed up I genuinely am.

"Say it again," Isaia orders, and my gaze drops to his

crotch. He's hard too. *Jesus Christ. What the fuck is this?*
"Say it!"

"Yes!" I blurt. "I want this."

"What exactly is it that you want?" Alexius says, pulling out and dipping the head of his cock back into me.

With my eyes pinned on Isaia's, I whisper to Alexius, "I want you to fuck me." I swallow. "While your brother watches."

"There you have it." Alexius drops the gun right next to me, and his fingers sink into my hips, jerking me back as he slams forward, his thick girth stretching me. It's an onslaught, and I'm moaning and gasping like a whore, all the sensations building to a point where it hurts.

Alexius' grip on my hip tightens, but his arm trembles. Is it still anger? Rage? Or is it him losing control? All I know is every time he slams into me, burying himself to the hilt, he's fucking euphoria into me, letting it consume me.

I cry out when he slaps my ass before driving back into me, so hard it hurts with a satisfying ache, sending waves of sensations down to my fucking toes.

"Do you hear that, brother?" Alexius says. "You hear her crying out for me?"

Isaia doesn't move, and Alexius pushes deeper, thrusting faster, fucking me deeper, pulling me down on his cock. I can't stop the moans that drip from my lips like toxic honey. I can't ignore the ecstasy that clings to my skin, penetrating my bones, the silk sheet rubbing against my knees and elbows, static crackling on my skin.

"You watching, brother?" Alexius says with rapid breathing, and my thighs tremble.

"Yeah, I'm watching," Isaia mutters, but his voice is different. It's low, gruff, but there's a tenor of something...*sensual* that ripples from his words.

"Good. I need you to watch every second. I need you to see how much she loves how I fuck her. It's because she's mine, and she knows it. I know it. Now it's time for you to know it, too."

Like a piston, Alexius starts to fuck me, skin slapping against skin, our rapid breaths growing louder, and sweat clings to the back of my neck. The friction of his cock and the vulnerability of being watched by his brother add fuel to the fire burning in my core, threatening to turn me into ash—a pile of fucking dirt, nothing but air.

My eyes find Isaia, and he's adjusting his crotch. Even Isaia can't deny it. No matter how much he thinks he hates his brother or how much he wants to kill him, he sees what Alexius and I are together.

Fire.

Our eyes meet for a second before mine roll closed, my body in complete surrender, with Alexius pummeling into me with unforgiving and unrelenting thrusts.

I fist the sheets, feeling the cold steel of the gun against my knuckles. I wrap my hand around it, holding my finger on the trigger. I didn't think it was possible, but I'm more turned on than I have ever been. Even that night at Mito watching Alexius play with another woman's pussy doesn't compare to this. The adrenaline. The danger. Fuck. Is it possible to get off on danger? To get off on the power it gives me while I hold it in my hand, Alexius' cock wrecking my pussy with delicious ferocity?

Yes. Yes, it is possible.

That's what Alexius is doing, what he's been doing all along. Getting off on the power he has over me. Just like the control he holds over me is my addiction, it is also his. That's how similar we are. That's how compatible we are. Each thriving on power…one surrendering it while the other holds it.

"Fuck," Alexius growls. "I love how hot your pussy is around my cock. You ready to come for me, my little slut?"

"Yes," I whimper. I'm so fucking ready.

"Who do you belong to?"

"You."

"Look at my brother when you say that. Who do you belong to?"

I glance up and into Isaia's eyes. "You."

"What is your name?" My ass slaps against him as he fucks me.

"Leandra," I murmur. "Leandra Del Rossa."

He snakes an arm around my hip, reaching between my legs and finding my clit, applying pressure that makes my entire body tremble. "Whose wife are you?"

"Yours." I'm still looking at Isaia.

"Who gets to fuck you? Who is the only one who will ever make you come?"

I whimper before sucking in a breath. "You. Only you. Always."

"Good girl." He circles my clit harder, faster. "Now, come for me, stray. Let my brother see how fucking beautiful you are when you come around my cock."

I detonate, and my body shudders as my climax rips me wide open. It's so intense, so powerful, tears well up in the corners of my eyes, and I scream—loud and desperate, needing relief from the pleasure crippling me with violent waves. My mind is bent, broken, and I'm nothing but coiled pleasure that has my body tied in knots.

"That's my girl," Alexius coos as my pussy pulses around his cock. I expect him to follow suit, to come inside me, but instead, he pulls out, and hot liquid spurts on my ass and back, Alexius jerking his dick, marking me with his cum.

I close my eyes, holding my breath, trying to come to terms with what the fuck just happened.

Now that the ecstasy is withering, fear is starting to trickle in again. There's no saying what will happen now, how we'll deal with this, because whatever this is, it's not right. It's not fucking normal.

But it's us.

For a moment while my mind is still shattered, I'm forced to be honest with myself by admitting something I've been denying for too long. The truth is, I would eventually forgive him for the tricked pregnancy. It's inevitable. What Alexius and I have can't be ignored, no matter what the outside factors might be. But after this, what happens now? This just turned into the most morally gray shit Alexius and I have ever done. It's fucked up, but the thrill still lingers in my veins, and it's indescribable.

But it's wrong. I can feel it corrupt me.

I have no idea where my strength comes from. It's like a burst of adrenaline floods my veins, and I grab the sheets, launching up, twisting around, and slap him across the face.

His palm is on his cheek, the smack slicing through the room, his dark gaze instantly gone, replaced with the blue iridescence I've come to love more than life itself.

"You bastard," I whisper, and his only response is solemn silence. "I'm your fucking wife," I say, rage rippling off my tongue. "Your wife. I'm not your goddamn toy, a possession you can play with whenever you want to prove a point. I'm not a prop for you to use whenever you feel like having a pissing contest with your brother."

His top lip curls up like he's contemplating whether to push a dagger through his own heart or mine.

I grab his hand, tears now streaming down my face, and place his palm flat against my belly. "I'm pregnant. I'm carrying your babies inside me. I'm going to be the mother of your children."

"I know that."

"Do you?" I push his hand harder against my stomach. "What you just did, what *we* just did, is twisted and warped beyond words. And it will never...*never* happen again."

"You fucking liked it."

"You're right. I did. That doesn't make it any less fucked up. We're going to be parents, Alexius. You're going to be a father. You'll be responsible for them, have to take care of them...*and* me." I place my palms on his cheeks. The cold, hard anger that was on his face moments ago is now gone. "You and me, we're going to be the people our kids look up to. And is this really who you want to be for your kids? A jealous, over-the-top, possessive fucker who can't control himself. A man who beats his brother and then fucks his wife in front of him because you somehow convinced yourself that you own me. Not love. Own. There's a big difference, and you need to realize that because soon you're going to hold your son or daughter in your arms, and I pray to God that when that day comes, you're a man worthy of that title." I let go of his cheeks. "Worthy of being a father."

I drop my hands at my sides, licking my lips. "I'm done with this shit. Done. Because I know I want to be a mother worthy of the title, too."

A stillness drops over us. It's cold as ice—overwhelming, weighted, dragging down around us with an unease that crawls in my blood. It's a wall blocking out everything other than the words I just spoke—the dose of reality I injected into both our veins.

My tears have stopped, but my heart silently cries, drowning my lungs while I hold my breath.

Alexius rights his pants and straightens his broad shoulders.

He looks over my shoulder at Isaia, and his expression remains stone. But I see the whirlpool of emotions in his eyes, the weight of it as reality sets in. His eyes meet mine for a single second before he turns and stomps out, the slam of the door behind him causing me to flinch.

I bite my tongue to keep myself from gasping, to stop the tears from resurfacing while my heart just...dies. Because deep down I know...nothing will ever be the same.

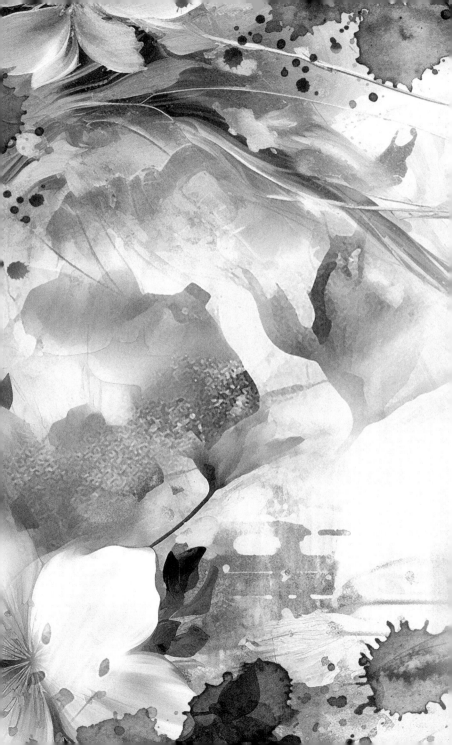

CHAPTER 11
LEANDRA

Tap water runs over my hands while I stare at my reflection. My mind is numb. But my body isn't. It aches everywhere, especially between my thighs. Alexius was ruthless and unrelenting. His touch was cruel and unkind like he didn't give a shit about me. All he cared about was fucking me, marking me in front of Isaia—a twisted display of ownership.

But no matter his intentions, he still made me come. My most sordid part liked it, and now I have to choose to believe he knew that, which is why he didn't stop. I refuse to think of the alternative—I refuse to let that thought take root. If it does, there's no telling what it'll destroy.

"You okay?" Isaia touches my shoulder, and I jolt, water splashing on my shirt.

"Shit. Yeah. I'm just..." I wipe my forehead with my arm. "I'm just on edge. Um...I thought you left?"

"I did. But I had to come back and see if you were okay."

I suck my bottom lip, unsure if I want him here or not. I'm a ticking time bomb right now, and I could burst into tears and collapse into a heap of misery at any moment. The last thing I want is to have anyone around to witness my breakdown.

"Did he hurt you?" Isaia's voice is soft, almost like he's afraid of the answer.

I shake my head. "No. Not physically, anyway." I reach up and touch his chin, studying his cuts and wounds, but Isaia leans away from my touch, grimacing.

"Sit," I order, indicating the edge of the tub, grabbing a hand towel. "Let me clean that."

"You don't have—"

"Sit down, Isaia."

His mouth pulls in a straight line as he hesitates, but then walks over to the tub and sits down, leaning with his elbows on his knees, clutching his fists together. "Shit went too far today."

"It did, but it's done now. We can't change it." I wet the towel then place it against the side of his face, lightly patting at the crusted blood.

"I'm sorry." He doesn't look at me. "For, um...for the part I played in all of it."

An image of him standing there while Alexius fucked me flashes in my head. He was hard as his body responded to the scene in front of him, his eyes dark with lust as he watched. The look on his face was that of dangerous desire and filthy intentions. Just like me, he lost himself in the moment of carnal sin, no matter how fucked up it was.

"It's okay," I breathe out. "Don't apologize. We were all kind of...out of it. High on adrenaline and endorphins and all that shit."

He's still not looking at me, keeping his eyes downcast. "I have to ask, and I need you to be honest with me."

I lean back.

"Did he do..." He clears his throat and shifts, running his palms down his jean-clad thighs. "Did he do anything to you that you didn't want him to?"

There's a sharp stab in my gut, and I swallow hard. "Are you asking me if he raped me?"

"Jesus," he mutters under his breath, rolling his head back, letting out a low groan like the thought pains him.

"No, Isaia. He didn't." It's the truth. "And I'm pretty sure you wouldn't have just stood there if he did."

"God, this is so fucked up."

"I'm serious." I start wiping along his jaw. "I know you. I know that if you doubted it for a second, you would have stopped him."

Isaia grabs my hand, stilling it next to his face. There's a heavy silence between us. So many unspoken words. But everything that needs to be said is heard in the quiet.

I squeeze his hand, ease my palm out of his grip, and continue cleaning his face.

"You're pregnant," he says, and I pause for a moment, holding my breath before nodding.

"Yes."

"You and Alexius are having a baby."

"Babies."

His gaze cuts to mine, his brows snapped together. "Twins?"

"Hmm-hmm."

"Wow. I wasn't sure whether I should congratulate you or not, but now I just kinda feel sorry for you."

I snicker. "I feel sorry for me, too."

"Was it planned?"

"Not by me."

His face pulls with confusion, and I decide to redirect. Isaia is already too caught up in my relationship with Alexius. There's already too much animosity between the brothers, and the last thing we need is for Isaia to know what Alexius did.

"I mean, it was a surprise...to both of us," I continue.

"Is he being an asshole about it? Is that what made you so upset with him?"

"God, no. In fact, it's because of him..." But I stop short, biting my tongue.

"Because of him, what?"

"I, um..." I reach for the scar behind my ear, then gather my hair and pull it over my shoulder. "We're both still trying to wrap our heads around it."

There's another deep silence between us, but the sound of the storm outside makes it bearable. Through the window, I can see the snow angrily carried by the rough winds, a white blanket forming on the outside windowsill. Some days, I wish I could get lost in the snow and pretend it's a different world. Today is one of those days.

Isaia keeps his head down while I take care of his wounds. The blood on his face is thick and sticky, making it difficult to clean without hurting him.

The more I inspect his wounds and nurse his cuts, the more guilt eats away at me, a dull ache fiercely gnawing at my stomach. I hate that I'm the cause of all this. If not for me, none of this would have happened. Alexius and Isaia wouldn't be hating each other right now.

"I'm sorry he did this to you."

"Don't. It's not your fault my brother is an asshole."

"Isn't it?" I look into his brown eyes, touching the wet fabric against the cut on his lower lip. "I'm the cause of this conflict between you and him."

"Nah. We've been going at each other's throats since I was old enough to call out his bullshit. Our parents groomed him to be the head of this family one day, and all that extra attention, constantly telling him he'll be in charge, has given him an ego the size of Texas, thinking he controls everyone around him."

"Maybe. But have you ever considered that maybe he's controlling because of the weighted responsibility he carries for this family?"

Isaia frowns at me. "Are you defending him?"

"He's my husband. I'd be a shitty wife if I didn't."

"Yeah, because he's been such an *amazing* husband to you," he sneers, sarcasm dripping from his words.

"Stop." I slap his shoulder lightly. "I think that

sometimes he overcompensates by making his presence known because he feels like the outsider."

Isaia snorts. "Ah, I can promise you that's not it. Alexius has no idea what it feels like to be an outsider in this family."

I lean my head to the side. "And you do? Because your brothers are in control of the Dark Sovereign, and you're not a part of that?"

His jaw tics, and he rubs his fists together, his shoulders tense and muscles taut. "I know it sounds petty, but it's not so much about me wanting the control they have, but more about being a part of something that defines this family." He shrugs. "Sharing something with my brothers."

My heart swells with empathy. He's not a man hungry for power; he's a brother and son who yearns to be a part of the family dynasty. Alexius and Nicoli have sat beside their father for years. Now Caelian has joined them, and that leaves Isaia on the sidelines.

"I mean," he straightens his shoulders, "I know Alexius and Nicoli want to get rid of my uncles, make the Dark Sovereign a Del Rossa legacy alone."

"So, Alexius plans on including you?"

"That's what he said, yes. But with Rome being back, it's not that simple anymore."

"Because Rome is taking his father's place?" I walk to the sink and rinse the towel, and Isaia cocks a brow.

"You're really clued-up about everything. Too clued-up."

I shrug. "Mirabella is quite...informed."

"Of course." He rolls his eyes. "I forgot she's like a ninja when it comes to snooping. Do you know how hard it was for my brothers and me to sneak girls into this house or come home drunk with Mira always seeing fucking everything? She was constantly blackmailing us." He grins and winces at the same time, touching his lip. "Ouch. Goddammit."

"You okay?"

"Yeah. It's a beast of a split, but thankfully not the first time I got my ass beaten by one of my brothers." He winks playfully. "What doesn't kill you..."

A fierce sense of blame roils inside me. And I hate it. I hate feeling responsible for the wedge between him and his brother that's growing bigger every day.

I stare down at my hands. "How do we fix this?"

"What? My face?"

"No." I snicker. "This...thing between you and him. You're brothers. You shouldn't want to kill each other all the time."

"Clearly, you didn't grow up with any siblings. Brothers want to kill each other all the damn time."

I toss the towel at him. "I'm serious."

"So am I." He smirks. "Do you know how many times the four of us have kicked each other's asses? Multiple times. It's what we do."

"You're not in love with me, are you?" I just fell out of the air with that one.

He scoffs. "You psychoanalyzing me now?"

"Maybe."

"I'd prefer you don't."

"You're not in love with me," I say again because I know I'm right.

"Yeah, well, everyone else seems to think I am."

"You don't."

He lowers his gaze, wiping at his hands. "For a while, I thought I was."

I lean against the vanity countertop, crossing my arms. "But?"

"But..." He stands, still clutching the bloodstained towel. "After the whole Micah thing, losing Melanie, and keeping my distance from you for a while, it somehow put things into perspective for me." He drops the towel in the sink and moves up to me. "From the moment I walked you down the aisle, I knew we had something. A connection. I didn't know what it was. I couldn't figure it out. And after everything that happened," he looks into my eyes, "the night you watched Melanie and me, and our little show on the patio with Alexius—"

My cheeks burn as I stare down at the floor, recalling that night.

"Hey." He touches my chin and forces me to look at him, his eyes warm and kind. "Don't do that. Don't be shy about it. We're all adults here. Sex is a big part of who we are as humans, and as long as you're not hurting anyone with your desires, you shouldn't spend your life being shy about it or feeling shame because of it. All you'll be doing is fighting against your own nature."

I clear my throat. "Yeah. I know."

"Good. At least that's one thing my brothers and I all agree on."

"Of course you do. How else would you all be able to share women?" I smirk, and he merely stares at me, unamused.

"So, anyway. I guess I was trying so hard to put a label on whatever it is you and I have, I ended up convincing myself that I'm in love with you."

"Which you're not."

"No." He shakes his head and takes my hand. "But I do care for you, Leandra. And I'm not wrong about this connection we share. It's there, but it's more like, I dunno, like we're twin souls or something."

I grin. "Twin souls? BFFs?"

"Not the time, smart-ass."

"Okay, okay." I hold up my arms in mocking surrender, and he smiles. A tiny dimple appears, and I realize that Isaia smiling isn't something I've seen a lot of. It's a good look for him, a shade of light cracking through his dark, hardened exterior.

But his smile fades as quickly as it appears. "I need to know that you're okay."

"I'm okay," I assure him.

He shakes his head. "You answered that too fast. I'm serious."

"So am I. I'm fine, Isaia. Really."

He reaches out and touches his thumb on my jaw, and there's a flash of something kind and tender in his eyes. "You're a bad liar, you know that?"

My eyes start to prickle, and I look away, biting my bottom lip to keep myself from crying.

He steps back. "Just know that I'll always be here for you. And when it comes to my asshole brother, I will always be there to defend you."

Isaia's words offer some comfort, and it's a reminder that he's been there for me all along. Always stepping in when I needed him. But doing so has also affected his relationship with Alexius, and it's a difficult pill for me to swallow.

I turn my back on him, staring down at the silver-clawed feet of the tub. The last thing I want right now is to lose the battle against the tears threatening to break through the facade I'm desperately trying to keep. "I don't need you to defend me when it comes to your brother."

"After what happened today, I'm not so sure about that."

"Alexius is." I crane my neck, staring up at the ceiling, searching for the right words. "He's slightly possessive when it comes to me."

"*Slightly*? My brother almost crossed a line today."

"Newsflash." I turn to face him again. "Your brother has been crossing and cutting lines with me like he's hitting cocaine."

"Do you want to leave?"

His question takes me by surprise, and I gnaw the inside of my cheek.

"If you want to leave, I'll help you."

"Isaia—"

"I'm serious. If you want to leave this place, leave this family, I'll help you."

I let out a deep sigh. "I'm not gonna lie, there are times I want nothing more than to leave and forget about everything that's happened here." I place my hand on my belly. "But leaving is not that simple anymore."

"I hate that my brother is hurting you."

"Me too."

"Asshole," Isaia mutters, placing his hands on his sides.

"Yeah. He is an asshole. But I love him. I love him more than I know how to deal with, and whenever he does something so fucking stupid or selfish, a part of me hopes I'll just wake up one morning and realize I don't love him anymore." I glance down at my hands, the hole in my heart a throbbing ache. "God knows it would be much easier if I'd stop loving him."

"You and me both."

Our eyes meet, and we both snicker, the moment giving us a slight reprieve from the weight that's been bearing down on our conversation. Out of the four Del Rossa brothers, Isaia always comes across as the dark horse. The tortured soul. But right now, at this moment, I'm catching a glimpse of a different Isaia—one who carries a light inside him, a light he hides so damn well. It makes it easy for me to want to confide in him. Almost too easy.

"I should probably go," Isaia says, brushing his hand through his disheveled hair. "You okay?"

"Yeah." I smile. "I'm okay."

He touches my elbow gently, his thumb brushing across my flesh. "I know I haven't been around lately, but that's going to change, starting today. So, if you need anything, I'm here."

"Thank you. But it's probably best if we keep our distance until things cool off."

"Nope. Not happening. I plan on being here for you, Leandra, and if my brother doesn't like that, he can go fuck himself."

"I don't want to cause more trouble between the two of you."

"Hey." He takes my shoulders and leans back, taking my gaze captive. "You didn't cause this. It's not your fault, and I won't let you blame yourself for it. So just...take it easy. For you and the babies."

I shoot him the warmest smile my cold soul can muster and merely nod.

"Good. Try to get some rest." He turns and walks out, and I have no idea how long I stay there staring out in front of me, yet not looking at anything. My mind is a maze, and I don't know which way to go or which path to take. I'm so sick and tired of always making the wrong decisions and going right instead of left or left instead of right. I'm always thinking about what would have happened if I had chosen differently.

What would have happened if I didn't run that day my father brought a friend home? What would have happened if I had chosen to lie to the cops that day? Maybe my father would have stopped his friend, realizing what he was doing was wrong, that he loved his little girl too much to whore her out for drug money. Maybe that would have been the day he changed for the better. Turned his life around so we could be a happy family. Maybe I should have given him a chance, and things would have been different.

Maybe...

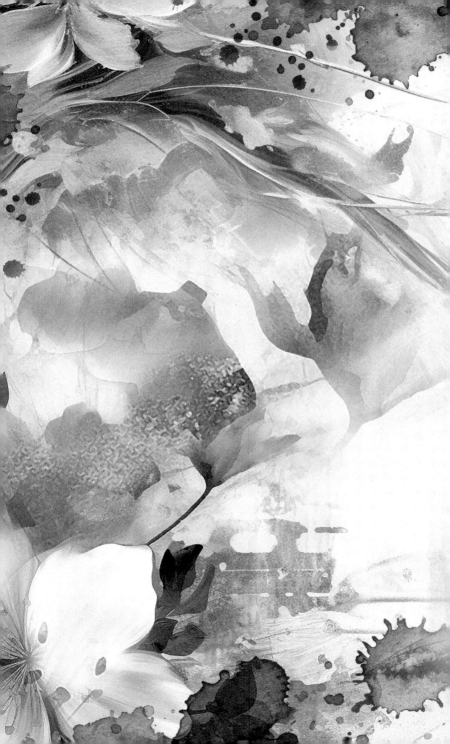

CHAPTER 12
LEANDRA

I haven't seen or heard from Alexius since the shit storm in my bedroom. He hasn't been on the estate since—that I know of. I've gone to his bedroom a dozen times, but there's no sign of him.

As the days drag on, it's not just my unease that's growing, but my belly, too. Every time I look at myself in the mirror, the round of my stomach seems bigger than it did before. My clothes no longer fit the way they used to. Everything is changing except for the sinking feeling in my gut. Alexius isn't here. He's gone, and I have no idea where he is. He's not taking my calls, and neither Caelian nor Isaia knows where he is. I suspect Nicoli knows, but he's not talking. Maximo still keeps an eye on me, but not to the degree he was before. It's like Alexius is giving me space.

Too much space.

At first, it felt like I could breathe again with him not around, like the dark cloud that hovered over me dissipated, but it was fleeting. A phantom relief. In the mornings when I wake up, there's that split second between dream and reality, a moment when my mind is trapped in a place where everything is okay. That Alexius is here, and we're together, and I could just turn around and find him next to me. Feel him. Smell him. Touch him.

But then reality would slam down on me like a thunderous weight of pain that penetrates my soul.

I'm alone. He's not here. If I turn around, I won't find him next to me. I can't nestle against him, smell him, touch him, or feel him. I can't wrap a leg over his waist to straddle him, wake him up with a quick morning fuck.

Alexius is not here. He's not here, and nothing about it is okay. I don't feel the freedom I thought I would without him clamping down my life. I don't feel free or light, but rather anchored to a misery that only grows stronger. Darker.

Something is wrong.

Of course, something is wrong. I can't remember when something was last right. But this feels like a different kind of wrong. Like he's left me. I can't explain it. There's this gaping hole inside my chest, and it's growing bigger every day without him around. His absence weighs heavily on my chest, and it's becoming increasingly harder to breathe. I'm terrified and anxious for reasons I can't articulate because it makes it all too real—like it's a step closer to being set in stone. Every day is an eternity without him here, and I can't sleep, I can't eat, I can barely keep a conversation without choking up.

I'm not supposed to miss him. I'm not supposed to want him to come back. I should pack my shit and run while he's not here to hold me prisoner anymore. This is what I've wanted, isn't it? To be able to leave, to be free of him. Yet now he's the one who left, and now I no longer want that freedom. Alexius has always been a mindfuck, but this is the worst one.

My mind is warped and bent, and I know I should still hate him after everything he's done. But I don't. Not even a little. In fact, the betrayal I felt, the anger, it doesn't compare to the pain I've endured since he left.

I'm constantly haunted by his absence, like I'm swathed in darkness, waiting for the black hole to swallow me.

Between dusk and dawn, there's a lifetime of loneliness. It's the time of day I dread the most. At night, everything feels a thousand times worse. The sound of the winter's howl, the whistle as the wind cuts and slashes against the house and windows creates a solemn foreboding in the middle of the night. But the winter is dead—even if there are a hundred different deafening sounds outside, it's all lifeless—just like these halls...just like me.

I wonder if he's at Myth, spending his time there instead of here. The thought makes my skin crawl. But how can I not think about it? Alexius is a hunter, a predator with a sexual prowess that's unparalleled. He's a skilled lover, and seduction seeps from his pores, making him lethal to any woman. Imagining him at the Del Rossa sex club with other women is not a petty insecurity.

Whenever I close my eyes, I have to will myself not to picture him sitting on a red velvet chair, a sexy woman with an hourglass figure and sleek blonde hair on her knees in front of him, sucking his cock and licking his balls. I see him bending over some pretty brunette, driving into her so hard her tits would bounce and her screams would peel the plaster off the goddamn walls.

Fuck!

I can't. It drives me crazy, turning my disturbing thoughts into murderous inclinations.

I bury my face in my palms, biting back the urge to scream as I drown out the light. The dark magnifies the longing and sharpens the blades stuck in my heart. Bone-numbing fear slithers across my skin as soon as the day turns black, and it doesn't leave until sunrise. But, even then, it leaves remnants of insecurity and uncertainty. What if he left me? The babies? I'd not only be alone but broken too. And it scares me. The thought of never seeing him again, never feeling his touch or his kiss, never feeling his warmth whenever I'm in his arms—it terrifies me. And I hate it so damn much. I hate it more than the days spent locked up in this room. I hate it more than the thought of Alexius coming inside me with the goal to fucking breed me. Trap me. Leave me with no way out.

I hate not being with him more than I hate everything else.

One would think I'm crazy for still loving him after everything that's happened. Maybe I am. Maybe I'm that psycho woman who would rather be a glutton for punishment than a wife without her husband. Maybe I'm the obsessed one, and not him. In the end, the heart wants what the heart wants, and mine wants him.

The emptiness is tiring, and I feel lost without him. Drifting. Roaming these halls like a ghost, no longer feeling like I fit in. We've spent weeks going at each other's throats, and I've been grasping at everything to continue fighting him. But now...now I'm starting to think I was wrong because what I felt then while locked in my room doesn't compare to what I'm feeling now. I need him with everything in me so he can keep me from drowning, because right now, I feel like I'm going under, and I don't know how to keep myself afloat.

The heartache is too much. It's debilitating, and with every passing minute, it only gets worse. There are times when I think my chest is being cracked in half, my stomach getting ripped out of me, the pain unbearable without him.

How did this happen? How did I go from wanting to leave to being desperate for him to come back?

Outside, the trees are bare, the grass and flowers are gone, and there's hardly any sign of life. There's a thick blanket of snow draped over the estate grounds. It's so white it hurts my eyes every time the sun peeks past the looming clouds. While staring out my bedroom window, I think about my dream, about Alexius chasing me through the trees. Even in my dream, I was conflicted. I wanted to run, but I wasn't sure I wanted to leave. I wanted to get away, but I didn't want him to let me go. I wanted him to catch me, and in my dream, he did. It felt so real, and disappointment flooded my system when I woke up realizing it was a dream, and not only was I alone, but Alexius and I were torn apart.

"You're awake."

I turn halfway and give a feeble attempt to smile at Mira before continuing to stare out the window. "Have you heard anything?"

"No. You?"

I tighten my arms around myself. "Nothing."

She slips in next to me, and usually, I'd feel comforted when she's close. But not today. Not since he left.

"And Nicoli won't budge. Neither will my brother."

"If Alexius doesn't want them to talk, they won't."

"Loyal bastards. They're pissing me off." Mira shifts from one leg to the other, crossing her arms.

"I'm sure they hate this as much as we do."

"I doubt that very much. Maximo loves showing me who has the higher rank between the two of us. And Nicoli just enjoys being a prick too much."

"Yet you can't—"

"I can't what?" she snaps, her pointed glare daring me to finish that sentence.

I frown at her, leaning my head to the side as I study her face—rose-blushed cheeks, delicate cheekbones, stunning green eyes framed with dark curled eyelashes, and pouty, heart-shaped lips always painted a sultry red. Mira is beautiful and not in an hourglass figure or a super thin runway model kind of way. More like a Marilyn Monroe kind of way. Timeless, classic, and a beauty that would never fade simply because of the elegance she exudes in such a natural way. I can see why Nicoli can't keep his eyes off her when they're together in a room. But I don't understand why he chooses to force this distance between them. It's like he's hellbent on acting like she doesn't exist.

"Oh, right. I almost forgot the reason I came looking for you." She turns to face me. "The doctor is here for your checkup."

"Here? Now?"

She nods. "He's waiting for you in the room Alexius set up."

"Oh, my God." I place my palm on my forehead. "I forgot about that. He told me he had that done since I'm not allowed off the estate."

Mira's eyes flash with pity, but I shrug it off. Me being trapped here has taken a back seat at the farthest corner of my mind right now. All I can think about is Alexius and where he could be and when he's coming back. *If* he's coming back.

I place a palm on my belly. "Alexius isn't here for the ultrasound." A profound sadness washes over me. "Mira," I look at her as I struggle to keep the tears at bay, "I'm a mess."

"Oh, God, no. Come here." She brings me in for a hug, brushing her palms down my back with comforting strokes. "You're not a mess. I think, considering the circumstances, you're far from it." She leans back and looks at me. "You're a strong woman, Leandra. You're still dragging your ass out of bed every morning, getting dressed, and smiling at everyone here while your heart is shattered, and that's true strength. God knows I wouldn't be able to do it."

"But I can't," I whimper, tears finally rolling down my cheeks. "I can't do this alone, Mira."

"No, no, no. Leandra, you will not go through this alone. I'll be here with you every step of the way."

"I know. But I need...I need him." My hands shake as I wipe tears from my cheeks, my emotions cracking me wide open. "Not long ago, all I wanted was to get away from him. I was angry. Hurt. And all I could think about was leaving and never wanting to see him again. But now," I wipe at my tears, "now that he's gone, I can't fathom the idea of doing this without him. I don't want to do this without him. And I'm so scared. So, so fucking scared. I need him, Mira." I choke on a sob. "I need Alexius, and I don't know what I'd do if he's no longer a part of my life. I love him so much, every part of me aches."

"I know you do." She smiles, reaching out and brushing away a tear on my jaw. "And everyone can see it. Everyone sees how much you love each other. Now, I don't know what happened, and I respect that you don't feel comfortable sharing it with me."

"It's not that I'm not comfortable with it," I say. "I just...I don't want to drag other people into our mess and cause more conflict within this family than I already have. Look what happened with Alexius and Isaia."

"Stop." She takes my hand, her eyes soft with sympathy. "Conflict is bound to happen when you have four, five male lions living under the same roof. It's a cesspool of testosterone, and them going at each other's throats is unavoidable. Don't beat yourself up about it, okay? You need to start focusing on yourself. Take care of yourself. You have two babies growing inside you, and that's what's most important in this entire equation." Her blonde hair slips down her shoulder as she leans her head to the side. "As I said, I don't know what happened between the two of you, but you need to sort it out and find a way to get past it. You both owe it to the children you'll be bringing into this world."

It's not an order or an accusation or meant as criticism. I can see it in her gentle eyes and soft expression. Her every word was spoken with love and compassion, meant to encourage.

I smile and pull her back in for a hug. "You are the best friend I could ever ask for."

"Remember that when I accidentally, on purpose, burn the pair of moccasins you're wearing."

"Hey." I look down at my feet. "These are warm and comfortable."

"No. Those are ugly and ancient."

"Ancient?" I lift a brow. "I bought these a month ago."

"Oh, my God. Was it one of those dodgy social media ads?"

I chuckle and lose the moccasins, pulling on a pair of black leather boots.

Mira's eyes shimmer, and her lips curl at the corners. "Better. Next week, we'll work on the tights."

"How about I just never shop on my own again?"

"Now, that's the best idea you've had in a really long time."

"Hmm-mm."

"Hey, listen," she weaves her dainty fingers through her blonde hair, "I know it won't make it any better or anything, but if you want, I could stay with you during the ultrasound. If you want."

There's a twinge in my chest, the thought of Alexius not being there pricking my already bleeding heart. But it is what it is, and no matter what happens between Alexius and me, I'll have to go on. I'll just have to survive—if not for me, for the lives growing inside me.

I give her the warmest smile my aching soul allows. "I would love that."

"If you don't mind, Mira, I'd like to go with Leandra."

Both Mira and I turn to find Isaia standing by the door.

"If that's okay with you, of course?" he asks, staring at me with his dark brown eyes. Eyes I've always found comfort in, and probably always will.

"I, um..."

"Oh, shit," Mira blurts and saunters to the door, heels clicking across the floors. "I forgot I have to talk to the chef about Christmas dinner. Isaia," she pats him on the chest, "be a gem and go with Leandra, would you?"

"I just said—"

"Thanks." She lifts on her toes, plants a kiss on his cheek, and then wipes the lipstick stain off with her thumb. "You're a star."

Isaia and I just smile and roll our eyes at Mira's attempt to not make this awkward.

"Thank you," I say, fiddling with my thumbs. "But you don't have to."

"I want to."

I sigh, my heart as heavy as my reluctance to even go for the damn ultrasound, but I muster a smile, reminding myself of what Mira said. This is not about me.

"Your face is healing well," I say as I walk out and close the door, joining him in the hall.

"Yeah." He touches his bottom lip, the large cut now only a tiny mark. The grotesque purple bruises have faded to a yellow-green shade, and I'm thankful Alexius didn't hurt him any worse than he did.

He holds out his arm, and I hook my hand in the curve. "Let's go meet my two nephews."

"Or your two nieces." I shrug.

His brows curve. "*Ooor*...my two nephews."

"Why not two nieces?"

"Two nieces will mean I have to kill a profound number of teenage boys, and I'd prefer to *not* do that since it'll pave my way to hell so much faster."

Our laughs fill the hall, and I welcome the comfort of it—a short reprieve from the bone-crushing anguish I've been living with. We walk into the room prepared with all the equipment needed, still laughing, and I stop when I see him.

"Alexius," I whisper. The stark white of the room sharpens the color of his eyes, highlighting the cerulean blue ring around his sapphire irises. My heart stops when our gazes meet, unable to beat as I take in the sight of him. With his hard, chiseled face and dark hair, he has a look that's effortlessly sexy, and I don't know how it's possible, but he's more striking than I remember. Regal. Powerful. Majestic. A force to be reckoned with and a man who commands without saying a single word.

"Alexius," I whisper.

He's standing at the back of the room, his stance wide and hands tucked in his slate gray pants. The fabric of his crisp white dress shirt flows over his shoulders, hugging the contour of his body, the collar unbuttoned, and sleeves rolled up mid-arm. Thick veins rim his arms, the muscles roped and defined.

I'm the girl at the diner again, seeing Alexius Del Rossa for the first time—experiencing the demand of his presence for the first time, and it makes me shift from one leg to the other.

Alexius lifts his chin, his full lips pulled in a thin line. "You can leave, brother."

"Oh, he was just...I didn't know." Oh, God. "Um, I just...we didn't think you'd be here."

He's still looking at Isaia. "Leave. Now."

Isaia turns to me, his pointed stare a loud, direct question, and I simply nod, letting him know it's okay, after which he leaves without sparing his brother a single glance.

The door closes, and Alexius moves. The soft rustle of his shirt and the weight of his footsteps is intimidating but familiar, and it gives me a trickle of hope.

I can feel the heat of his eyes on me as he comes

closer, his presence a powerful charge that, to some, is heavy and cold, but to me, it's warm and inviting, making me lean into it, wanting it to envelop me.

My heartbeat echoes in my ears, and I hold my breath as he takes another step. I can smell him—the wild spice of his cologne mixed with a scent uniquely him. I miss having it on me. I want it to steal my air, so he's the only thing I breathe.

"Are you okay?" The tenor of his voice has me taking a sharp inhale.

"No." I swallow. "Where have you been?"

He squares his shoulders, leveling me with a confident stare. "I've been taking care of a few things."

"Things you can't take care of while you're here?"

"I'm here now."

"That's not—"

"Mr. and Mrs. Del Rossa," the doctor greets as he walks in. "Sorry to have you waiting. I had an urgent phone call."

Alexius presses his lips together, and when he severs the connection by looking away, I want to cry. "Doctor, I pay you a fuckton of money to take care of the mother of my children and to be available to us twenty-four-fucking-seven. So I'd appreciate it that whenever you're here, you pretend like you have no goddamn life out there. Understood?"

A sheen of sweat gathers above the doctor's mustache. "I do apologize, Mr. Del Rossa. It won't happen again."

"Good." Alexius moves to stand on the other side of

the examination table and looks my way. "I'd like to see my children now."

His jaw has a tic, and hard lines crease his features. And while our eyes remain locked, there's only one thought trapped inside my head...

He didn't refer to me as his wife, and he always refers to me as his wife.

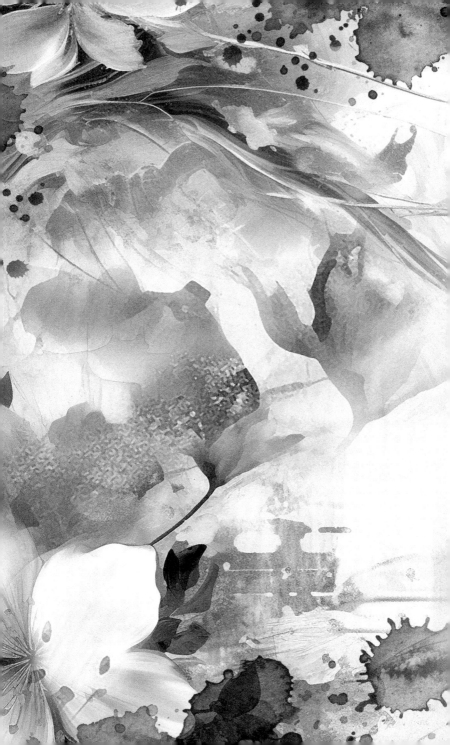

CHAPTER 13
LEANDRA

There are no words to describe what I'm feeling. My heart is full even though it's bleeding. How is that possible? How can I feel complete and torn at the same time? I have no idea, but I'm looking at the monitor, and I see two tiny figures so clearly, and I can hear their heartbeats. It's the most beautiful sound I've ever heard. With each thump, the broken pieces of me slip back in place. The gaping hole I've felt for weeks narrows, and the void dwindles, and I haven't felt this whole in so long. It's almost...magical.

My world has been turned upside down and inside out, but while I stare at the image of my growing babies, all I feel is this immense wonder and love, bursting with new hope for the future. How could I not when the two little beings I'm carrying are a part of me and a part of the man I love? Everything else fades away, and nothing else matters. The past? Inconsequential. Old grievances? Trivial. My own pain? Insignificant.

After the first ultrasound, I was overcome with fear. But now, all I feel is awestruck by the life growing inside me. I feel hope, and life no longer seems so dark. I don't know what changed. Maybe it's the way Alexius clutches my hand, his fingers interlaced with mine. He squeezes lightly every time the doctor points at the screen, telling us what we're seeing, how our babies are growing.

Maybe it's because he's here. No. Not maybe.

It *is* because he's here. It's not just seeing my babies and hearing their heartbeats that make me feel complete. It's him, too. It's because we're together.

I glance up at him, and my heart expands. It's easy for Alexius to hide his emotions with his unreadable expression. He always has me guessing what he's feeling and thinking. But now, he can barely disguise the awe and wonder in his eyes as he stares at the monitor. Everything I feel reflects in his blue irises, and he looks at me like I'm everything. Like I'm all he needs. We're no longer two pieces of this love story. We're one, and the life inside me is proof of that.

"Everything looks great," the doctor says, and Alexius and I look at him. "So far, you have a healthy pregnancy, and your babies are growing just fine. Have you decided if you'd like to know the genders or keep it a surprise?"

My breath catches in my throat, and Alexius' eyes grow wide. "You can see that?"

"It's still early at fourteen weeks, and it's never one-hundred-percent accurate, so I always caution my patients against having their mind set on the gender based on what we see on the ultrasound. But I'm seventy-five percent sure of the gender of this little one here." He points at the monitor. "The other one is a little shy today, but hopefully, he or she will give us a better view at the next ultrasound." He looks at us. "So, do you want to know?"

Alexius looks at me questioningly, and I'm sure my heart is about to leap out of my chest. I shrug. "I don't know. Do you want to know?"

Alexius pulls a palm down his face, his eyes fixed on the monitor. "I think I do." He looks at me. "Do you?"

I'm bursting at the seams to know whether we're having at least one boy or girl. My curiosity gets the better of me, so I nod. "I think I do, too."

The doctor smiles, still pointing at the baby in question. "It looks like you'll be having at least one little girl."

I suck in a breath, and the room goes quiet. "A girl?"

"Looks like it," the doctor confirms, and I look at Alexius, who's still staring at the monitor, speechless.

"Oh, my God." I swallow back tears.

"A girl," Alexius whispers like he's almost afraid to say it out loud, his eyes gleaming with what looks like shock and amazement.

The doctor removes the transducer from my belly, wiping away the remaining gel. "I'll see you again in four weeks' time. If you have any questions or concerns, you have my number."

"Thank you, Doctor," I say, and Alexius simply nods as the doctor leaves the room, almost knocking over one of the staff standing outside the door with a clean set of towels.

"Not now," Alexius barks, and the poor man scurries out like a pack of rabid dogs was just sent after him.

I give him a disapproving stare. "Was that really necessary?"

Alexius lets out a low grunt, and I merely shake my head, not wanting anything to ruin this moment. "I can't believe it. This is so surreal." My heart is racing, bubbles of excitement popping inside my stomach. "One of them is a girl," I whisper in disbelief, and I want to cry and laugh simultaneously. "We're having a little girl."

"Yeah." Alexius lets go of my hand and turns away, staring out in front of him with his palm over his mouth.

I pull my shirt back down and throw my feet off the side of the bed as I sit up. "Are you okay?"

He doesn't turn to face me, and the sinking feeling slowly trickles back.

"Alexius, say something."

"I, ah..." he turns to face me but doesn't look at me, "I have to go."

"No!" I leap off the bed and put myself between Alexius and the door. "No. I'm not letting you leave again. Not before we talk."

He still can't look at me and turns away, stalking to the other side of the room.

"Where have you been?" I ask, pushing myself away from the door.

"I told you. I've been taking care of some things."

"And what things need taking care of with you not being here with your family?"

"Leandra," he rubs his temples, "I can't do this now."

"You don't have a choice. We're doing this now," I demand. "And stop giving me some bullshit excuse about dealing with things. You're avoiding me. You're avoiding talking about what happened. But disappearing and pretending we don't have shit to work through will only make it worse."

"How in the name of fuck can things get any worse?" he yells, finally looking at me, his eyes wild and fierce, but their radiance is gone. "Tell me how things can get worse, Leandra."

"By letting it fester," I snap. "If we don't fix this now—"

"We?" He arches his brows. "*We?* There is nothing *we* need to fix."

"How can you say that?"

"Because *you* didn't do anything wrong." His voice slams against the ceiling. "I fucked up! Not you. Me."

I stare down at my hands, fidgeting with my fingers. "I don't think we're beyond fixing. We still have something worth saving."

"How? Huh? How the fuck do we fix this?" He slams his fist into his chest. "I hurt you. I fucking hurt you, and I don't know if it's something we'd ever get past."

"First, I'm assuming you're referring to what happened with Isaia, because you didn't feel any guilt after getting me pregnant and locking me up in my room. So, no. You didn't hurt me. Not that day, anyway.

163

Second," I step forward, both desperation and determination pulsing through my veins, "after what we just shared, after seeing our babies, hearing their heartbeats, knowing we're having a little girl, I know we can get past it. Just don't disappear on me again."

"I had to leave." His wipes his fingers down the side of his mouth and over his chin. "I had to get the hell away from you because I can't look at you without thinking about what I almost did, how close I came to hurting the one person I love more than anything in the entire goddamn world."

"If it's your conscience fucking with your head, maybe you should try apologizing. It's the only thing that lulls that inner voice reminding us of our regrets."

He gives me a deadpan look.

"Yeah, I know." I cross my arms. "A Del Rossa never apologizes."

"It was never my intention to hurt you."

"I know that."

"I wanted to kill my own brother, for Christ's sake." His jaw is clenched as he spits out the words. "And not in some juvenile brother-kicks-younger-brother's-ass way. I wanted to really kill him. Coat my hands in his blood after tearing his motherfucking heart out. Even now," he drops his arms at his side, "when you walked in here with him, I nearly cracked my fucking teeth trying not to lose my shit with him again."

"Alexius, listen," I step closer, "you need to stop. Isaia is not in love with me."

He scoffs, placing his hands on his hips.

"He's really not," I continue. "He thought he was, but he realized that what he feels for me is a very strong friendship. But it's not love." I shake my head lightly. "I can't explain it, and neither can he, but we've had this special bond ever since he walked me down the aisle. But he's not in love with me, I swear it. To him I'm more like the sister he never had."

"Somehow that still doesn't make me want to kill him any less," he bites out, his jaw clenched. "I don't think you understand the magnitude of what I feel for you, how protective I am of you, how determined I am to give you everything you want."

My heart skips a beat.

"Ask me for ashes, and I will burn the world to the ground. Ask me for blood, and I will slaughter every man from here to Bangkok and bring you their hearts. There is nothing I wouldn't do for you."

I rush to him, reaching up and cupping his cheeks in my palm. "Just love me, Alexius. That's all I want."

"Me loving you *is* the problem," he says, placing his hands over mine. "I didn't see it before now. Lying to you, switching your birth control and getting you pregnant, I didn't regret doing that because I love you. Locking you in your room, keeping you here like a captive, I didn't regret that either because I love you." He eases my hands from his face, his thumbs pressing gently in my palms. "Beating my brother, holding a gun to his head while fucking you in front of him like you're nothing but a goddamn animal...I regret that *because* I love you." He scoffs and lets go of my hand, taking a step back as he

165

rubs the back of his neck. "And today, hearing my babies' heartbeats, seeing their tiny little figures on that screen, finding out I'm having a daughter," he lifts his brows, a tormented hue of blue glimmering in his irises, "what kind of father will I be to a little girl if this is how I treat their mother?"

To see the pain in his eyes is unbearable; it's twisting my insides. I want to take it away. I want to touch the sadness I see in him and drown it, destroy and take it away even if it means carrying it myself.

"I know a lot has happened," I murmur, trying to calm the storm with a gentle tone. "I know it's going to take time—"

"What is this, anyway?" he interrupts me. "For weeks, all you wanted was to get away from me. And now you, what?" He gestures toward me. "You had a change of heart? A moment of enlightenment?" His voice is laced with sarcasm, and it fucking irks me.

"I was angry, and rightfully so. Yes, you hurt me with everything you've done, but while you were gone, shutting me out, I realized that it doesn't matter what happened or what lines were crossed. I love you. I fucking love you, and nothing will change that." I stomp my foot, and I'm aware of how childish that might be, but I'm so frustrated, angry, scared, and fucking annoyed because just a few moments ago, I was high on excitement and filled with hope, only to have it squashed.

I half expect his mask of indifference to settle on his features, but there's this faraway look in his eyes, as if he's somewhere else. "Love is not the butterflies you feel when you're with someone. It's the brokenness you experience when you're apart."

My heart hiccups, and I place a palm on my chest. "That's beautiful."

He looks at me and shrugs. "It's something my mom said to me once."

"She's a wise woman."

"Yeah." He takes a sharp inhale. "But I'm pretty sure it's not that simple."

"Nothing about our marriage, about our relationship, is simple, Alexius. But there's one thing that became painfully clear and simple to me in this room today." I walk closer again, refusing to look anywhere except in his eyes. "I would rather live with the burden of loving you than suffer without you."

Abruptly, he reaches out and pulls me against him, the air bursting from my lungs, and I quiver with a sudden surge of urgency to have him claim me again—to bend my body to his will and make me his filthy little slut again.

His fingers weave into my hair, and my lips part as I welcome his possession. His eyes are molten silver, and he pins me with a fervent stare of a thousand different shades of blue. I recognize the desire that burns within their depths, and it makes me hyperaware of my own need, arousal pooling between my legs.

He drags a finger leisurely down my chest, over the swell of my breast, stilling for just a moment when he reaches the peak of my pebbled nipple. I hold my breath, anticipating his next move, wanting him to palm my breast, suck the hard nub, and ravage my body as only he can. But his gaze falls lower, his hand now tracing down my abdomen and flattening his palm on my stomach. "Your belly has grown."

"It has. I've also grown impatient." It's a challenge, and he sees it as such, pulling his lips in a snarl, his blue eyes flashing with a familiar hunger I've come to recognize so easily.

"You are everything to me, Leandra." His voice is low and rough. "Nothing will ever change that. But—"

"But nothing," I say. "You are mine, and I am yours. That's all that matters, and if you don't see it, then you're the stupidest fucking man I know."

His mouth collides with mine, his kiss fire on my lips, and I return it with everything I have in me. It's not just about loving him or about him loving me. It's about needing each other, unable to exist without one another. He needs to understand that what we have is more important, stronger than any 'what ifs' held in the past.

My palms are flush against his chest, and a moan echoes off my lips onto his when he rolls his hips, his cock hard and ready, and I can't stop myself from reaching between us, palming his thick shaft. He lets out a labored breath, his lips parted, and wraps his fingers around my wrist as if it's an attempt to stop me, but he doesn't. Instead, he spreads his palm over the top of my hand, urging me to stroke him harder, faster, as he thrusts his length deeper into my eager hand.

"I can't control myself with you," he says against my lips.

"I don't want you to."

"I hurt you the last time."

I pull back, jerking my hand, and slap him across the face. "Stop!" I grip his cock harder in my palm and lick my lips as I lean closer. "Were you so fucking possessed that you missed the part where you made me come?"

His eyes search mine, his lips glistening from our heated kiss.

"Were you so caught up in the madness you didn't realize I liked it?"

"What was there to like? I lost my shit, and I used you to prove a point to my brother. It was fucked up."

I continue to stroke his dick through his pants, lifting my shoulder as I press harder. "Someone once told me if you want to do something simply because it thrills you, you do it. The world is unraveling, and we have every right to unravel with it."

He licks his lips, and I can feel his body vibrate, his eyes dark and turbulent.

I loosen his pants and snake my hand inside. The second I wrap my fingers around his smooth cock, he hisses, shoving himself deeper into my palm.

"At Mito, you told me I've been a predator all along. You were right. I'm not prey. I'm just like you, and together we do fucked-up so goddamn well."

Precum beads on the tip of his cock, and I rub my thumb over it. My body is nothing but flames. My panties are soaked, and my pussy throbs, needing to feel him inside me more than I need my next breath.

I force my hand in deeper, palming his balls, and he

snarls while biting his bottom lip as he leans his forehead against mine, his eyes rolling closed.

"Unravel with me, Alexius."

He grabs my hand, stopping me from stroking him, his expression feral.

I lick my lips. "Now, give me what you promised. Love me until death us do part."

His mouth is on mine once more. His kiss is hard and desperate, like he's trying to taste my soul. Our tongues dance and duel while our lips claim unapologetically. His breathing is rapid and labored as he pulls back. "Take off your pants. Do it now."

I obey and pull my pants off, kicking them to the side. He takes the hem of my shirt and pulls it over my head as he forces me to move backward. I gasp when I feel the cold wall against my back, and Alexius drops to his knees in front of me, his hand guiding my leg over his shoulder, his lips tracing up my inner thigh.

I'm all sensation, and my instinct is to close my eyes and lean my head back, but instead, I thread my fingers through his soft hair, slanting my head so I can look at him and relish the sight of such a powerful man on his knees for me.

I brace myself by gripping his hair tighter, his lips brushing against my smooth sex. My legs start to shake, my core tight and slick, and I moan out loud when he snakes his tongue into my pussy, licking a long, leisurely stroke through my slit, then flattening his tongue deep in my cleft.

"Alexius," I whimper.

"Shh." The vibrations of his lips ripple to my core. "Keep quiet."

I suck my bottom lip, watching him roll his tongue as he eats me out. He clamps his lips around my clit and sucks hard, causing me to swallow a moan. It's intense, almost too much, and I have to lean my head against the wall, closing my eyes as I arch my back. I push his head closer, burying his face deeper into my cunt. There's a low growl that reverberates from his throat, causes my core to quiver, and I'm so close—so fucking close, and I feel it starting in my toes, my muscles tense and tight, desperate for release.

I buck my hips against his face, and he slips a finger inside me. "Oh, my God," I whisper breathlessly, rocking myself into his mouth.

"That's right." He dips his tongue where his finger enters me and drags up before flicking it against my clit. "Fuck my face, stray."

"Jesus." I look down at him and try to spread my legs wider, thrusting my hips downward and rocking my wet pussy onto his face. He moans against my sensitive flesh, his finger pumping faster as I grind into him, my clit throbbing.

"Alexius, I need your cock."

"I want you to come on my tongue."

"And I need you to fuck me."

Abruptly, he grips my thighs with his fingers biting into my flesh, pulling me down harder onto his face. He sucks my clit hard, and I can't stop it. I cry out, my body convulsing with pleasure, and I claw at his hair, pulling and pushing, fucking his face and riding out the orgasm that leaves my body and mind in fragments of ecstasy.

His tongue doesn't stop, his finger pumping my pussy, milking every last drop of my orgasm. Finally, my muscles relax, and if it weren't for his arms wrapping around my waist, I'd collapse because I have no strength left in me.

Alexius stands, his lips glistening with my cum. "Please fuck me," I whisper, even though I can barely stand. "I need to feel you inside me again."

He places both hands on the sides of my neck, easing down my naked shoulders, leaning his forehead against mine. "Not today, stray. Not today."

Before I can say anything, he pushes away and walks straight out the door without looking back.

CHAPTER 14
ALEXIUS

I t's good to be home. Hotels are the worst. I could have stayed at Myth's penthouse suite, but after what happened with Leandra and Isaia, a sex club was the last place I wanted to be. Being away from her, unable to touch her, kiss her, slide my cock inside her welcoming cunt is torture enough without being surrounded by kinky fuckery. But I suppose for a glass-is-half-full kind of person it worked out well, since me not being here kept Rome from frequenting the estate, which meant it kept Leandra out of his sights. He knows the best way to fuck with me is through her, even if it's just for shits and giggles.

God. I've become so fucking transparent since falling for my wife—and in my line of business, that's not a good thing.

I've never been so much in my own head before, having my emotions control me. Damn Isaia. Little shit. I'm probably going to hell for not feeling remorse about kicking his ass. And God knows, I don't regret fucking my wife in front of him, either. I wanted him to see it, how Leandra's body bends to my will and only mine. How I slam into her pussy, my cock the only dick she's ever had inside her, and that's the way it's going to stay.

This stupid fucking game between us started the night she watched Isaia fuck—the night I found her in the bathtub playing with her pussy, soapsuds clinging to her wet skin, her hard nipples teasing into view as the water rippled around her. I was instantly hard when I saw her, my balls tight and blood rushing to my dick. I couldn't stop myself from toying with her that night, watching her carry herself to orgasm, then squirting jizz on her cheek. That was the night everything started, and my obsession with her ever since has grown into something that now consumes me.

I've seen the way he looks at her. I've seen the desire in his eyes. The lust. My brothers and I loved to share, and it fucked with his head when I didn't want to share her.

Once was enough, and it was the hardest thing I've ever had to do, but I did it for her—to help her defeat her demons and realize that her desires aren't the same as the perversions of her parents. I saw something in her that night in the tub. I saw a temptress waiting to be unleashed—a siren who needed to be set free so she could wreak havoc around her. Around me. And by God, I fucking love her chaos just like she loves my madness. It's that same madness that detonated when I walked into that room to find my brother next to my wife, holding her in his arms, and she looked so peaceful, so at ease...and it turned my vision red. I saw blood and carnage, and I wanted to slam my fist through my brother's chest and tear his heart out. The jealousy was a bitter, vile taste on my tongue that day. It wreaked havoc in me and tore away at my humanity until there was nothing left but a monster who craved blood.

I wanted to kill him. I've never wanted to kill anyone as much as I did my own brother. Like I needed another reason to go to hell.

The leather of my chair creaks as I lean back, staring at the blank wall of my office, trying to sort through my thoughts like thousands of unpacked boxes.

I left because I wanted to give her space, and I needed some reprieve from the fucking guilt that was only pissing me off. I'm a Del Rossa. We don't feel guilt. We don't feel remorse. We rule, we dominate, we take. We don't fucking mope around like lost boys...which is exactly what I did in that goddamn hotel room—getting drunk and acting like a brooding teenager.

I wasn't planning on coming back today—probably not anytime soon, either—but when the doctor called confirming the appointment, I knew I had to be here. I missed the first ultrasound because my wife was too scared to tell me. There was no chance in hell I'd miss this one too, so I came. And when she walked into that room, and I laid eyes on her, I swear to God my heart fucking stopped. She's more beautiful than the image of her that remained in my head the entire time I was gone. Her belly has grown, her breasts round and fuller, her body shaping and adapting as my babies grow inside her. It's the most amazing thing—and apparently, my dick loves it too, because her pregnant body had my cock aching like a motherfucker. It still does, and my balls hate me, too.

I run my thumb along my lower lip, still tasting her cum on my tongue. My eyes roll closed at the memory of her thrusting her hips into my face while I licked up every last drop. The delicate sound of her moans and how it grows louder as her pleasure crests. It was incredible, the confidence she showed in knowing what she wants by fucking my face like it was the last living thing she'd ever do. The way she slid back and forth on my tongue, gripping my hair, forcing me closer, deeper. Her thighs trembled as she climaxed, her pussy gushing as pleasure ripped from her core. She's nothing short of amazing, and among the trillion cells in my body, there's not a single one that wants any other woman but my wife. Leandra is all I want. I have to have her all the damn time. I could have her a million times over and over, and it would still not be enough.

I love her to the point of madness. I would spill blood for her, kill and maim for her. What I feel for her is just too damn powerful...which is why everything is so fucked up.

My phone vibrates on my desk, my lawyer's name flashing on the screen.

I answer, "Is it taken care of?...I don't give a fuck how much red tape is around this potential epic shit-storm, you need to stop this," I bark into the phone's receiver. "I don't care how you do it. Just get it done. And do not call me again until you do." I hang up, toss my phone on my desk, and squeeze my fingers on the bridge of my nose. "Fuck!"

"Problems in paradise?" Nicoli strolls in, looking like he just got home from a vacation. My twin brother never lets anything rattle his cage, always acting calm, cool, and collected. It fucking annoys the shit out of me some days...and that someday is today.

I lean back in my chair, tapping an impatient finger on the armrest. "I'm buried up to my eyeballs in shit right now."

"You got things sorted with Leandra?"

I look out the window. "I'm not sure."

"How can you not be sure? You either have shit sorted, or you don't."

"It's not that simple."

"Ah, yes. It is."

"For you, everything is simple." I pull a hand through my hair. "Too fucking simple."

He cocks his head to the side, narrowing his eyes as he scrutinizes me. "Have you ever considered that maybe you overcomplicate everything?"

I snort. "What? Am I supposed to take everything in stride like you?"

"Maybe."

"Someone needs to take shit seriously around here. And since none of you assholes want to step up, I'm the fucker who has to."

"Bullshit." He grins at me. "You have to because

you're the firstborn Del Rossa. God, best decision I ever made."

"What decision?"

"Letting you go out the birth canal first."

I try not to laugh, but looking at Nicoli makes it impossible not to.

"Asshole," I mutter.

"Seriously, though." He lights a cigarette, inhales deeply, then lets the smoke trickle out the side of his mouth for a bit before blowing it out in a plume. "Will you be able to sort shit out with Leandra?"

"I don't know. Maybe."

"She still pissed at you for locking her up?"

"No." I get up, round my desk, and lean against the edge at the front, crossing my arms. "In fact, it seems like she might have gotten over it."

"What?" He looks at me pointedly. "She's over it?"

I shrug. "I think so. She, um," I rub my temple, "she wants to *fix* things."

Nicoli's eyes narrow, suspicion clinging to his top lip. "Don't trust it."

"What?"

"It's a trap."

I frown. "A trap? How?"

"Women don't get over shit that fast. They say they do, pretend like everything's fine, long forgotten and forgiven. Then one day you forget to put the damn toilet seat down, and all that long forgotten and forgiven crap comes back and pummels you to be the lowest piece of shit ever."

"Oh, my God." I drag my palms down my face. "Leandra's not like that."

"All women are like that." He puts his cigarette in the ashtray and gets up, pouring himself a glass of whiskey. "You locked her up, for Christ's sake, after you got her pregnant without her consent." He drags out the T, putting more emphasis on it. "And then some other shit happened with our dearest younger brother."

"It's not—"

"No!" His hand shoots up. "I don't want details. You tried rearranging our little brother's face, but that's as much as I want to know. The less I know, the less Mira will be up my ass wanting information out of me."

"I wasn't about to tell you."

"Theeeen," he starts pacing, "you disappear for fuck knows how long without as much as a note for your pregnant wife saying where you are, why you left, and most importantly when you'll be back, because we all know women need a timestamp on everything. Date. Hour. Minute. To the fucking second."

"Jesus," I mutter. "What's up your ass?"

He cranes his head and closes his eyes, breathing out a sigh. "Between the time I walked in here and the part where you said Leandra has supposedly forgiven you, I realized that it's been too long since I had my dick stuffed in pussy."

I roll my eyes and brush past him, pouring myself some whiskey. "Go to Myth, then. Or do everyone a favor and fuck Mira. Get it out of your system."

Everything goes quiet. It's the kind of silence that can

crack bone, and I can practically feel Nicoli's glare burning holes in my skull.

"If you weren't my brother, my knife would be lodged in your jugular right now." And if that doesn't kill me, the poison laced in his voice will. It's the one thing that rattles his cage. Mirabella.

I take a big gulp of whiskey, rolling it around with my tongue, letting it linger on my tastebuds before swallowing, feeling it sting as it settles in my stomach. "I fucked up," I say without turning to face my brother. "I *really* fucked up, and my wife wants to fix it. So, either she's incredibly foolish and naive, or I'm just one lucky son of a bitch." I'm speaking more to myself than I am to Nicoli, then chase my words with more whiskey.

Nicoli comes up behind me and places a reassuring hand on my shoulder. "If you're the one who fucked up, and your wife seems to think it's fixable," he squeezes, "then you fucking fix it."

I slam back the rest of my drink, sucking air through my teeth as the alcohol stings, then pour myself another. "Here's another little piece of information I'm sure you'll find amusing as fuck."

"I can't wait to hear it."

I turn to face him as he sits back down, taking the last draw of his cigarette.

"I'm having a daughter."

Nicoli freezes, his fingers hovering over the ashtray. "Say that again."

I shake my head, already knowing he's about to take a

piss at me. "The doctor was able to see the sex of one of the babies, and it's a girl."

"So, you're not only going to be a father, but you're going to have a daughter?"

"Yes."

"A girl?"

"We're going in circles."

"A girl?"

"Nicoli, snap out of it."

And then he bursts out laughing. And it's not just a chuckle or a snicker. It's a full-belly laugh, and by the looks of it, it's hurting his face.

"Holy shit," he says through a fit of laughter. "You're going to have a girl."

I stare at him, deadpan. "I fail to see the joke in this."

"Oh, it's there." He leans his head back, his laughter rolling in every direction. "See," he finally gathers himself and sits up straight, "when you have a boy, you only have to worry about one penis. When you have a girl, you have to worry about all the cocks running around town."

"You're insane."

"And you are fucked." He continues to laugh, and soon my frown turns into a smile and then a snicker. I mean, he's not wrong. If I don't want men to even breathe in my wife's direction, I sure as shit won't let any teenage boy with a hard-on close to my daughter.

I rub my fingers along my forehead. "I think the universe reckons I haven't spilled enough blood yet and decided to give me more motivation."

"I cannot wait to see your face the first time a boy knocks on this door."

"I'm afraid you won't get the honor to see my face that day because the little shit won't get through the damn gates."

"Oh, man," Nicoli sighs. "I haven't laughed this hard in ages."

"I'm glad my life amuses you, brother." I sit across from him and watch the jackass as he pulls his shit together, shaking the laughing fit. "On a different, more somber note."

Nicoli smirks. "More somber than your life right now?"

"Here's a thought. Go fuck yourself."

"Okay, fine," he throws his hands in the air, "let's pull on our serious faces. What was that phone call about?"

Maximo stomps into my office, his cheeks red from the cold, snow stuck to his jacket. "We might have a potential problem?"

My eyes widen. "Potential problem?"

"A big-ass potential problem."

His pointed look tells me exactly what, or rather who, this potential problem is.

Nicoli raises a brow. "What's going on?"

Shit. I wipe a palm down my face. "I wasn't planning on saying anything about this to anyone," I say. "But since you're here, I might as well."

"What is it?"

"We've been trying to deal with a situation that's a personal matter to me and not official Dark Sovereign business, hence why I wasn't planning on including anyone else if not necessary."

Nicoli motions with his arm, growing impatient. "Get on with it already."

Maximo and I give each other a knowing look, and I shift in my seat. "Federico Dinali."

"That's Leandra's dad. You told me about him. He's in prison, right? Drugs. Child pornography. Grooming. Overall sick bastard."

"And about to get parole." The words burn like acid in my mouth.

"What?" Nicoli scowls. "Parole?"

"Yes," I reply, rubbing my hand across the armrest, the leather smooth beneath my palm while my blood boils and melts my veins. "That's the other reason I haven't been around. I've been working with our lawyers to ensure that fucker doesn't see the outside of that prison wall."

"And you don't want Leandra to find out," Nicoli says.

I tap my fingers on the leather. "She can't know."

"We agree on that." He leans with his elbows on his knees, rubbing his hands together. "Were you able to put a stop to his parole?"

"Not yet." I look at Maximo. "What's the potential problem we might have?"

He slips his hands in his jacket pockets, worry lines forming grooves on his forehead, and whenever Maximo worries, I get an ulcer.

"Apparently, Federico has been walking around

prison puffing his chest like a motherfucking peacock, bragging about his daughter being married to a Del Rossa."

"What?" An instant hit of adrenaline rushes through me as I leap to my feet. "How in the name of ever-loving fuck would he know that?"

"That's not the worst part."

My eyes almost bulge out of my skull. "How is that not the worst part?"

"According to our guy on the inside, there are whispers about Federico making deals and using the Del Rossa name to strengthen his street credit."

"Jesus Christ!" I slam both fists into my desk, pens and files clattering on the wood. "This is what I've been trying to avoid."

Nicoli stands. "So, this fucker is already using his daughter's last name to get ahead." He turns to face Maximo. "Is our inside guy solid? Can we count on him to tell the truth?'

Maximo nods. "Sam is solid."

"Who the fuck is Sam?" Nicoli's brows are curved with question marks.

"A guy whose ass was glued to the seats of one of our casinos." I rest against the edge of the desk. "We had a target we needed to eliminate, and Sam had debt he needed to pay. It was supposed to be simple, but he got caught and had his ass tossed into jail. So, we offered him protection between those walls in exchange for him being our eyes and ears in the place."

"Sam?" Nicoli's lips spread in a thin line like he's trying to put a face to the name. "Do I know this Sam?"

I shrug. "I don't know. His cousin works as a waitress at the diner where Leandra used to work. Wendy, I think her name is. Shit," I blurt, roughing both hands through my hair. "I knew this would happen. I knew if that low-life cunt found out about his daughter's new last name, he'd be a problem."

Maximo steps up. "Any word from the lawyers?"

"I spoke to them earlier. They've been jumping through fucking hoops trying to find something to make sure this fucker stays locked up, but nothing's sticking."

"Anyone on our payroll who can help?" Nicoli asks. "A judge? A psych doctor? Jesus?"

I shake my head. "I've called in every favor, but it's like there's a giant brick wall waiting around every corner."

"This is bullshit." Maximo yanks off his jacket and throws it over the back of the couch. "We have the best lawyers in the goddamn city on this, but they can't find a way to keep this bastard behind bars?"

"It doesn't make sense." Nicoli stares at the wall behind me. "For this guy to be able to find a way around our lawyers, he must have some kick-ass legal representation."

"Something's not right," I mutter. "I can't help shake the feeling that it's not this fucker's lawyers we're up against."

"You're right."

All three of us look at the door, Rome's tall frame filling the entryway. "It's not his lawyer you're up against. It's my dad."

CHAPTER 15

ALEXIUS

I'm not sure if it's hysteria or just a giant motherfucking "ah-ha" moment when I burst out laughing.

"Of course, it's our dear Uncle Roberto. My God, how did I miss that?"

"My dad's been upping his game," Rome says as he strolls into my office. Just like the rest of us, except for Isaia and Maximo, Rome always looks immaculate in well-tailored suits, Italian leather shoes, and the cut of his dress shirt fitting his physique. The stock market has treated him well. "He's cashing in every favor owed to him," he continues. "Blackmailing every sorry son of a bitch he has dirt on so he can fuck you over."

"I didn't even know his reach went that far. The legal system? Judges?" I lift a brow. "I hate to say it, but I'm impressed."

"I told you not to underestimate my old man. He's a different kind of beast when cornered." Rome pours himself some whiskey, sits next to me, and takes a sip from his glass, closing his eyes as he appreciates the smooth taste.

He straightens his blue tie down his chest. "The fact that he reached out to me and groveled, begging me to come back home after I've caused him nothing but embarrassment, proves just how desperate he is."

"Desperate has been your father's middle name for years."

"Can someone please tell me what the fuck is going on here?" Nicoli's face twists in confusion as he studies both me and Rome. "You two hate each other, or am I missing something?"

Rome and I glance at one another before I look back at my brother. "Turns out our cousin here isn't the enemy but rather an ally."

"So, you two have been, what? Docking dicks this entire time?"

Maximo stifles a laugh while I merely glare at my twin, deciding it's safer not to provoke him into saying more stupid shit. "When he gatecrashed our meeting wanting to claim his father's spot in the Dark Sovereign, I was just as surprised as you."

"Your surprised faces had to be real," Rome chimes in. "I couldn't risk coming to you beforehand. As I said, my dad is desperate and like a fucking Rottweiler, smelling bullshit a mile away."

"So...what?" Nicoli pulls up his shoulders. "You and my brother sat down with some tea and macaroons afterward, scheming?"

"Well, not tea," Rome replies flatly, and Nicoli shoots him an unamused look.

"Listen," I move to the edge of the couch, "Rome approached me and told me that his father asked him to come back and join the family business."

"*Our* family business," Nicoli sneers. "He's not getting Isaia's spot."

"I don't want Isaia's spot," Rome interjects. "Do you really think I came back because I suddenly want to be a part of all this shit after I left to be fucking free of it all?"

"You're a Savelli," Nicoli barks. "Who knows with you lot?"

"Need I remind you that your mother is a Savelli, too?"

"Need I remind you that I have a loaded gun and an itchy finger?"

"Oh, you mean this finger?" Rome flips him off, and Nicoli bares his teeth. "I can assure you, I don't want any part in Dark Sovereign business, and I have no desire to sit at that goddamn table."

"Then why did you come back? Why go through all this trouble to pretend to fall for your father's bullshit, only to tell Alexius about it?"

"I'm trying to do the right thing."

Nicoli stretches his arm along the back of the couch. "Yeah, and what's that?"

"If you remember correctly, I was there on your father's birthday seventeen years ago, listening to my dad speak about how he plans to take out your entire fucking bloodline. That was when I decided I'd break free from this goddamn family the first opportunity I got."

"Pussy," Nicoli mutters.

"Family is supposed to protect each other, not kill each other."

"Yeah, well, we're special," Nicoli says while lighting another cigarette. "And you're still a pussy."

"Call me whatever the fuck you want—"

"Cuntface."

"Nicoli," I warn, and he snarls in my direction. "Every question you're asking now, I've already asked. Every doubt you have, I've had it threefold. So far, the only thing our cousin has done to piss me off is talk to my wife."

Rome grins. "It's so easy to get under your skin."

"Touch my wife, and you lose your spleen. As easy as that."

"Is that what you tried to do to Isaia? Tried to pull out his spleen through his face?" Rome grins, and Nicoli snorts.

"How about we just keep my wife out of this, shall we?"

"Yeah. I'm rather fond of my spleen, thank you." Nicoli leans his head back, opening his mouth and letting the smoke trickle out, spreading like tendrils, drifting upward, weakening into faint wisps.

"I'm afraid we can't do that." Rome's face tightens, and the atmosphere in the room turns as heavy as the frown Maximo's had on his face for the last fifteen minutes. "It's why I came over here. There's been some new developments. Or rather, my dad seems to want to up his game."

"He wants to get my wife's psychotic pervert dad out of prison. How in the name of fuck does he want to top that?"

Rome slams back the rest of his drink and places his glass down, the sound rocking through the sudden silence. I don't like the sudden shift in him. My skin prickles with an awareness, a warning that has me wary, knowing I'm not going to like a single word that comes out of his mouth next.

"What is it, Rome?"

He shifts in his seat, not looking in my direction like he's uncomfortable. Good. He might be my cousin and on our side...for now. But I'm still the fucking king who demands respect and the tyrant who ruins those who don't show it.

Rome taps his finger on the armrest. "You're having a daughter."

A chill surges through me and settles deep. "How the fuck do you know that?"

"It seems my dad's reach doesn't stop at your gates, I'm afraid."

My mind goes nuclear. It's a goddamn atomic blast that bursts through my insides, and I leap to my feet. "What the fuck are you saying?"

Maximo is next to me in a nanosecond, glaring down at Rome, ready to choke answers out of him. "Speak."

Rome stands to face us, moving the sides of his jacket back and sliding his hands into his pants pockets.

"Someone in your house is feeding my dad information, and he just got a call about you and Leandra having a little girl."

"Someone who?" I demand.

"I don't know. I didn't even know he had someone on his payroll."

"Then find out!" Maximo is barely able to restrain the anger tightening the tendons and thickening the veins in his neck. "You better give me a goddamn name, Rome."

"I said, I don't know."

"Then I guess I'll have to start killing everyone in this goddamn house!"

"Enough!" I snap. "We'll figure out who it is, Maximo. But right now, I want to know what my uncle intends to do with the information." I turn to face Rome. "If it were simple as having a mole inside my house, you would have told me this over the phone. But you wanted to see me in person, which leads me to believe there's more."

"There is." He draws in a breath, and I know I'm about to lose my shit. "My dad knows where to aim so it hits the hardest. He knows the only way to get to you is through your wife."

I ball my fists.

"The plan is to get Leandra's dad out of prison and shove him back into her life to stir shit. Federico is already going around prison telling everyone and their mother that his son-in-law is Alexius Del Rossa. Now, imagine the kind of influence that gives him."

"You're not telling me anything I don't know yet."

"I know I've said this to you before, but my dad's hate for you has consumed him. Especially after he got that anonymous letter confirming what he suspected, that you killed Jimmy."

"I didn't kill Jimmy," I lie with the straightest fucking face ever.

Rome's forehead creases as he scowls at me with a silent *we-all-know-you-did-it* look. I lift my chin and stare him down. No one intimidates me. I'll never confess. My brothers will never tell. When we vow to take something to the grave, that's exactly where it goes, no matter what.

"Your father has always been jealous because he wants to own the Dark Sovereign."

"That's where it all started," Rome says, his voice steady and controlled. "For years, he had to watch you be groomed for the position he covets more than anything. Then it was your stunt with the recording—"

"Stunt?" I shoot him an incredulous look. "You say that like I wronged him in some way when he was the fucker who planned on killing us all."

"That's not what I'm saying. But my dad saw it as a pissing contest, one he lost."

"It's not my brother's fault your dad has peanut-sized balls." Nicoli slaps his hand on the leather armrest. "It is what it is. No use in starting a war about it."

"This war started years ago," I say.

Rome nods. "You made it clear you plan to get rid of him."

"Because he doesn't deserve to be a part of the Dark

Sovereign legacy." I can't stop the malice that pours from my lips. My hate for him seeps from my soul, and I know that I will never be rid of it...not until I plow his corpse into the fucking ground.

"I get that. Believe me, no one is more aware of my dad's faults than I am. But did you honestly think he'd just sit back and let you kick him out? That he would pack his bags and leave with his tail between his legs? No. Of course, he's going to retaliate, fight for what he's always felt is his."

"But it is not his!" I shout, maddened by Roberto's nerve to think he can challenge me. "The Dark Sovereign is not his, and it will never be. Not as long as I breathe."

"Believe me, he's well aware of that."

"If he plans on killing me," I spread my arms, pushing out my chest, "then let him come. Let him give it his best fucking shot. I have all the motivation in the world to drive a stake through his heart before he can even touch me. But let's say by some miracle he accomplishes this impossible endeavor by taking my life. I am not afraid to die. And I have three brothers who will continue this war without me."

"He knows that, too," Rome says, deadpan. "Which is why he plans on killing you...without taking your life."

"Killing you without taking your life?" Nicoli grimaces. "A riddle. Seriously? So, you're not just a pussy. You're a nerd, too."

Rome glares at Nicoli, then looks at me, pulling a hand through his hair. "There's only one thing worse than death for a man with a family, and that's losing his loved ones and being forced to live without them."

Ice fills my gut. A red haze explodes in my vision, and my anger is a roar that rips the air from my lungs, blood rushing to my head. Outside, there's a storm approaching, and the rumbling thunder is an echo of the madness that slams against my chest. I grab Rome by the collar, jerking him close so he can feel the fire on my breath. "If you, anyone, harms a single hair on her head, I will wipe out every last Savelli, no matter how far down the bloodline they are."

"Hey," Rome grabs my wrists, "I'm not the enemy here, remember?"

"How long have you known about this?"

He jerks free, nostrils flaring and dark eyes glaring. "We were discussing his new plans when he got the call about you having a daughter."

"What plans?" I growl.

Rome wipes his mouth with the back of his hand, his cautioned gaze cutting to mine. "His plan to use her father to get close to her."

"How the fuck would he do that? Except that there's not a chance in hell I'd let that sick fuck near her, she wouldn't want anything to do with him."

"She won't have a choice," he snaps. "The plan is to have Federico blackmail her, get her alone with him, away from you so they—"

"Can kidnap her. Hold her for ransom until all his demands have been met." Nicoli finishes the sentence as he stands, buttoning his suit jacket. "Your dad sure as fuck lacks some originality. That's the oldest trick in the book."

"Not kidnap her, no." Rome's eyes turn dark. "Kill her."

If I were a bomb, this would be the moment I'd explode, tear people's limbs from their bodies and have their intestines cover the walls. "Hell would freeze over before I let anything happen to her."

"I have a suggestion," Rome says, and I can hardly contain my anger long enough to listen, my fists clenching and unclenching, my blood a vicious swoosh of venom.

"What is it?" Maximo asks.

"Her father."

"What about him?" I snap.

"Stop trying to put a stop to his parole."

"Not a chance."

"You're only delaying the inevitable," he says in earnest. "Federico will be free sooner or later. My dad will make sure of it."

I lose my tie and pull it from around my neck while I pace. "If you think I'm just going to sit here and do nothing so that sick fucker can walk the streets and sink his claws back into my wife, you're as dumb as you are ugly."

"What I'm saying is," Rome starts, "if we focus our attention on the details of his parole instead of trying to stop it, we can get the upper hand."

"How so?" Nicoli lights another cigarette, the coal turning into burning embers as he drags it in deep.

Rome looks my way, and I'm pretty sure he can feel the ripples of my displease and rage. "The way I see it, Federico Dinali can't do much harm if we get to him before my dad does."

"Man's got a point," Nicoli says. "With Dinali out of the picture, it's one less fucker to worry about."

I look at Maximo at the same time he looks in my direction. The knowing look he gives me tells me where he stands, what his opinion is of Rome's idea. It's a stupid fucking idea, but it's the best one we've got right now.

I grab my phone off the desk and dial a number, my nostrils flaring as I glare at Rome who seems confident in this plan of his. "Pull back," I say into the receiver. "Call it off. Let the parole happen, but I want to know every last detail, from his last meal served in prison, the last shit he takes in that place, right down to the second he walks out," I bark at my lawyer. "I want to know everything."

I hang up, my pulse racing, and warning stabbing a thousand blades in my skull. "This plan better fucking work."

CHAPTER 16
LEANDRA

I wake to darkness and suffocating heat. Sweat clings to my forehead, and a sheet of moisture covers my chest. The sheets are twisted around me, and I struggle to get out of them, my breaths coming in short gasps. That's when I hear it, the sound of ice cubes clinking in a glass. I stop moving and listen, awareness trickling in, and I reach out for the lamp.

"Don't."

I freeze. "Alexius."

"You should have said no." His voice is like the roll of thunder in the dark. "The day at your apartment, you should have said no."

"Would you have accepted it if I said no?"

"Probably not." There's a second of silence. "Definitely not."

I shift on the bed, narrowing my eyes, trying to see through the darkness. "What are you doing?"

Ice cubes clink again, and I know he's on the couch

across from the bed. "I'm just sitting here watching you sleep."

"Why?"

"That's all I'm allowing myself at the moment."

My skin prickles. "Is there something else you'd rather be doing?"

Silence is his only reply, and there's a delicate stir inside me.

"Can I turn on the light?"

"No."

"I want to see you."

No response.

I narrow my eyes, blinking, trying to see him. "Then I'll just get up and find you."

"Don't," he warns.

"Why not?"

"I'm already struggling to control myself by just watching you sleep. If you come closer, that will no longer be the case."

My fingers grip the sheets, heat spreading through my core, and I'm overcome with how badly I want him. "What would happen then?"

I hear the ice. "I'd want to touch."

My breath turns rapid, and I reach up my neck, brushing my fingertips across my skin, the silk of my nightgown soft against my flesh. "Then touch me."

"If I touch you, I'll only want more." He scoffs. "That's the problem with me. Nothing is ever enough for me when it comes to you. The more you give me, the more I want."

He leans forward and into the soft light of the estate's nightlights weaving through the curtains. I hold my breath when the light catches the blue shades in his eyes —sparkling sapphires looking right at me.

"First, all I wanted was a wife with no strings attached." He lifts the glass to his mouth, his throat bobbing as he swallows. "Then I wanted your virginity, and as soon as I tore through your innocence, I wanted your every wicked desire. And that still wasn't enough. It still isn't."

"Alexius—"

"Then I wanted you bound to me forever, so I got you pregnant. Locked you in a room." His elbows are on his knees, dark hair draping down the side of his face. "My greed almost destroyed us."

"You did not destroy us."

"I said almost." His voice is a low timbre of power, vibrating to every bone in my body.

The moisture on my skin starts to burn, and the heat becomes too much, so I kick the sheets down to my feet before pulling my fingers through my hair, smoothing the tresses over my shoulder.

I bite my lip. "What else do you need from me?"

He leans his head to the side, leveling me with his fiery stare, twirling the glass between his fingers. "Too much."

"That's not up to you to decide," I murmur, my body starting to buzz with a mix of adrenaline and need. I'm so hungry for his touch, his kiss, his possession, it's slowly building, growing strong enough to give me the courage and confidence I need to show him that I know what I want.

I lean back against the headboard, pull up my knees, and let the silk of my nightgown slip down my thighs. His gaze drops to my legs for a moment, then locks with mine again.

I trace a finger along my collarbone. "Maybe that's been your problem all along. You don't give me the chance to make my own decisions."

"Because I like to get what I want."

"And you think my choices would go against what it is you want?"

"I'm not the kind of man who leaves anything to chance."

"And I don't like my choices being taken from me." My finger traces along the strap of my nightgown, my nail gliding along my flesh. "Perhaps we need to find mutual ground. Some place where you're in control, and I have the freedom to choose for myself."

My back arches as I trail a finger over the swell of my breast, my nipple hardening against the soft silk. His blue irises turn to steel, his eyes an iridescence of hunger as he studies me.

He places his glass down and stands, his frame impossibly large within the darkness as he stalks closer, his features striking as he moves deeper into the light, a king clothed in authority who has me chained to him and bathed in magnetism that will always keep me captive. He stops by the end of the bed, and I finally reach out, switching on the dim light. "What are you proposing?"

"When it comes to our lives together, being husband and wife, I get the freedom to have my own opinion, make my own decisions." I reach between my legs, spreading my knees apart, and a flame erupts in my core when he looks at where I touch myself, slipping my hand inside my panties. "But when it comes to our most wicked desires, you control everything. You're the dictator, and I am merely your filthy...little...slut."

He spreads his arms wide, gripping the posts of the bed. "Are you wet?"

"Yes." I drag a finger through my slit, bucking my hips. "Very."

"Take off your panties."

"Is that a yes?" I challenge. "Do we have a deal?"

He slays me with a stare that turns my insides into liquid fire, and my breathing becomes labored. "Take off your panties, stray."

I obey, biting my lower lip and slipping my underwear over my thighs and down my legs, making a show of it as I drop it on top of the sheets. He lifts a brow when I close my legs, purposefully denying him what he wants to see.

His nostrils flare, and he takes my panties, bunching them up in his palm, bringing them up to his nose and inhaling deep. He closes his eyes, and I watch him savor the scent of my arousal, and I can feel the wetness start to coat my inner thighs.

"The smell of your pussy makes me want to hunt you, eat you, fucking devour you." His top lip curls in a snarl as he tosses the panties on the floor. "Turn around and get on your knees."

My chest tightens, my lungs unable to pull the air in deep enough as I turn my back toward him. I can feel his eyes on me. It's a white-hot flame on the back of my neck. My hair bounces off my shoulders as I pull the dress over my head, and I glance halfway over my shoulder at him, watching him unbutton his shirt. "Do we have a deal?"

"Lay down on your stomach."

"Do we have a deal?"

I gasp when he grabs my hair and yanks my head back, his cheek flush against mine. "I'm in control here, remember?"

"But—"

"Now lay the fuck down."

With a jerk, he lets go of my hair, and my skin is an inferno of sensation, my pussy aching and nipples yearning to be touched, the sheets brushing against them as I lie down, propping myself up on my elbows.

"Spread your legs," he commands behind me, that familiar low tenor forcing shivers up my spine, and I can hardly breathe right while doing what he says.

"Wider."

The muscles in my inner thighs stretch as I spread my legs as wide as I can, my pussy lips open and sensitive as the cold air laps against my heated, wet flesh.

"I love looking at your cunt, watching it glisten, growing wetter the longer I stare at it."

My fingers claw at the sheets, and I lean my forehead against the soft silk when I feel his touch on my calf.

"Is this what you want, stray?"

"Yes."

"I'm not talking about sex." His fingertip drags over the back of my knees. "I'm talking about this. Us." His finger slides down to my ankle again. "Me."

"Yes," I repeat, this time with more conviction. "You are what I want."

"Even after everything I've done?"

My heart hiccups, and I clutch the sheet tighter. "Yes." My answer is soft, but it's true.

"Are you sure, stray?" I hear him unzip his pants and the swoosh of fabric as he drops them to the floor. "Are you one hundred percent sure? Because this is who I am," he says. "I will never stop being obsessed with you. I will never stop being a possessive, jealous, and maddening bastard when it comes to you."

I flip my hair to the side. "What are you saying?"

The bed dips, and I whimper when he takes my right leg, lifting it so he can plant a gentle kiss on my ankle. "I'm saying...I'll try." Another kiss. "I'm not saying I'll succeed and that I won't fuck up, but I'll try."

"That's all I'm asking for," I murmur, and he eases my leg back down. "I love you, Alexius. I fell in love with all of you, even the possessive, jealous parts." His hand glides across my skin up the back of my thigh. "You warned me that loving you would be a burden, but it's a burden I'll gladly carry for the rest of my life because being without you is just no longer possible for me." Tears sting the back of my eyes, his touch a leisurely ripple of sensation as he continues over the swell of my ass. "I just...I want to be someone to you and not some...thing."

"You are so much more than that."

"Can I turn around? I want to look at you."

"No." His fingers bite into my thighs. "I need to say it like this. You're not just someone to me, stray. You're everyone. Everything. I could lose everyone else in this world right now, and I'd be okay because I have you. But if I lose you, every other person in my life would mean nothing to me because it's all you. Just you."

I settle back down, a tear slipping onto the sheet, causing a dark circle to spread through the silk. "And I'm nothing if I'm not yours," I whisper.

Both his hands cup my ass, sliding down, his fingers tightening around the arc of my ass, squeezing and easing them apart. "Good, because you will never be anyone else's. Not in this lifetime or the next."

His thumbs brush along the outline of my pussy lips, and a moan slips from my mouth.

"This cunt is mine. And this little hole," he presses a finger against the tight ring of my ass, "will be mine, too. Soon."

I shiver, an ache spreading to every corner of my body, and I don't know if it's the weight of the moment or desire. Maybe a little of both. It's been too long since he's claimed me, and paired with his heart's confession, it has catapulted me into a frenzy of emotion and desire. I'm already writhing on the sheets, and he's barely touched me.

"Alexius?"

"Yes, stray." His fingers prod and play everywhere except where I yearn for it.

"Please, I need you."

"I know you do," he says behind me. "I can see it. Your pussy is all swollen and pink. And so fucking wet."

"Then fuck me."

"I want to play with you just a little longer." His hands press against my cleft, pushing outward, forcing my legs farther apart. "I love looking at your cunt."

My clit quivers, and I press down on the mattress, needing the pressure.

"Oh, no, you don't." He slips his hand underneath me, my sex now against his palm. "If you feel the need to fuck something, you fuck me. Whether it's my hand, my thigh, my face, or my cock. You don't fuck anything else."

My legs are spread impossibly wide, and when he slowly sinks a finger into my hole, I moan, fisting the sheets tighter, pushing my hips down, and grinding my pubic bone against his palm. The sensation is indescribable. Every inch of my body is hypersensitive to the subtlest touch. Even my hair slipping down my shoulder, brushing along my collarbone, is intense, his finger easing out and back into me.

"I've missed you," he growls behind me. "I've missed your body, your moans."

"And yet you choose to drag this out when you could be fucking me senseless right now."

"I'm not dragging it out. I'm savoring." He moans when he sinks a second finger into me as if he can feel the pleasure it gives me. "Your pussy is so warm and tight, baby."

I continue to rock myself against his palm. "You're torturing me." My hips flex, and I push down, taking his fingers deeper, spreading my pussy wider. "Please, Alexius. I need you so much it hurts."

He moves to hover over me, the tip of his cock brushing along the crease of my ass as he leans down, placing delicate kisses all along my spine, his tongue painting my skin with delicate strokes. "I love the way your skin tastes and how you shiver whenever I touch you." His fingers continue their slow rhythm, and I'm sinking into mindless oblivion where nothing but his touch matters.

Abruptly, his fingers pull out of me, removing his hand from under me, leaving me empty and aching. "Beg," he commands, settling his arms on either side of my waist, towering over me, the head of his dick nudging at my entrance. "Beg for my cock."

"Alexius, please." I'm drowning. I'm suffocating. "I need you inside me."

He keeps his cock at my entrance, placing more kisses on my back. "Why?"

"Because I need you."

"Why?"

"God, Alexius. Please."

"Why do you need me?"

My body is in so much agony. It's like I'm being torn apart simply by not having him. "Because I love you."

"Why else?" He peppers soft kisses along my shoulder blades.

"Jesus," I moan, trying to push down so I can take him inside me, but he merely rears back, denying me.

"Why else?"

I fist my hands, tears burning my eyes, every bone aching. "Because it fucking hurts if I don't have you."

He enters me with one swift slide of his cock, and I twist underneath him, moaning as he stretches me. "It hurts me, too, when I don't have you, stray," he whispers against the back of my ear. "That's how I felt every single minute you hated me."

"I never hated you."

"That's what it felt like to me." He flexes, pulling out and sinking back into me.

"But I didn't," I breathe out.

"Just like I never thought of you as a possession."

"It felt like you did."

He moves, balancing on his arms, kissing gently behind my ear, and rasps, "But I didn't."

"What are you saying?"

He spears into me with a hard thrust, causing me to cry out. Then he stills. "I'm saying that sometimes what we feel because of someone else's actions or words is not always the truth. Emotions, feelings have so many gray areas, it's easy to get lost within what's real and what's not." This time he pulls out completely, steadies himself on one arm, and wraps his other hand around my throat, driving into me hard and deep. "But this, what you feel now, this is real. My love for you will always be real, no matter how many times I fuck up. Do you understand that?"

"I do."

"Good. Now swear that you'll never deny me this body of yours again."

"I swear," I whimper, his hand tightening around my throat.

"Swear you'll never doubt my love for you again."

"I swear it, Alexius. Never."

"That's my baby girl." He kisses my shoulder, lapping his tongue across my skin while he fucks me, and I lean my head to the side, needing his tongue and lips everywhere on my skin.

"You have to promise me something, too."

"Anything."

"Never shut me out again. Ever." This time the tears spill free while my body is consumed with the feel of him inside me. "Never shut me out and leave...again."

He moves his hips in a way that drives me crazy. It's a rhythm I know so well. And his thick girth fills me, his cock reaching the deepest part of my core, and it feels like I'm being stretched to the brink with his every thrust.

"I swear it." His thrusts turn frenzied. And the sound of his heavy grunts and rapid breaths are like ecstasy to my system. I try to rock back, lifting my hips off the mattress, giving him more access to enter me deeper, but his control over my body in this position is absolute, and he gives me no room to move, no chance to challenge the way he chooses to fuck me.

I'm helpless and entirely at his mercy, but it's the way

I want it. It's how I need it. "Fuck me harder," I plead. "Please."

"God, I love it when you're desperate to be fucked." His cock throbs inside me, and he does as I ask, slamming into me, his pelvis slapping against my ass, the sound of skin hitting skin intoxicating the air.

My orgasm starts to trickle down my spine, my pussy clenching around him, and I struggle to keep my legs stretched wide as he pounds me into the mattress.

"Do not fucking close your legs." Alexius lets go of my throat and pushes himself up, twisting to the side, and reaches for my thigh, forcing it wider so he can fuck me deeper. "I want to fuck you so hard you'll feel me for days."

"Alexius, I need to come."

"Come, baby," he grits out breathlessly. "Drench my cock in your cum."

"Fuck!" I cry, my body squeezing him tight as pleasure erupts deep inside my core.

He doesn't let up. He doesn't slow down as my orgasm crests, my screams filling the open space around us, and he rocks into me relentlessly. It would hurt if it weren't the most pleasure I've ever felt. His cock would tear me apart. But I'm so wet, my pussy so slick with my cum gushing out of me, his dick pummels into me with ease.

He lets go of my thigh and presses his palm on my waist, pinning me down so I can't move. "I'm going to fill you up good, slut," he growls. "Do you want it? Tell me you want my cum."

"Yes," I say, out of breath. "I want your cum inside me. Every last drop, please."

"Jesus. Fuck." His hips jerk while he's buried to the hilt inside me, and his breaths are sharp snarls and low rumbles.

His body is rigid, and I can feel his girth swell as he comes, his cock throbbing as he spurts his hot cum inside me.

He sits up, and I flinch when he pulls out of me. His hands are on my ass, and he spreads me wide. I peek over my shoulder to look at him, his gaze fixed between my legs. "I want to see my cum drip out of your pussy."

I clench my inner walls, and he bites his lower lip when I feel hot liquid drip from my sex.

"God, look at that. My cum creaming your pussy." He reaches down and scoops it up with his fingers, shoving it back inside me. "I want it all inside you."

I smile and lean my head down on the bed. "I'm already pregnant."

"I don't give a fuck. My cum inside you is the hottest goddamn thing."

He wraps his fingers around my waist, and with a swift move, he turns me over and pulls me into his arms. I curl into him, welcoming his familiar warmth—and I'm at ease for the first time in so long. Comforted by his presence.

"I love you," he whispers against my hair.

I smile and nestle closer. "I love you, too."

Laying my head on his chest, I can hear his heartbeat, and it's the most beautiful sound.

"Leandra."

"Yeah?"

His chest stops moving. He's holding his breath, and I feel his muscles tense.

"What is it?" I shift and look up at him, his jaw set and firm. "Alexius?"

When our eyes meet, he cups my cheeks and pulls me close, our lips colliding in a desperate kiss that has the power to erase the entire world around us. His tongue is hot and wet, like velvet against mine, and I wish he could kiss me forever because I won't ever get enough of his taste. But this one feels different. He's not claiming. His kiss isn't consuming or possessing.

His kiss is desperate, urgent, and I feel it penetrating my soul. I don't think he's ever kissed me like this before.

A moan slips from my lips when he pulls back, placing his forehead against mine. "I'm sorry," he whispers, and my heart stops. "I'm so...fucking...sorry."

CHAPTER 17
ALEXIUS

"I'm so fucking sorry." I mean every single syllable. It's the only thing I could say. It's something I've wanted to say since she slapped the bejesus out of me after I fucked her in front of Isaia. I had the blood of many on my hands, but when she looked at me with fractured eyes, I truly knew what it meant to be the villain.

I wanted to say it a thousand times over and over. And after I heard my babies' heartbeats, I wanted to scream the words that kept burning the tip of my tongue and plaguing my conscience. But my pride kept me chained up, and I couldn't do what I knew I needed to.

That's why I sat in the dark for over an hour watching her sleep, her hair fanned out over the pillow, her chest rising and falling in a calm rhythm...my babies growing inside her belly. The shadows tried to hide her from me, but I could see her silhouette in the white silk nightgown. Or maybe I'm just used to the dark because

I've been basking in it for almost my entire life—that's until a poor waitress from the other side of town gave me a taste of the light.

Before she woke, I sat there musing over my uncle's plans to harm her and how I would slaughter everyone who dared to come near her, a part of me wondered... what if?

What if something had to happen to her? What if something had to happen to me? What if I never get the chance to tell her how fucking sorry I am for hurting her?

Until now, it's only ever been words. Words with meaning that didn't apply to us. A Del Rossa never apologizes. We don't relent, and we don't wallow in guilt. At least that's how it was...before her.

They're the hardest words I've ever had to say— harder than saying goodbye to my father—but I had to find a way to make it right, even if she had forgiven me.

Apologizing is the only way I could make her see that my love for her is stronger than my life within the Dark Sovereign.

"I love you," she whispers, and I swear to God I feel those words sink into my soul.

"I don't deserve your love, but I'll take it anyway." I brush my cheek against hers. Her hair smells like orange blossom and coconut, and I thread my fingers through the soft tresses, tucking them behind her ear. "I love you, too, stray. More than anything in this entire goddamn world." I drag my lips down to hers and kiss her lightly, a mere brush of lips and a colliding of warm breaths. "Being apart from you was the hardest thing I've ever had to go through."

She leans into my touch, closing her eyes. "I thought it was what I wanted, but I was wrong. I couldn't breathe without you, and I never want to go through that again."

The selfish bastard in me loves hearing her say that because there's no chance I'll ever put myself through that torture again.

"We'll never be apart again. I swear it." I reach down, placing a palm on her belly. "You and these babies are my life now. My sole existence is to protect you and give the three of you the world." I've never been more serious in my life. "You are my world now. Just you and nothing else."

Her beautiful, plump lips pull in a smile. "You know how much I love your dirty mouth, but hearing you say all these heartfelt words," she shifts and slides over me, straddling my hips, "it does things to me."

God, she's been a vision before. But now, with the gentle swell of her belly and full breasts, she's a goddess.

I lift my hips, and a groan rumbles in my throat as she slides her wet cunt along my cock, igniting a deep lust that hums in my balls. "Should I start writing you love letters and reciting poems?"

"As much as I love your words of affection, I think I prefer the filthy ones more."

I grab her waist, digging my fingers into her flesh and forcing her to move her hips. "So, instead of telling you how much I love you, I should tell you how obsessed I am with this cunt of yours?" I buck and pull her down, so my shaft fits perfectly between her pussy lips.

"Oh, yes," she moans and rocks on top of me, gliding my dick along her creases. "More."

"When I'm not with you, all I think about is seeing your pussy swallow my cock." I reach for her breasts and massage them lightly, loving how they fill more of my palm now. "And how I can't wait to watch these tits bounce while I fuck you."

"Hmm."

"God, I want to make you come just by rubbing my cock between your folds."

"I want to come with you inside me."

"I know, baby." My hands are on her waist again, and I lift her, watching as she reaches down, her eyes urgent, her long, delicate fingers wrapping around my shaft, positioning it by her center. I give her just the tip of my cock even though I want to pummel inside her and fuck her raw. But instead, I practice restraint so I can look at her beautiful face overcome with lust, her lips parted, and cheeks flushed. I give her a little more and tilt my head, watching her smooth, glistening pussy clench down on me before focusing my gaze on her face as she takes me, her body shivering and chest rising, her eyes closing in pleasure the moment I'm fully seated inside her.

"That's it, stray. You're such a good little slut taking all of me," I murmur, holding her hips firmly in place. The feeling is exquisite, her wet walls engulfing me, and I move my hips upward, needing to be deeper.

"God, I love your cock," she says, squeezing her tits

together as she straightens her elbows, moving her hips in slow circles, grinding on me. "It feels so good to have you inside me."

I clamp my fingers down on her hips. "Then stop fucking around and ride my dick like it's the last time you'll ever feel it inside you."

She steadies herself with her hands on my abdomen and starts to move, slides up and down my length, her breasts bouncing with each thrust.

My abs pull taut, my thighs straining as I buck to meet her, the sound of our wet skin filling the room.

"Oh, fuck," she gasps.

"Do not fucking come. You're not done riding me yet," I demand, clenching my jaw and biting my lower lip while watching her fuck me with wild movements, looking down at her pussy. "Fuck, I love watching your wet, slutty cunt swallow my dick."

She moans and pushes herself down, rocking her hips while grinding against my pubic bone before lifting back up. This time I thrust upward, slamming back into her, and she cries out. "Alexius, I'm going to come."

"Not yet." Again, I buck, straining my hips to pound back into her.

"Fuck!" she cries, her arms shaking and legs trembling. "Please." She smacks back down onto me and twists her waist, and my entire body goes rigid as my balls pull tight and my cock swells.

"Jesus, woman," I curse and bite my fingers deeper into her waist, throwing my head back and arching my back off the sheets. "Come. You have to come before I do."

"Oh, God," she cries out, and I groan until my load erupts from my cock in a rush, spilling my hot cum into her, her body shivering as she explodes around my cock, both of us coming at the same time.

Her pussy tightens. My cock jerks. And I'm buried to the hilt inside her while she bounces and grinds, riding out her orgasm. It's fucking beautiful, seeing the hard lines of ecstasy on her face, a soft sheen of sweat glimmering on her chest.

She drops onto my chest, breathing rapidly, her hot breath on my skin, and I wrap my arms around her. "God, I love your pussy," I say breathlessly, and she lets out a winded chuckle. "And I'm not even kidding if I say I want to fuck you over and over, every goddamn day, for the rest of my life."

"I'm totally okay with that, Mr. Del Rossa." She trails a lazy finger along my chest, waking goosebumps along my flesh.

"Good." I take her hand and bring it to my lips, kissing it gently. "You need to rest," I say, shifting her off me and onto the mattress.

"I need to shower first."

But I stop her from getting out of bed. "Lay still. Let me take care of you."

I grab a towel from the bathroom, and Leandra keeps still as I clean between her legs, wiping her thighs clean, her pussy red and swollen. "We'll probably have to start taking it easy with you being pregnant."

"We can still have sex. The doctor says it's completely safe during pregnancy."

I still and lift a brow. "I don't mean we should stop. Good God, no. Do you want to kill me?"

She lets out a gentle laugh.

"What I mean is, just...be a little more careful."

I pull the sheet over her as she turns on her side, and I start a trail of tender kisses over her shoulder, collarbone, and neck, stopping below her ear. "Until death do us part."

CHAPTER 18
LEANDRA

Things have been simpler since the tension between Alexius and me has been severed. I've moved back into his room, and he's been there every night, making love to me and sleeping with his hand on my belly.

His touch is gentler, and so is the way he fucks me. He's becoming increasingly cautious when it comes to my body and the babies and tries to control himself the best he can with me.

I love his softer side, but I miss the fiery, carnal explosion when our twisted desires take control. The way he dominates me, giving me the pain I crave and the humiliation I need to be consumed. But I know it's only temporary. Once the babies are born, we'll...unravel yet again.

Even though Alexius and I have made up, and we're finally on the same page again, there's still an ominous current in the air around the house, especially when the brothers are together, disappearing into the Dark Sovereign meeting room. I can't help but feel like Alexius is hiding something from me—that they're all hiding something from Mira and me. But for now, I'm done fighting, done digging into things that don't directly affect the babies or me. Alexius will always have his secrets, and Dark Sovereign business will never be pillow talk for us.

Mirabella and I are wrapping presents for the local children's home, and I try to avoid her knowing looks, but I can feel her curious gaze on me.

"Yes, Mira?" I say with a grin.

"So, you and Alexius are okay?"

"We are." I place the lid on the box and tie the red ribbon around it. "We're okay."

"Good. I was a little worried if you had to run away, I would have to travel halfway around the world to see my niece and nephew...or niece. Have you thought about a name yet?" She shrugs. "For the girl, at least."

"It's not something we've had a chance to discuss yet."

"You know what would make a beautiful name?"

I eye her with suspicion. "Let me guess. Mirabella?"

"Ew, no." She wrinkles her nose and starts stacking a few presents on top of each other, placing them on the other table so we have more workspace. "I've always loved the name Aria. I think it would be the perfect name for your little girl."

"Aria." I say the name, wanting to hear the sound of it with my voice. "That is a beautiful name. I love it, actually. But don't you want to keep it as an option if you have a daughter one day?"

She presses her red lips together, folding a blue boy's t-shirt into a box. "If I have a girl, I want to name her Natalia, after my mother."

My heart constricts. "That's a beautiful name, Mira," I say, noticing the light shimmer in her green eyes. I know what it feels like to lose a parent. What I don't know is how it feels to lose a loving parent.

She brushes a finger below her eye, sweeping away a bead of moisture. "I'm not getting my hopes up, though. Who knows if I'll ever get married."

"Don't be silly." I toss a piece of torn and bundled-up wrapping paper at her. "There's no chance a beautiful woman like yourself will grow old as a spinster."

"Clearly, you have forgotten what a hound my brother is. At school, guys simply talked to me and they'd have a broken face the next day. The school's star quarterback somehow gathered the nerve to ask me out. God, I was so excited, and Liam Collins was so hot. But he never showed, and I thought I was stood up." She clears her throat. "The following day, everyone heard that Liam was in some sort of accident and broke his leg in two different places. But I knew the truth. It had my brother and the Del Rossa brothers written all over it. After that, guys didn't even dare to breathe in my direction."

"Whoa." I'm shocked. "That's...insane."

"Right? When I came walking down the hall, guys

would turn around just to avoid eye contact with me. It was like I had leprosy or something."

I twirl a string of blue ribbon around my finger. "Considering how you lost your parents and older brother, I guess I can understand why Maximo is so protective of you. He doesn't want to lose you too."

"How do you do that?"

"Do what?"

"Always see the good behind everyone's actions?"

I shrug. "I don't know. Maybe it's my way of convincing myself that people aren't just all bad, that there's at least one pure intention behind a hundred bad ones."

"Clearly you haven't lived in this house long enough or had a single adult conversation with my brother."

I snicker. "Or your brother just felt like none of those high school jocks were good enough for his little sister."

She takes the ribbon from my hand and starts twirling it around her own finger. "Or he's just a selfish asshole who's trying to ruin my life by eating all my potential boyfriends alive."

"I haven't seen him chewing at Nicoli's heels yet."

"Shut up." Mira shoots me a warning glare, and I merely smile, turning my focus back to the task at hand.

"How many presents have we wrapped already?"

Mira counts the stacks. "Thirty-one, which means we have fifty-nine more to go."

"We're going to need some help if we want these wrapped by tomorrow night." I blow a strand of hair from my face. "A lot of help."

"Let's take a break," she says, weaving her fingers through her hair and brushing it behind her ears. "I'll ask some staff members to continue here while we finalize the Christmas dinner menu."

I don't object because I'm convinced I've developed an acute case of carpal tunnel by now.

We walk to the living room, where we find the chef waiting for us with some menu options. From baked brie bites, camembert wreath with crusty bread, and sweet potato soup with holly croutons as appetizers, to slow-roasted striploin in red wine and port with creamy mashed potato, maple-glazed ham, and traditional roasted Vermont turkey.

"The options are endless," I say, reading through every menu numbered from one to eight. "I'm so grateful this decision isn't solely mine to make."

Mira leans her head to the side as she studies the menus. "Let's go with two, three, and seven."

My eyes widen. "Three? Are we going with *three* menus? What, do you plan on feeding a village?"

"On Christmas, the men in this house are a village."

It's hard for me to fathom that much food on one table. Not only didn't we celebrate Christmas when I was a child, but I still ate my dry noodles instead of a meal prepared for a special occasion.

Nicoli and Caelian come sauntering in, both with a drink in hand, their sleeves rolled up to their elbows, and their collars loosened. "What are you two up to?" Caelian asks.

"We're just finalizing the Christmas dinner menu," Mira replies.

Caelian steps up behind Mira and looks over her shoulder at the menus. "Which did you choose?"

"You'll just have to wait and see." Mira hands the menus back to the chef and thanks him, her gaze drifting in Nicoli's direction, and their eyes meet for only half a second, but it's enough to make her cheeks blush with a shy glow.

Nicoli clears his throat. "What's on the menu tonight? I'm starving."

"I told the chef to surprise us. Leandra and I have been busy all day with the presents for the children's home."

"It's ironic, don't you think?" Caelian falls back on the couch, spreading his arm along the back. "Our family donating Christmas gifts to charity bought with money made from," he lifts his shoulders, "doing what we do."

Mira stares at him, deadpan, placing her hand on her hip. "Oh, you mean the money you make by running illegal casinos and sex clubs?"

"Not running, princess." Caelian smirks, tipping his glass at her. "Owning."

"Good God." Mira rolls her eyes.

"Hey, I don't see you complaining when you buy twenty pairs of those Louis Batone boots."

"It's Louis Vuitton, dumbass," she corrects him with a sneer.

"Batone, Vuitton. Same thing."

She slants her head to the side. "Not even close."

Alexius strolls in, and my heart flutters as I watch him walk my way.

"Hey, beautiful," he says and gives me a peck on the cheek, then places his palm on my belly. "How are you feeling today?"

"Good." I smile.

He tips my chin upward, studying me. "Did you rest?"

"Alexius, I'm fine."

"Just making sure." He kisses my jaw, making my body tingle, a spark traveling downward between my thighs.

"Seriously," Caelian starts, "everyone's aware that all is well again in the land of Alexius and Leandra. No need to gross us out with all this PDA. Get a room. God knows, there's more than enough to choose from in this house."

"Will Isaia be joining us tonight?" Nicoli asks, standing by the fireplace, the glimmer of the flames dancing off his features.

"I'm here." Isaia walks in, and I catch myself smiling when I see him. "Please tell me we're having good old-fashioned grilled steak tonight. I can't stomach another fancy-ass meal." He sits next to Caelian and takes Caelian's drink, swallowing the last bit.

"Excuse you, you little fucker." Caelian slaps Isaia on the back of the head, and everyone laughs.

The atmosphere is light and warm. Peaceful for a change. There are no dark clouds looming over us, no worries about spiraling tensions between anyone. It's the first time in so long that the air isn't gloomy and bleak.

When Mr. Del Rossa died, there was a shift in this house which everyone felt. Sadness cleaved through this family, and grief draped the walls. It was hard to breathe and not smell the sorrow.

Now, it's like they're a family again—like *we're* a family.

I look out into the foyer at the large Christmas tree lit up by lights that cling like a thousand fireflies to the branches. I feel the magic in the air—how it warms my blood and fills my heart. For a few moments, I'm that little girl again, the one who lay awake at night wondering what that excitement felt like—the excitement of wondering what you'd find under the tree on Christmas morning, wondering if the house would smell like cinnamon and pine when you woke up.

"Where are you, stray?" Alexius leans closer, his breath caressing my ear.

"I'm..." I press my lips together, smiling as I look up at him. "I'm right where I want to be."

He kisses me again, and his brothers cause a stir with their whining in the background. Alexius pulls away and licks his lips. "Jealous fuckers," he tells them, and Caelian throws a scatter pillow at him.

A while back, I didn't think the magic of Christmas could fill these halls. But it does. And so does hope. Love. Laughter.

It's not perfect, and I doubt it'll ever be perfect. But this might just be...home.

We're halfway through dinner when Alexius gets a text, and judging by the scowl on his face, it's not anything good.

My first instinct is to ask what it is, but I remind myself of my place—that when it comes to the family business, I have no place.

Alexius looks across the table at Nicoli. Anyone with half a brain can see that something passes between them, and I know I'll be going to bed alone tonight.

Alexius places his hand over mine. "I have to—"

"I know." I smile when he lifts my hand and presses his lips against my skin.

Maximo appears in the doorway, and there's a storm in his eyes as he stares straight at Alexius. The ice in his demeanor slithers down my neck, chills pricking my skin.

Alexius stands, fastens his suit jacket, and excuses himself from the table, Nicoli and Caelian following suit.

"Isaia." Alexius glances at his brother, still seated at the table, and with a simple nod, he tells Isaia to join them. To outsiders, it would be an insignificant moment. But to everyone in this room, it speaks louder than words blasting through a megaphone at three in the morning.

"My brother sure knows how to kill the mood." Mira slips in next to me, crossing her arms. "Whenever he silently demands Alexius' attention, it's never good."

"You think it's Dark Sovereign business?"

"It has to be, or Alexius wouldn't have his brothers join them." She takes the last sip of her red wine and stands. "So, since our dinner just came to an abrupt end and you won't be having sex tonight, how about we go wrap some presents?"

CHAPTER 19
ALEXIUS

This is probably the most challenging decision I've ever had to make. I'm staring at a stack of files, and I can recite every name mentioned by heart.

Timothy Sutherland. Leroy Jones. Samantha Vanguard. Hillary Rose. Kira Ward.

And the list goes on.

I've been going through these for weeks, looking at photographs and reading the horrific details of each case.

I know we're hardly saints, but there are bigger monsters than us out there in this fucked-up world. It's no wonder parents don't let their children play in parks anymore or ride their bicycles to the grocery store around the corner.

Fathers no longer show their daughters any sort of affection in public out of fear it might be misinterpreted, and moms rush their kids home whenever an old man on the street hands out candy.

Society has been mind-fucked by countless heinous acts of psychopaths, not just killing and hurting our children but destroying trust in humanity. It's because our world is sick. It's festering, rotting from its core, and killing the good one gruesome act at a time—one psycho fuck at a time.

Leaders and philanthropists spend their time and money trying to find ways to stop global warming while our children are targets for the sickest motherfuckers that live and breathe among us. Why the fuck bother saving the planet when we can't save our children? And why are the rich so obsessed with making Mars habitable? So we can fuck up that planet too?

Good God, the negativity is pouring out of me like toxic vapor.

"Our uncle sure had to pull a fuckton of strings to make this happen." I lean back in my chair.

Caelian swirls the ice in his tumbler. "He probably took it up the ass more than once."

"So, what do you want to do?" Maximo leans against the wall, arms crossed in front of his chest.

"I don't know." I pull a palm down my face. "This is not just business. It's personal. Really fucking personal."

"Let me do it." Nicoli takes a long drag of his cigarette, the tip lighting up with golden embers. "I'm feeling a little tense tonight, and disemboweling someone always lets me work off some steam."

Caelian grimaces. "Psycho freak."

Isaia stands by the window, staring at nothing but the black night. He hasn't said a word since we closed my office door. It's a lot to take in, especially since he has a personal investment in this, too.

"Isaia, what do you think?" I swivel my chair to face him straight.

He doesn't turn around, and his shoulders move as he breathes. "Did he touch her?"

I shift in my seat. "She got away before he could."

"He didn't hurt her?"

"Not physically. Emotionally, they both screwed her up good."

Finally, he turns and leans back against the windowsill. I can practically smell the rage oozing out of him. His leather jacket creaks as he straightens his arms, fingers clutching the ledge. "I think you and I both know what needs to be done."

A knowing look passes between us, and my insides coil. "Yeah. We do."

"Are you two fucking insane?" Nicoli cuts his glare between Isaia and me. "She's pregnant. You can't dump this shit on her now. I say we deal with it, and she never has to know."

"I love your plan, brother. I really do," I say. "There's nothing I want more than to finish this and not drag her into it. More than anything, I want to protect her—"

"Then don't fucking tell her. It's not rocket science, man."

"I've already taken too many choices away from her. I can't do that again, especially not with something like this."

"That's bullshit!" Nicoli shoots to his feet, his eyes

blazing. "We make the hard decisions to protect the people we love. If keeping them safe and out of harm's way means we have to choose for them, then that's what we do. We get our hands dirty, brother, and we do fucked-up shit without blinking for the ones we care for. If it means they hate us, then so fucking be it because all that matters is keeping them safe!" His voice slams like thunder against the walls, and everyone's staring at him, staggered because Nicoli hardly ever loses his shit like he just did.

I lean with my elbows on my desk. "Where the hell is this coming from?"

Nicoli's nostrils flare, and there's a brief glance between him and Maximo, and suspicion prickles the back of my neck. But whatever it is, it has to wait.

I get up and button my suit jacket. "Believe me, no one is more concerned about her well-being than I am, and no matter how much I want to make this decision for her," I glance at Isaia, and he nods his approval, "I can't. Not this time."

Leandra

"Leandra?"

I look up and find Alexius filling the entryway with

his large frame, his black suit and tie casting a spotlight of authority over him. "Can I talk to you for a moment?"

"Sure."

I push the wrapped present to the side and smile at Mira before walking over to him. He places a gentle hand at the curve of my back, and I suck in a breath only to have it burst from my lungs when Alexius pushes me up against the wall, pressing his lips hard against mine, kissing me hard, his tongue breaking through the crease of my lips and sweeping through my mouth.

"Mmm," I groan into our kiss, struggling to keep my legs steady. I can hardly think straight while he's kissing me stupid, his hand sliding up the back of my thigh, squeezing my ass in his palms, and lightly nipping my bottom lip between his teeth.

"What was that for?" I murmur breathlessly.

His finger traces along the curve of my jaw, his forehead touching mine. "Do you trust me?"

"Well, that's a loaded question," I tease, but he levels me with his stern gaze, and my stomach turns. "What's going on?"

"I know I've hardly given you any reason to, but I need to know if you trust me."

"That depends." I search his eyes. "Are you planning on locking me up again?"

"Don't even joke about that." He lowers his head, watching as he smooths the fabric of my shirt between his fingers. "I'm serious, stray. There's something I need to show you." His dark brows knit together, his blue eyes stern, his cheeks sharp and carved. "But first, I need to know if you trust me."

"Alexius, you're scaring me."

"For once, I want to do the right thing when it comes to you." He pulls his lips back in a snarl, hissing as he places his hand on my chest, his fingers touching the base of my throat. The tendons in his neck are strained, the thick vein pulsing fast. I can't tell if he's angry or anxious. Maybe both. "No matter how I feel about it or how badly I want to make this decision for you."

"What are you talking about?"

"Goddammit!"

With a jerk, he pulls away, turns his back on me, and paces. I have no idea what the hell is going on, but I'm scared. Warning sets my nerves alight, fear twisting my stomach. "Alexius."

"Leandra. Do you. Trust me?" His eyes flash with an urgency that penetrates my bones, his features solemn but stern. Whatever is happening, it's serious, and it has my husband more on edge than I've ever seen him.

"Yes," I breathe out. "I trust you."

Our gazes lock, and I'm not sure if it's a relief or fear I see within the blue shades of his eyes. He holds out his hand for me to take, and I place my palm in his, his fingers gently closing, then squeezing lightly. "I need to show you something."

"I don't know if I should be nervous or scared right now."

"Just—" He presses his lips together and touches my cheek. "Trust your gut."

I'm trying to keep my breathing steady as I follow him, his hand clutching mine tightly. We're walking through the foyer, past the steps to the back of the house and down a long corridor. With every step, my heart beats faster, and my senses heighten. There's an energy around Alexius, and I can't place it. But whatever it is, it's radiating off him in waves that make the hairs on the back of my neck stand on end.

The corridor leads to a black door at the far end, a gold-plated doorknob glinting under the fading light. It's one of those doors you see in horror movies, the ones that lead to a basement filled with torture devices and dead bodies.

I'm shaking by the time we reach the door, and I'm sure my heart skips a beat when Alexius turns the knob, the latch clicking open, revealing a flight of stairs leading downward, with dim lights against the walls.

"You okay?" he asks when he feels my hand tremble in his.

"Yes. No."

"I won't let anything happen to you. I swear it. You're safe."

"Safe from what? Alexius, just tell me."

"It's better if you see for yourself." He starts down the stairs, but I pull him back.

"No. Tell me now, please. What's down there?"

He hesitates for a moment, his blue irises searching mine, and it's easy to see how conflicted he is. My God, if whatever is down there has him so unsure, so on edge, it'll probably fucking destroy me.

245

He reaches for my other hand, holding it tight, placing a gentle kiss inside my palm, and I swear I almost drown with a single breath. "I promised you that I'll try, remember?"

"Try what?"

"To let you make your own decisions. To not make them for you." He leans closer, and I can smell the whiskey on his breath mixed with his wild spice cologne as he kisses me. It's so soft, so gentle. For a moment, I wonder if he's kissing me or merely breathing against my lips. It settles me a little, calming my nerves even though my heart is still racing like crazy.

He pulls back and tucks a strand of hair behind my ear. "This is me keeping that promise."

I swallow hard. "What is down there?"

Alexius stills, staring at me like he's scared I'll break. Like I'm a porcelain doll and he's searching for the cracks.

"Alexius?"

"Please trust me," he says softly and urges me to move by holding my hand tight in his as we descend the stairs. I have no idea what's waiting for us at the bottom, but something tells me it's not a puppy.

It's humid, and a musty smell drifts from the concrete walls. There are no windows, and the air grows thicker with each step. My heart is racing so fast I'm sure Alexius can feel my pulse against his palm.

We take the last step, and I lose my balance, stumbling into Alexius' side. He grabs my elbow and steadies me, wiping tresses of hair from my face. "You okay?"

I nod, and we continue around a sharp corner, walking into a large, open room. Nicoli is the first person I see standing on the left, his cigarette glowing brightly in the dimly lit area.

Caelian and Isaia are both standing on an elevated platform, the other half of the room cast in complete darkness.

It's the look on Isaia's face that threads fear through my veins. With his hands tucked into his jeans pockets, his shoulders squared, it's as clear as daylight that he's nervous—and that makes me nervous. If it wasn't for Alexius tightening his hold on my hand, this would be the part where I bolt and rush in the other direction. It's when I glance over my shoulder that I notice Maximo behind us. I have no idea where he came from, but then again, I never do. The man is like a phantom, and super fucking quiet. It's like he's in permanent stealth mode all the damn time.

I jolt when Nicoli speaks. "There's still time to change your mind, brother."

Alexius lets out a grunt, and I narrow my eyes at him. "Change your mind about what?"

"About letting you decide if he lives or dies."

My eyes widen. "If who lives or dies?"

Alexius nods in Nicoli's direction. There's a loud crack of electricity rumbling through the walls, and the entire room is suddenly lit up. I hold up my hand, shielding my eyes from the blinding light, but as my vision adjusts, the scene in front of me unfolds little by little...and my heart fucking stops.

"Dad?"

CHAPTER 20
LEANDRA

F ear is a complex emotion. It can either give you the motivation you need to be stronger or kick your ass and make you run in the other direction.

Right now...it's kicking my ass, but I can't run. My feet are planted on the concrete floor, my insides pulverized, and I'm not sure if I want to scream or throw up.

"No," I whisper.

"Leandra—" Alexius tries to pull me close, but I'm frozen solid. I stare at the man tied to a large metal chair, the chains around his feet glinting under the light. It's my father. How can that be him?

His head is hanging down, blood dripping in ribbons from his nose and onto his torn, pale blue shirt, seeping through the woven fiber of the cotton fabric. His dark hair is matted against his forehead, and sweat beads down the side of his face.

It's when he lifts his head and our eyes meet that I truly feel the horror of this moment—a moment I didn't think would ever come. I've never thought about the day I'd see him again because a part of me hoped he was gone for good.

His jaw hangs crooked, thick strings of spit and blood dribbling from the corner of his mouth. But his gaze is a dark pool of vacant amusement as he stares at me. Suddenly, I'm back in the past. I'm that little girl again—the girl staring up at her dad, wondering what it is that he wants her to do with his friend. I'm the girl who ran from her father that day...which is exactly what I need to do now.

"No. No. No." I take a hesitant step back...and another. "What the fuck is this?"

"Listen to me." Alexius reaches for me, but I jerk away.

I point at my dad, still staring right at me. "He's supposed to be in prison."

"Your father got out on parole."

"Parole?" I snap my gaze to Alexius. "That's not possible."

"My uncle made it possible."

"What?" I take another step back, struggling to keep my heart from crawling out my throat. "Why would...what does your uncle have to do with my father?"

"He set up the whole thing and pulled every string to get your father out."

"I don't understand." From the corner of my eye, I see

Isaia get off the platform, slowly approaching. "Um... why...why would Roberto do that?"

Alexius inches closer, like he's afraid I might run if he moves too fast. "My uncle only did this because he knows the best way to get to me is through you."

I shake my head lightly, unable to form a coherent thought. "What are you saying?"

"I'm saying you're not just my wife, stray. You're my weakness too, and my uncle knows it. He knows there is only one thing that would be far worse than death for me, and that's losing you."

The acidic taste of bile rises up my throat, leaving a rotten taste in my mouth. Nausea follows it, and I clutch the fabric of my shirt over my belly, struggling to breathe through the bitterness.

Alexius drags a hand through his hair, brushing it out of his face. "Word got to your father that you're a Del Rossa now. A Dark Sovereign wife. He started using that to his advantage, making deals and forming alliances, saying his son-in-law is Alexius Del Rossa."

"Oh, my God." I suck in a breath, but the air doesn't reach my lungs, my gaze cutting back to the man in the chair. I don't even want to think of him as my father. It's too close, too personal like that. I hardly recognize him. He's older than I remember but not as skinny. Clearly, he's been fed more in prison than he fed himself when he was free. He didn't care for food back then, only caring about his next goddamn fix. He thought his daughter didn't care for food either.

There's a sharp pain in my gut, and even though we

just had dinner, I can remember what it felt like having to go to sleep hungry every night. I remember clutching my tummy, hoping the hunger pangs would die and the grumbling noises would stop. I would wake up in the morning, my stomach burning with nausea and my head throbbing.

A pained whimper escapes me, and I have to plant my palm in front of my mouth. "This isn't happening," I mutter.

"Your father told everyone about you and me and how he has access to the Dark Sovereign through you. It's given him a fuckton of street credit, Leandra. And the plan was for him to get close to you, blackmail you, extort you as far as he could, and then..." Alexius stops short, his throat bobbing as he swallows.

"Then what? Kidnap me. Kill me. What?"

"It doesn't matter. All that matters is that I won't let anyone fucking hurt you or take you from me. Roberto managed to get your father out on parole, but he fucked up by underestimating us, and we found a way through the cracks in his plan."

Rome walks in, the collar of his black trench coat straightened to cover his neck. The confusion I feel is sickening, and I'm sure all the blood in my body has been drained.

"Rome helped us," Alexius explains. "He knew of his father's plans and agreed to help us so we can protect you." He moves close and places his hands on my shoulders as if shielding me. "I need you to understand that I would much rather have put a bullet in your father's head and end his miserable existence than put you in this position. The last thing I want is to put you through this. But I made you a promise, and that's why he's here. That's why you get to decide today."

"Decide what?" I search his face, my heart pounding like it's moments away from ripping through my chest.

He steps up close, cupping my face in both his palms, forcing me to look at him as he wipes tears from my cheeks. "We have two options here, Leandra. We have the ties to make him disappear, make sure where he's going no one will ever find him. Or we kill him."

My heart splits open, adrenaline flooding my veins. "Kill him? You want me to decide what happens to him?"

"Yes."

"No."

"You have to, Leandra."

"No!" I cry. "I'm not God, Alexius."

"Yet he played God over more than two dozen kids' lives without fucking blinking."

"I know what he did," I snap back at him. "I was there, remember? I'm the little girl he tried to whore out to his friend."

"Yeah, and you ran. You made a split-second decision and ran. Thank God for that. But do you know who wasn't that lucky? Who didn't get away?"

Tears lap across my lips and down my chin.

"Brandon Morris," Alexius bites out, barely containing his anger. "He didn't run. He couldn't run. Instead, he got to star in underaged porn along with Pippa Coleman, two days after her tenth birthday."

My stomach churns. "Stop."

"Kendal Roberts couldn't run. So she got locked up in a room with a man the same age as her motherfucking grandfather."

"Alexius," Isaia calls. "Stop."

"No. She needs to hear this." His eyes slay me as he pins his red-hot gaze on mine, his jaw set and nostrils flaring. "Nathan Garrison couldn't run. He tried to fight back, but that cost him an eye because he got his face bashed against a wall before some sick fuck raped him."

I look at the man in the chair, the words coming out of Alexius' mouth erasing everything familiar about him. The longer I listen to my husband listing these heinous crimes, the torturing of so many children, the less this man looks like my father, and the more he takes on the features of a monster. His depravities rot away his flesh, the scales of his sickness covering him in shadows. Even his eyes seem to turn black, his cheeks a sickening gray.

"Sophie Reed couldn't run," Alexius continues. "So she ended up with a needle in her arm and woke up in a pool of her own blood staining the dirty sheets she slept on."

I move closer to where the monster sits, my thoughts stacking up like a row of dominos, every block morphing my fear into empowerment.

"Samantha Vanguard. Hillary Rose." Alexius' voice rolls like thunder in the distance. "Timothy Sutherland. Leroy Jones. Kira Ward. Mia Lancaster. They all disappeared. They were never found. And for the last fifteen fucking years, their families have been living with this open wound that oozes with suffering because they never got any damn closure." His angered tone echoes around the room, crashing against the concrete walls. "You wanna know what all these kids have in common?" Alexius snarls and points at my father. "Him. He groomed them, whored them, assaulted them, kidnapped and sold them. For what? Not for food for his starving daughter. No. For drugs. To get high. And the worst part is, they couldn't convict him of all the crimes. Lack of evidence, they said. For the missing kids, they said no body, no crime. It's disgusting."

I was so young I didn't know the details of my father's case or understand any of it. All I understood was the accusations my mother would spit my way, telling me everything was my fault, that my father left because of me, and that she was unhappy because of me. I believed it then, but now...I know better.

I stop in front of the monster and can practically smell the sulfur leaking from his blackened soul like pus from an infected sore and leprosy that's eaten away his humanity over the years.

Up close, I can see all the scars on his face. Prison hasn't been kind to him, not that he deserves any level of kindness.

His jaw hangs awkwardly to the side and makes a crunching, slurping sound as he tries to speak but fails.

Alexius moves in next to me but doesn't reach for me or touch me as I stare down at the monster. "Nicoli broke his jaw. We thought it best if the fucker couldn't talk to

257

you. Fuck knows what he'd be spitting at you if he could talk."

I'm thankful for that. I've managed to forget the sound of his voice over the years, and I'd rather not be reminded and forced to think of all the vile things he said to me whenever I mentioned that I was hungry or cold or when I was sick with a fever. Or the sound of his disgusting grunts when he was fucking my mother in the living room while I was locked in the bathroom, listening to their sex parties and orgies with people he'd get off the street.

But none of that matters anymore. My own pain isn't the driving force. It's the names—all the names Alexius had said.

I glower down at the monster, feeling nothing but hate and disgust. "For so long, I wondered whether things would have been different if I didn't run that day." I clench my fists. "If I had just waited another ten, twenty, thirty seconds. Would you have gone through with it if I had given you more time to change your mind? Would you have stopped your friend?" Tears drip down my cheeks, the salty drops lapping between my lips. "If I had waited just a few more seconds...would you have seen all your mistakes? Would you have had some kind of divine revelation, turned your life around, and become a real father who loved his daughter more than he loved his next goddamn fix?" I hiss, my lips curving into a snarl as I keep my eyes on his. There's no change in his expression as he listens to me speak, no signs of regret or remorse. It's all just hard lines of evil, a man bathed in the vile acts of a monster.

Alexius pulls a gun from behind his back, and I don't even flinch at the sight. I'm no longer scared. I no longer feel fear. What I *do* feel is this deeply rooted hunger for...vengeance.

"It's your decision, stray," he says, placing the gun's muzzle against the monster's temple, his finger firmly on the trigger.

For a moment, I look up at Isaia, his worried gaze silently asking if I'm okay, and I reply with a barely perceptible nod.

"I know you have it in you, stray. You're not that helpless little girl anymore," Alexius murmurs, and I look at him, his face stricken and eyes determined. "You're my queen," he breathes. "You are...a Del Rossa."

It's a rubber band that snaps. A resolve that slams against my bones. His words reach all the way to my soul, my veins exploding with an energy that floods my system, and strength that burns my blood.

Alexius is right. I'm not Leandra Dinali anymore. I'm no longer the woman Alexius found in that shitty apartment, saving me from a fate determined by a past molded and shaped by my parents.

I'm me. Leandra Del Rossa.

I lean down, bringing my face close to his, tilting my head to the side as I make sure he looks me in the eye. I want him to see me, to *really* see me. I want him to see that the little girl he said was the biggest mistake of his life, the daughter he called a waste of space and a leech, a pathetic piece of shit who would never be something, is now...something. I'm more than something. I'm strong. I'm fierce. I'm gentle and kind. I'm a friend. A wife and soon-to-be mother. I'm...a Del Rossa.

I lean closer, smelling the rancid stench of blood and the flesh of a man who will burn in hell. "Say hi to Mom for me."

I straighten and look at Alexius. "Do it."

He nods, and I turn around, walking in the other direction, wanting my back to be the last thing the monster sees before he finally pays for his sins.

A loud crack erupts. It's a thunderclap that slams against every bone in my body, sending a tremor shaking down my spine. It's the death rattle of a demon. A sound I'll never forget because in the rumbling echo is the final confession of a monster.

CHAPTER 21
ALEXIUS

A bullet wound to the skull is too merciful for a psycho fuck like him. I should have let Nicoli have him for a few hours. Let my brother torture him by slicing his flesh off with a fucking potato peeler. I've seen what my twin is capable of, and he would have given this fucker the slow, painful death he deserved.

But this isn't about him or Nicoli's twisted taste for torture. This isn't about handing out fair judgment to a monster like Federico. This is about my wife. It's about what's best for her, what she needs. And the man I just shot in the head is...no, *was* still her father.

Blood oozes from his head, seeping into the concrete. It's thick and vile and carries the pain of those he wronged. Of the children whose lives he ruined. Everything that's wrong with the world is bleeding out on my goddamn floor right now.

"I would have done a much better job." Nicoli steps

in next to me, staring down at the body. "At least I would have made a show out of it."

"Believe me, killing him with a single bullet was not my first choice either."

"I know this was some epic moment and all," Rome starts, "but my dad is on his way here. He knows you have Federico. Well," he glances at the body, "*had* Federico."

"Why the fuck would he walk into the lion's den when he knows we have Federico, which also means we now know his plan?" Caelian asks, raising a brow.

Isaia scoffs. "Our uncle is ballsy. I'll give him that."

Rome shakes his head. "Just because you managed to snatch up this dead fucker here doesn't mean you know anything. Plus, he has me. He knows I won't let you touch him."

Nicoli's dark brows curve at the edges. "Would you?" He moves closer to Rome, sizing him up with a leveled stare. "You say you're on our side, but if push comes to shove and foreplay turns into full-on fucking, will you save your dad when he's staring down the barrel of my gun?"

"My dad's made his choices," Rome grits out.

"He's your blood."

"And a father who tried to make a cold-blooded killer out of me. You have no fucking idea what my father put me through, the shit he made me do before I finally managed to get the fuck away from him." Rome inches closer, his jaw set and eyes wide. "So, to answer your question. No. I won't save him. I won't plead his case and ask for mercy because he wouldn't show me the same courtesy if our roles were reversed. I came back to stop my father from ruining more lives. To fucking help you."

Tension ripples off them in waves, and Nicoli leans closer into Rome's face, their gazes fixed and eyes glowing with unspoken threats. Nicoli still doesn't trust our cousin, and I don't blame him. For a family as close as ours, it's hard to imagine that a son would betray his father. But you can't exactly compare Rome's father with ours. Roberto is a scaly, sly motherfucker who doesn't know the value of family. Makes sense for his son not to see the value either.

"Nicoli," I snap. "Back off. Our cousin knows if he tries to save his father, we'll bury him as well."

Nicoli grunts, followed by a cocky smirk, before moving away from Rome. "So, what's the plan? Are we just going to let our uncle waltz in here?"

"Security won't allow him on the estate." Maximo pulls out his phone, fingers gliding across the screen.

"No. Let him in when he gets here," I say and look at Nicoli, then Caelian and Isaia. "It's time we settle this shit once and for all. Maximo, make arrangements to get Mira and Leandra out of the house. I don't want them here when shit goes down."

"On it."

I start toward the exit.

"Where are you going?" Caelian calls after me.

"Give me a few. I need to go speak with my wife."

"Are you serious? Roberto is on his way here."

I pivot, slapping Caelian with a glare that can

incinerate stone. "I'm fully aware that there's a war looming on my goddamn doorstep, brother, but right now, all that matters to me is to make sure Leandra is okay. The world can blow up in fucking flames around me at this very moment. I don't give a shit. All I care about is her. So you all can manage without me for a few goddamn minutes while I go check on my wife!"

The echo of my outburst still reverberates off the walls when I turn around and stomp off. My brothers need to come to terms with the fact that the Dark Sovereign is no longer my only responsibility, just as I have. It's no longer the only thing that defines me, and as much as I tried to fight that realization myself, it's just the way it is. My heart has grown stronger since I fell in love with Leandra, and now it rules me. My wife trumps everything else in my life—including the family business.

I find Leandra in the bathroom with nothing but a towel wrapped around her, waiting for the tub to fill. Leaning against the doorframe, I watch her silently for a moment. Her back is turned toward me, her long, dark hair pulled up in a messy bun. From here, I can see how tense her shoulders are, the way she pulls them up just a little. The hot steam around her licks her skin and leaves a faint sheen of moisture on her back.

My eyes trace the curve of her body. Even the fabric of the towel has wrought itself into her shape. I'm an asshole, no doubt about it. My swollen cock proves it. I'm not supposed to be hard for her while aware of her struggle because of what she just went through. But her flawless skin beckons me closer, and she sucks in a breath when I place my palms on her naked shoulders.

"Stray."

"For so long, I've wondered what would have happened if I didn't run that day," she says softly. "I've spent so many nights thinking about whether I made the right choice."

"I've come across some evil fuckers out there, Leandra. Trust me when I say your father was incapable of changing." I brush my fingers along her glowing ivory skin. "If you had stayed, something far worse would have happened to you that day. And think of all the children you saved by turning your father in. Think of all the lives you protected by making that one split-second decision."

"There's at least comfort in that thought."

"Are you okay?"

"I am." She reaches up and places a hand on one of mine resting on her shoulder. "Thank you."

"Right now, I can't think of a single thing you need to thank me for."

"You kept your promise," she murmurs, and my heart constricts. "I know it had to be hard for you to do."

I place a gentle kiss on the nape of her neck. "If it were up to me, I would have taken care of him myself, and you would never have had to go through this. The last thing I want is for you to hurt."

"It doesn't hurt." She glances over her shoulder, her expression calm and eyes liquid. "It doesn't hurt at all. It's like burying my mother all over. Am I incapable of feeling grief? Am I broken?"

"No. You're incapable of wasting your emotions on those who don't deserve it. And that makes you strong, not broken." I kiss the back of her head, closing my eyes, wishing there was a way to make her see inside me, to give her a glimpse of herself through my eyes. "You're the strongest person I know, stray. Even after all you've been through and the cruelty the world has shown you, you haven't lost your heart or your kindness. Your ability to forgive."

"Maybe that's why I don't feel anything for my parents. I haven't forgiven them."

I drag my hand from her shoulder down her chest, where her heart beats beneath my palm. "They don't deserve your forgiveness, and your heart knows it. God, I'm not even sure I deserve your forgiveness after what I've put you through."

"My heart seems to think you do," she whispers, and my entire fucking world lights up. What I did tonight was risky, but deep down, I knew she would be strong enough to handle it. I saw the wall of strength in her the day I walked into her apartment with my *mutually beneficial* offer—an offer that put everything in motion for us to end up here in a world where we would only ever need each other.

"I have a confession to make." I lean into her, tracing a delicate line with the tip of my nose down the side of her neck, inhaling deeply. She smells of vanilla, and it's an intoxicating fusion with the lavender-scented bath oil that lathers on the water.

"What is it?" She leans her head to the side, her skin gleaming under the bathroom light.

"I loved watching you go from scared and uncertain to a beautiful goddess of war." I press my lips on her naked shoulder. "My own fucking Athena. God, you're perfect." I loosen the towel around her and let it drop to the floor and watch as it pools around her feet. Looking down at her naked body, I drink her in—the shape of her calves, her thighs, the firm rounds of her ass, and the tempting curve of her back. "I'm probably a sick son of a bitch for saying this," I run a finger from the base of her spine, along every vertebra, up the middle of her back, "but you were fucking exquisite in your vengeance."

She leans her weight back into me, her soft breaths quickening. "Are you trying to seduce me, Mr. Del Rossa? After I told you to kill a monster less than an hour ago?"

I grin against her skin and snake my hand around her waist, tracing a fingertip along her belly. "It's fucked up, I know. But you and me...we do fucked up really well."

"I can't argue that." She raises her arm, reaching her hand behind my head, and sways her ass against my hard cock. "You just killed a man, and now you want to fuck me?"

My hand dips low and cups her sex. A soft moan rushes past her lips. "I want to make you come. Show you there's pleasure in justice." My fingertip finds her clit, and I start with soft circles, and it causes her to tremble against me. Her head drops back, resting against my chest, her delicate throat bobbing as she swallows. "Is that what you want, stray? You want me to make you feel good?"

"Yes," she breathes, and I reach deeper into her slit, sliding my finger through her wet folds, spreading her arousal along the crease of her cunt. I kiss her neck, lapping my tongue along her flesh, tasting the sweetness of her skin. "You were fucking incredible. So strong. So fucking exquisite." Her hips move, and I know she wants more. More of my touch. More friction. Pressure. She needs to feel good after what happened. She fucking deserves to feel good, and I'll die a happy man knowing I'm the one who knows how to give it to her.

"Alexius?"

"Yes, baby girl?"

"Make me come, please."

Winding an arm around her waist, I pull her closer as her legs start to tremble, clutching her tight as I find her clit again, this time working it harder and faster, teasing that bundle of nerves until her gentle breaths turn into wild whimpers.

Her wetness coats my fingers and palm, her swollen flesh warm and eager for my touch. She's so slick and ready, the scent of her arousal fucking with my control. My cock is damn hard; I want to be inside her. I want to fuck her. I want to slam into her so hard she'll forget how to breathe. But this isn't about me. Not tonight. This is all about her. What she needs from me. And right now, she needs this release far more than I do.

I bend my legs slightly, reaching deeper between her thighs, finding her entrance, and sinking a finger into her.

"Oh, God," she cries, her ass grinding against my aching cock. "I'm close."

I groan and speed up my movements, placing more pressure against her clit, massaging harder and faster.

"Yes," she moans. "Don't stop."

"I won't stop until your pussy creams my palm, stray. I want your cum on my fingers, and then I want to watch it coat your inner thighs."

She's no longer holding herself up. I keep her pinned against me, loving how she leans all her weight into me while I stroke her cunt, listening to her moans fill the room.

"Come for me. And say my name while you do."

"Hmm–mm," she moans, sucking her bottom lip into her mouth. Her pussy clenches around my finger, her body shaking as she chases the pleasure.

"My name, stray." My voice is a dark timbre of warning, and her head lolls from side to side.

"Alexius." Fuck, my name is a goddamn melody on her lips.

"Again." I press hard on her clit, my fingers moving fast, working her body into a frenzy.

"Oh, God. Alexius, I'm coming."

"That's my girl."

Her body goes rigid against mine, and her orgasm crests. Every muscle pulls tight as I carry her through the pleasure, erasing all the pain with euphoria. There is not a single sound in this entire goddamn world that's as beautiful as her moans and whimpers while she comes.

"Alexius," she says, out of breath, and I grab her waist, spinning her around as I drop to my knees, my gaze level with her smooth cunt.

"I want to see how wet you are."

"Jesus," she says breathlessly, steadying herself by weaving her fingers through my hair.

With my thumbs, I spread her pussy open, her clit blushing and swollen, her folds glistening with temptation. It's fucking beautiful.

I work my fingers through her slit, opening it wide so I can see every inch of her, see her wetness cling to her thighs. "Fuck, your pussy looks delicious all coated in your cum." I can't stop myself. It's too fucking tempting, so I slip my tongue through her wet pussy, lapping up her sweetness. Her taste only spins me into a frenzy, a crazed need to bury myself in her.

I reach around her and cup her ass in my palms as I eat her cunt with greedy licks, her fingers pulling at my hair.

"I need you." She moves her hips and grinds her pussy deeper into my face. "I need you to fuck me...please."

Abruptly, I straighten, slamming my mouth on hers, forcing her taste from my tongue to hers as she tugs and pulls at my pants, trying to free my cock. We're swallowing each other's moans when she pulls my dick free, wrapping her palm around my naked shaft.

A growl tears from my throat, and I hoist her into my arms, her legs wrapping around me as I carry her across the room, placing her on the bathroom countertop. Perfume bottles and bath oils fall and clang behind her. But we don't stop. We grab and claw, kiss and bite, our primal needs pushing to the forefront and taking control.

Her hand is on my cock and lines it up with her entrance. I pull her closer to the edge, pushing forward and spearing into her.

"Oh, fuck." Her lips part, her breath dancing like fire along my cheek. I clutch the counter's edge with one hand, my other arm wrapped around her waist, plunging into her over and over, her body jerking against mine with every thrust. "You feel so fucking good inside me, Alexius. Don't stop."

"I'm not stopping, stray. Not until your body takes every drop of my cum."

She reaches for my hand on her waist and jerks it up to her throat.

"No." Instead of squeezing, I brush my fingers across her skin. "I'm not choking you, stray. You're pregnant."

"Don't choke me. I just need to feel your hand there. Just a little. You know I like it when you fuck me rough."

"Jesus Christ," I curse and force her back, pinning her shoulders against the mirror, her body arched and tits bouncing while I pound into her slick cunt, all warm and tight.

"Yes!" she cries. "Like that. God, don't stop. Please don't stop."

Every muscle in my ass pulls taut as I fuck her with quick, incessant, wild thrusts, grinding into her.

"Can I come?"

"You better come before I do."

With a violent shudder, her pussy walls clamp down around my cock, pulsing as her orgasm peaks. Her body tenses, her thighs squeezing my sides so hard she stalls me and fucks with my rhythm. I pull her back up, and she throws her arms around my neck as I pull her close, her body flush against mine, and I sink so deep into her that I come instantly, the pleasure bursting through my veins.

"I love you," she mutters through panting breaths, my cock jerking, pouring my cum inside her.

"I love you, too." I'm breathless, but I claim her mouth, willing to give my last breath just to kiss her.

My cock slips out of her, and I pull her into my arms, carrying her over to the tub, setting her down and helping her step in. I kiss her cheek as I crouch down beside her, splashing the water over her chest. To others, this strong connection I have with this woman is insanity, but to me, it's life. It's air. It's the blood that keeps me alive.

I place my forehead against the side of her face, closing my eyes as her presence intoxicates me. "I want to burn down the world for you, stray. Rid it of all the monsters for you."

"I know. And I love you for it."

There are a few seconds of silence, enough time for reality to bleed back in and pull us out of the moment.

"I need you and Mirabella to leave."

"What?" She pulls away, staring at me with confusion.

"Maximo is arranging for you to be taken to a safe place. Just for tonight."

"Why? What else is happening tonight?"

I reach out, tucking a wet strand behind her ear. "Tonight, I end a war."

CHAPTER 22

ALEXIUS

"They're safe," Maximo confirms as he comes toward me. "They're at—"

"Don't tell me." I stop him. "No one can know where they are except you."

He nods, and I place a hand on his shoulder.

"I've never thought of you as anything other than a brother. You and Mirabella are as much a part of this family as the rest of us. Your loyalty has not gone unnoticed."

"My loyalty is out of love and respect for this family."

"*Your* family," I urge, squeezing his shoulder. "As far as I'm concerned, we're blood, and nothing will change that. But I need you to promise me that whatever goes down tonight, Leandra's and Mira's safety come first. If a decision needs to be made, you choose them above all else. Even me."

"It's not gonna come to that. I won't let it."

"Just," I sigh, "promise me you'll protect them. Protect my children. If anything has to happen—"

He cuts me off, slapping his hand on my shoulder and gripping it tightly, looking me straight in the eye, his voice low as he says, "I promise, Alexius. I will protect them."

"Thank you," I breathe out, and Maximo's phone chimes with a message.

He pulls it out and slides his finger across the screen before cutting his gaze to mine. "They're here."

"Good. Let's get this over with." I unlock the doors to the Dark Sovereign room, sliding them into pocket walls. Every time I walk in here, I'm hit with nostalgia, the smell of fresh, polished furniture reminding me of my father and how I sat beside him, taking in every word, every decision with the hope that I'd one day be able to make him proud as head of this family. But the more I walk in his shoes, the more I realize I won't ever be able to fill his shoes. I'll never be Vincenzo Del Rossa. But I am his son, and I will be the best leader I know how to be without sacrificing the happiness of those I love.

Nicoli, Caelian, and Isaia walk in behind me. Nicoli's usual smirk is absent, replaced with sharp edges and hard lines. Caelian has a cigarette dangling from his mouth and a fervent gleam in his eyes as if excited about shit finally hitting the fan. Isaia glances my way as he slips in behind Nicoli, and I notice the reluctance in his eyes. I know what he's thinking. "Isaia," I call. "You do not stand at the back. You're also a part of this family, so take your place next to Caelian."

He hesitates but then moves in next to Caelian. No matter the differences between Isaia and myself, this feels right, having him here and including him. Hopefully, if tonight goes well, this is how it will be from now on.

"Security is escorting them in," Maximo says, standing guard by the entry.

"Tell them to back down as soon as they enter the house."

"What?" Maximo's brows curve. "No."

"Tell them to back down," I repeat, lowering my voice. "We're settling this like men tonight, and not a bunch of pussies hiding behind a wall of bulletproof-wearing security guys."

"I think that's the best pep-talk I've ever heard." Nicoli grins, his energy contagious.

Nicoli exhales a plume of smoke. "Is it strange that I'm a little turned on right now from all this tension? My spine's all tingly."

"Just keep it in your pants. No one wants to see your ugly dick tonight," Isaia says, lacking the grin to go with that dose of sarcasm.

I trace my finger along the gold DS engraved into my black tufted chair—my father's chair—before taking a seat. If my father was here, what would he say? What would he want me to do? The Dark Sovereign started out as carved in five. Three Del Rossas. Two Savellis. An uneven number to ensure we never end in a deadlock. It was supposed to be the merging of two strong families, a joining that made us as powerful and influential as we are today. But my uncle's greed fucked that up, creating a rift between us. If Roberto were to retain his place within the Dark Sovereign, it will only be a matter of time before he sells us out to the highest bidder and gathers more allies who will eventually support his cause of getting rid of every Del Rossa. That's what he's been trying to do for years. He doesn't want five around this table. He wants one. Him.

Over my dead goddamn body.

Rome enters the room first, specks of snow glistening on his black trench coat. We greet each other with a curt nod and a knowing look. I glance at Maximo, a silent sign for him to do as we planned, and he stomps out just as Roberto walks in looking like the smug, fat bastard he is. Not even an Armani suit can make him look less repulsive.

"I see we're all here." He stops short, and his cruel gaze finds Isaia. "What are you doing here, if I may ask?"

"You may not," I interject. "He's my brother, so his place is here with the rest of us."

"He has no place here. There are only five."

"Then what the fuck are you doing here? You no longer have a place here since your son took yours."

Roberto scoffs. "I'm merely here for support. Teaching my son the ins and outs, showing him the reins."

Ricardo comes walking in, pale as a fucking ghost and eyes bewildered.

"Look who finally decided to show up," I say, leaning back in my chair, glowering at the coward who hardly ever shows his face around here.

Nicoli snorts. "He's never here because, just like the rest of us, he knows he doesn't belong here, do you, Uncle?"

Ricardo barely makes eye contact with Nicoli, cautiously glancing at Roberto from under his dark brows.

"Fuck knows why someone would think you have something valuable to offer," Nicoli continues. "You're just here to fill a seat. But lucky for you, we have far better-suited candidates to take your place. So do us all a favor and fuck off."

"Is that any way to speak to your uncle?" Roberto snaps, his eyes lit with disdain.

"No," Nicoli says, stalking closer. "It's the way to talk to a coward and his backstabbing, low-life piece of shit brother who has an ass for brains because everything that comes out of your mouth is complete and utter shit."

I hear Caelian snort behind me, and I watch in silence as my twin brother and uncle keep their glares locked in a silent battle of power. It's Roberto who looks away first. Of course, it is. We all know he doesn't have the balls to take on any of us, especially not Nicoli.

"So," Roberto turns to me, "where is your lovely wife this evening?"

"Vacation."

"Oh, well, that's too bad. I hoped to congratulate her on her father's early parole."

I bite the inside of my cheek, trying to keep my composure and not lose my shit so early in the conversation. "No need to congratulate her. You might

281

want to pay your respects since he's dead." I shrug. "You know, from one piece of shit to another."

His expression falters. "What do you mean he's dead?"

"What I mean is I planted a bullet in his skull."

"You killed your wife's father? I have to say, Alexius, that's cruel even for you."

"Cut the bullshit. We all know you're behind it. You arranged for Federico Dinali to be granted parole."

"Why on Earth would I do that?"

I want to wipe that smug grin off his face. Patronizing fucker knows how to turn my blood to fire. "I know about your plan, Roberto."

"What plan? Seriously, Alexius, you're not making any sense." He straightens his sleeves.

"The plan to have that perverted son of a bitch go around town telling everyone he has ties with the Del Rossa family. To have him get close to my wife, blackmail her, keep her in your sights until you're ready to strike."

Silence passes, and he doesn't even fucking blink. My chest burns with cruelty aimed at my uncle, a savage need to cut his throat and watch him choke on his blood, a brutal desire to hear him scream from the pain caused by the tip of my blade grating down his spine.

"That's preposterous," he snarls. "This is exactly why you shouldn't sit in that goddamn chair. You're a conniving little shit who will conjure up lies so your actions are justified."

I scoff. "I don't need to justify anything. I have all I

need to get rid of you. The recording of how you planned on killing my father. Your plan to kill my wife."

"Kill your wife? That's insane." His fat fingers struggle to button his suit jacket. "How did you come up with these blatant lies?"

"A little birdie told me."

"A what?"

I cut my gaze to Rome, who steps closer, his shoulders squared, nothing but pure resolve painted on his features. "I told him."

Roberto's eyes flash with shock, and I'm sure all the blood just drained from his body. A sheen of sweat beads along his eyebrows as he turns to look at Rome. "You?"

Oh, this is one substantial motherfucking biblical moment, watching the surprise on Roberto's face as he stares at his son, the shadow of betrayal clouding his expression. "Is this your doing, son?"

Rome licks his lips, straightening as he pulls on the hardened demeanor of a son who carries the secrets of a boy who has been wronged by the man who's supposed to protect him. "I can't stand back and watch you ruin their lives as you've ruined mine."

"What?" Roberto's eyes flash with a scheming glint. "Jesus, son. What lies have you told them?"

"I told them the truth."

Roberto shakes his head lightly, sucking his bottom lip into his disgusting mouth. "Then I guess you've told them about your problem?" he says with a smooth but fake tone of disappointment.

Rome narrows his eyes. "What problem?"

"It pains me to bring up this delicate matter, son, but I can't have you go around slandering my name and making up stories."

"Oh, believe me, no one can slander your shitty name as much as my brothers and me," Nicoli remarks with a cocky grin.

Roberto shoots him a deadpan look, then returns his fake sympathetic stare at his son. "You're a compulsive liar, Rome. And you have been since you were a little boy, always making up stories, trying to stir conflict."

Rome starts to laugh, a cackle of mocking amusement. I remain silent as I watch the dominoes start to fall in place, and I'd be a liar if I said I'm not enjoying every goddamn moment of it.

"You really think they'll believe you?" Rome asks, pointing at us while glaring at his father.

"It's the truth."

"You've burned this bridge, Dad. No one trusts you anymore because you're a greedy, sick, two-timing asshole who doesn't deserve a goddamn bowl to piss in."

"Amen," Nicoli chimes in. "I'm starting to like our cousin."

Roberto stalks up to Rome, who is almost a foot taller than his old man. "You are a liar. And the truth is, you're a fucking disappointment. I should have kill—"

"Since we're on the topic of lies," I cut him off, rounding my desk, wanting to be in my uncle's face when I say this. "You were right, Uncle."

"Right about what?"

"About Jimmy." I shrug. "I did kill Jimmy. I shot him right after I cut his finger off."

Roberto's cheeks turn bright red, and his nostrils flare. "I knew it. I knew you killed Jimmy. You couldn't stand him."

"Because just like you, he was a low-life piece of shit who didn't deserve to be a part of this family."

"He was my son!" Spit flies from between his teeth. "You killed my son."

"No. His arrogance is what killed him. And he was not your son. You have one son, and he's standing right there." I point at Rome, who now stands next to Nicoli. "He's your blood, yet he can't stand you either. For weeks he fooled you, pretending to be on your side and helping you keep a hold on the Dark Sovereign by taking your place. But he would rather betray you than be your fucking puppet. I'd say that makes you a real shitty father, don't you agree?"

"Like your father was a goddamn saint," he sneers. "As if you'll do better. Oh, talking about fatherhood, I hear you're having a little girl. Congratulations." His lips curl at the edges in a malicious grin, his eyes almost vibrant with ill intent.

"About that." I snap my fingers, and Maximo walks in with the traitor who has been feeding my uncle information, forcing his ass into a chair next to me. "I found your rat. You should really pick them better, Uncle. This one is as subtle as a heart attack, pretending to bring us a clean set of towels after my doctor almost trampled over him. Fucker was standing outside the door eavesdropping for twenty minutes and didn't realize he was being recorded on a security camera."

The vein in Roberto's neck bulges, his lips pursed, and guilt creased along his forehead as he stares in shock at the fucker sobbing, tugging at his tied hands.

Nicoli hands me his knife, and I move to settle behind the rat who starts to piss himself, the rancid stench of urine and fear a sharp precursor of death. "When will you realize that you can't outsmart us, Uncle? That, no matter how hard you try, you just don't have what we Del Rossas have." I let out a low snarl, reach over, and slice the blade clean through the rat's throat. "Power," I say without blinking, and the gargling sound of the fucker choking on his own blood is music to my ears. There is no mercy shown to traitors. Never.

"Jesus," Roberto mutters, his eyes wide with shock. "You're a fucking psychopath."

"And you're in over your head." I wipe the bloody blade clean on my sleeves and start to circle Roberto like a predator in the mood to play with his prey. "First, you tried to take what's not yours by plotting to have my father killed, then wiping out the Del Rossa bloodline by killing my brothers and me. Time after time, I sat in this room listening to you argue with my father about changing the rules, changing our legacy by getting more allies on board because you're too greedy for your own good." I scoff. "It's funny, really, how a man who has no idea how to wield power wants more of it."

Roberto stares at the dead rat, whose head hangs

eerily to the side, blood still pouring from the wound onto my expensive goddamn carpet.

"You should have walked away when I gave you the chance, Roberto. You should have just cut your losses and disappeared. But no. You had to try to fuck with me by bringing Rome here to take your place so you could still have an influence on what happens around here." I shrug. "But little did you know that Rome wasn't eating the bullshit you were feeding him, and your entire plan to kill my wife got shot to shit."

"You do not deserve to lead the Dark Sovereign," he bites out, his jaw clenched and veins bulging at his temples. "You are nothing but a spoiled fucking brat who desperately sought his father's approval. Even now, with your father dead and buried, you're still so goddamn desperate to prove you have what it takes. It's pathetic."

I hand Nicoli's knife back to him, and shift in behind my chair, tracing my fingers along the gold weaved letters. "What's pathetic, dear uncle, is that even after almost twenty fucking years of plotting, you're now farther from this seat than you've ever been. In fact, I'm going to make sure your name is erased from every document, every piece of paper, every article, every little fucking thing that ties you to the Dark Sovereign. You are a disgrace to this family. You are a sorry excuse for a man and father, and I will make it my life's mission to ensure that I expunge you from this fucking world entirely, and it'll be as if you never existed."

Roberto's lips twitch, his eyes dark with the kind of rage that turns men into irresponsible fuckers.

Adrenaline floods my system, the back of my neck prickling with warning that shoots to every nerve. There's a violent glint as we both draw our guns, aiming them at each other. My heart is pounding, and I hear my brothers draw their guns behind me.

I smirk. "This is where you realize that you're truly and completely fucked."

"I should have killed you in your sleep when you were a fucking baby."

"Lucky for me, you didn't have the balls. You still don't."

Sweat drips down Roberto's face as he keeps his gun aimed at me, and the way his eyes turn void, he knows as well as I do that there's no way he's walking out of this alive.

"You know what?" Roberto's top lip curls into a snarl. "I won't kill you."

"Smart move."

"I'd rather die knowing you have to live with the reality that I killed someone you loved."

My mind splinters. Horror slams into my chest, and air rushes from my lungs. I scream as Roberto moves his aim, the sharp crack of a gunshot crashing straight through my gut, ice shattering through my veins as I watch Nicoli stagger back, blood spreading like crimson tentacles seeping through his white shirt.

I'm still screaming, rage and shock pulsing, gripping every muscle, every molecule, every fucking thought as I spin around, aim at Roberto's face and pull the trigger.

Every sound is muted, and Roberto falls back in slow

motion, half his face gone. Everything goes blank, and I don't know how I got there, but I'm on my knees next to my brother, my ears ringing, my heart pounding. My hands are on his chest, blood seeping through the creases of my fingers and coating my hands. I know I'm saying something. I'm telling him to hold on. Begging him to stay with me. Pleading for him not to fucking die. But I don't hear a single word that comes out of my mouth.

The first thing I hear is the roar that ruptures from my chest, followed by the wail that destroys me from the inside out...and that's when Nicoli closes his eyes.

CHAPTER 23
LEANDRA

"Where are we going?" I ask Alexius, who looks dapper all dressed in black. Black suit, black shirt, black tie. I don't think I'll ever get used to what a beautiful creature my husband is.

"You'll see soon enough," he replies, his voice all low and mysterious.

"We'll be home before midnight, right?"

"Of course, we won't." He arches his brow as if I had just asked the world's dumbest question.

I shift in the passenger seat of Alexius' car. "It's my first time out since having the twins. You have to ease me into it. I'm already choking on anxiety here."

"They're safe with Mirabella. Plus, Isaia is around if she needs any help. There's nothing to worry about."

"I know. But I can't help it. I don't like leaving them. What if Aria gets hungry? You know she's a fussy eater and hates the bottle."

"She'll be fine."

"What if Alessio's colic acts up again?"

"He'll be fine, too. Stop worrying."

I scoff. "It feels like I haven't stopped worrying since they were born."

"Which is why you need tonight. For the last ten weeks, you've been nothing short of amazing, being the best mother our babies can ask for." He takes my hand while keeping his eyes on the road, lifts it to his lips, and kisses it tenderly. "But tonight, I want you to remember that you're not just a mother and a wife. You're a woman with needs and desires too." A wicked glint in his blue eyes sends a shiver of excitement down my spine.

"What are you up to, Mr. Del Rossa?"

He places his hand on my thigh, his fingers slipping the red fabric upward and igniting a flush of goosebumps on my skin. "Reminding you that you and I, we're meant to unravel."

It's like he flicked a switch, my body going from nervous tremors to fervent quivers within a split second.

It's been a long time—too long—since Alexius and I indulged. We played it safe during the pregnancy, but while vanilla sex was satisfying, it didn't quite satiate us fully. I've only recently recovered from a hard labor with the twins, who were born four weeks early. And I now finally got a green light from the doctor saying Alexius and I can return to our 'normal' sexual lifestyle. Normal. Alexius and I've never had a normal sex life. At least not according to society's tight-laced tastes.

I glance out the windows as we take a turn down a

long path, large oak trees skirting the sides of the road. It's a full moon tonight, casting its glow on the world and making the tree branches seem alive as it reaches through the light. There's a thrilling energy in the car with us, excitement popping in my belly like bubbles of champagne as we pull up to a brass-plated gate that creaks open. A double-story, Victorian-style mansion comes into view, and Alexius circles around past the driveway, pulling up at the back of the building.

"What is this place?"

"Here." He hands me a box wrapped in gold foil and gets out of the car. I smile as I open the box, revealing the same black lace masquerade mask he gave me the night at Mito in Italy. My heart stutters thinking about that night, about the ecstasy that lingered in my veins for long after we left that club. It was one of the best nights of my life.

Wait...is this...

My door opens, and Alexius gives me his hand, helping me out of the car. I find my footing and stare at the large building, my heart about to leap out of my chest. "Is this—"

"Welcome to Club Myth."

"Oh, my God, are you serious?" I'm nothing but molecules of excitement, my gaze darting around every inch of the estate lit up by so many lights.

Alexius shoots me a roguish grin. "I am."

"But you said you'd never bring me here."

"I know what I said." He removes my mask from the box, eases it over my eyes, and moves in behind me, gently tying it before clipping it into my hair. All the memories of that night in Italy come crashing back, and my body is set alight with anticipation trying to imagine what it is Alexius has in store for us tonight.

He snakes his arm around my waist, pulling me close, breathing along the shell of my ear. "There are rules."

"Of course there are." I bite my lip, my insides stirring with simmering heat.

"The club is closed tonight to anyone who did not receive an exclusive invitation."

"Ooh. Well, that sure sounds interesting."

"It's a private...*event,* if you will, hosted by one of our most important clients."

I lean back into him. "What type of party is it?"

"You'll see." He grinds his hips, and my lips part when I feel his cock is already hard. "Now, you don't speak. At all. Not even when spoken to. The only person who knows who we are is Gabriel King."

"Your associate?"

"Sort of, yes." He places a kiss on the nape of my neck, and I close my eyes. "He's the most discreet person I know, and I fully trust that our presence here tonight is something he'll take to the grave."

"Any other rules, Mr. Del Rossa?" I purr, swaying my ass against his crotch.

He hisses in my ear and jerks me tighter against him, touching his lips below my ear. "As always, no one touches you, and you don't touch another man."

"Can I touch another woman?" I challenge with a sultry twist in my voice.

"Oh, now, that is something I think I'll be able to live

with." His voice is low, a seductive tenor that sends tremors down my legs, my core already needing to be filled.

His hand travels up my middle and slips inside the low neckline, cupping my breast with gentle fingers. "You look ravishing in red, stray."

"Thank you, husband, but you forgot to make an essential request."

"And what is that?'

I lean my face to the side and glance up at him through thick lashes, his sapphire-blue eyes penetrating mine. "I'm wearing panties."

His lush lips curl in a sexy as fuck grin. "I can take care of that." Dropping down and crouching right there behind me in the parking lot, he slips his hands underneath my knee-length dress, pulling my panties down my legs. I gasp, and I'm already wet even though he's barely touched me. Will I ever become immune to his touch?

I hope not.

Straightening, he tucks my panties in his jacket pocket. "Better?"

"Much."

"For God's sake, don't drop anything. I'd hate to have to kill someone in my own damn club."

I let out a laugh, and he pulls me close, staring into my eyes hungrily as he touches my chin with his thumb and forefinger. "Are you ready to unravel with me, stray?"

"Always."

My heels click across the paved walkway, and I'm

both excited and nervous as Alexius clutches my hand tightly. The double doors open, and we enter the building, chills zapping up and down my skin.

There's no way I can stop myself from gasping as I take it all in. High, coffered ceilings with crown moldings create the illusion of endless space, and the double-story chandelier lights scatter off the rows of crystals, reflecting on the stark white walls and marbled floors like drops of gold.

"This place is exquisite, Alexius," I remark in awe.

"We like to hide our sins with wealth." He smirks, and I nudge him lightly. A man wearing the same full-black attire as Alexius waits for us at the edge of the stairs.

"Gabriel," Alexius greets, and they shake hands.

Gabriel simply looks my way and nods, and I remember Alexius' rule. *Do not speak to anyone.* My guess is our host is aware of this rule, which is why he chooses silence when greeting me. For a moment, I'm stunned by Gabriel's cobalt blue eyes illuminated by the chandelier's light. Not even his mask can suppress their brilliance. There's a force around this man that makes it hard to look away; a powerful authority that reaches for you, demanding all your attention.

"We're about to start. Please follow me."

I glance at Alexius as we walk down the flight of stairs, the gold rails decorated with intricate filigree. There's a door to our right that we enter, walking into an area that's dimly lit, the paneled walls a bold velvet red. We're at a top level, standing by the railing and gazing down at a group of women listening intently to the hostess, and by the sound of it, she's telling them the rules.

"As I said before, you do not choose your Dom. The Dom chooses his submissive." I'm sure if melted chocolate had a sound, it would be this woman's voice. "There are six Doms here tonight, and as there are so many of you, some of you will not get to go up those stairs tonight, depending if you get chosen or not. I feel it necessary to stress the fact that if you are unhappy with the one who chose you, you are free to leave. But if you do, you will never be allowed to attend again, and once you walk out of here tonight, you will live like this place does not exist."

The small crowd of women nod their understanding. Everyone is dressed in black and shades of red, except for one wearing a crisp, ivory-colored dress, the rhinestones in her white lace mask shimmering under the soft lights.

I sneak a glance at Gabriel standing on the other side of Alexius. His gaze is transfixed on the girl in white, and I can practically feel the pulse of his desire for her.

Six men dressed in black suits and wearing masks line up by a round, pristinely polished mahogany table set underneath an exquisite black crystal chandelier. This room is charged with so much sexual energy it's hard for me to stand still and not clench my thighs every two minutes.

The woman standing next to the one in white separates from the crowd, her dark burgundy dress swooshing around her ankles as she makes her way to the middle.

I'm holding my breath in anticipation, watching her get on the table, gracefully lying back and spreading her legs. She's not wearing any underwear, and from up here, we can see her pussy glistening underneath the chandelier.

I swallow, my core starting to tingle with need, and I tighten my grip on Alexius' hand. He squeezes back, a silent acknowledgment that he feels my energy, my sexual tension climbing with every passing second. God, I love how he knows me.

Once the woman on the table is comfortable, the first masked man steps up, and my breathing turns rapid, watching as he looks down between her legs, his hands resting comfortably on her inner thighs. She's already panting, writhing on the mahogany, her gentle moans growing louder as he leans down, gently blowing on her naked folds.

My wetness spreads along my crease, and I gasp, my insides turning into a thousand tingling knots the moment he starts eating her cunt. He takes his time sampling her, his head bobbing between her thighs. The woman cries out, bucking off the table when the first man straightens and walks away.

"Why is he walking away?" I whisper.

"I told you to keep quiet," Alexius scolds me. "This is how the Doms choose their submissives. Every man gets a chance, and the one who feels the most connected to her takes her for the evening."

Oh, God. I think my blood just turned to fucking fire.

A second man moves into place, his hands starting at her ankles, gently easing up her legs, straightening his arms as he reaches for her pussy, spreading her folds wide. He's biting his bottom lip, and I'm squirming where I stand, trying to press my thighs together, the ache growing stronger.

This man is going down on her like her pussy is the last fucking meal, reaching up and cupping her breast as he roughs his lips and tongue between her legs. He's not gentle. Doesn't take it slow. He's like a savage, and before long, she's coming, her cries reaching the ceiling.

Holy fuck.

I touch the scar behind my ear, my entire body burning with need. It's as if liquid spreads through my chest, my legs growing weaker as my arousal grows stronger.

I'm convinced this man will choose her, judging by the way he just made her come. But he doesn't. It's the fifth man who tastes her pussy who ends up extending his hand, choosing her as his partner for the evening.

Alexius looks at me, his lips curved seductively. I'm so damn wet and needy, ready for him to fuck me right here, right now, not giving a shit about the erotic ritual of Dominants and submissives taking place on the lower level.

The woman in white is chosen for the table next, and I smile when I see Gabriel descending the stairs.

I lean close to Alexius. "If you'd rather not fuck me

against this banister, I'd suggest you take me somewhere else right now."

"You don't want to watch the rest of the girls get their pussies licked?"

I turn and trace a finger down his black silk tie. "I'd rather get my own pussy licked."

My breath lashes from my lungs as Alexius pushes my back against the iron banister. He's on his knees in front of me, lifts the front of my skirt, and my eyes roll closed, the girl on the table below moaning at the same time Alexius covers my pussy with his mouth.

I stretch my arms across the railing, wrapping my fingers around the iron. With his expert fingers, he spreads my folds open for him, his tongue darting out and flicking against my clit.

"Oh, God." I forget to breathe, his tongue swirling around the outline of my pussy before diving inside, licking up my slit, sending sparks through my bones. Again, I have to remind myself to breathe, lolling my head back and side to side, my body climbing as Alexius' velvet tongue licks, his lips enclosing my sensitive nub, sucking, sending sparks of electricity up my core.

I glance down at him, biting my lip as I watch him. I want to see his mouth fuck my pussy. I want to see my cum slick on his lips and around his mouth. "Fuck," I curse breathlessly.

Mesmerized, I keep my eyes on him, his tongue teasing at my entrance, then licking up my soaked sex. He pulls away and stares up at me, the darkness and shadows dancing across his blue eyes. "Look down. Look at them."

I do as he says, glancing around the room. So many masked faces, some staring up at us, the others staring at the couple on the table. Lust and twisted desires fill the space like thick smoke. Everyone here has come with a need to have a fantasy fulfilled, and watching us is part of that fantasy. Watching the woman on the table getting tongued is part of that fantasy. Pussies are wet, and cocks are hard because everyone in this room loves watching.

"Mmm," he groans against my sensitive flesh, working his tongue faster. "My pretty little slut."

It's like four magic words, catapulting me toward a pleasure meant only for sinners.

My hips start to move as he eats my pussy with greedy licks, and I throw my head back, my hair hanging down and over the railing. I can't hold it back. I can't stop it. The sensation is too much. The tension in the room is too much. It's everywhere, coating my skin and filling my lungs with every breath.

"Alexius," I breathe out. "I need to—"

He jerks away and drops the skirt of my dress, my climax gone and my body in sheer agony. "What the hell?"

He wipes my arousal from his mouth with the back of his hand, his tongue swiping along his lips. "You don't get to come yet."

"Are you trying to kill me?"

There's a sly grin on his face, and I'm inclined to

think that right now, my husband is an asshole for not letting me come.

My thighs are wet. My pussy is throbbing. And every muscle in my body is complaining as Alexius leads me out of the large room and down a dark hallway. Light strips are attached to the floor like a thousand fireflies are flanking the hall, soft music playing through the ceiling speakers. For so long, I only imagined what this place looked like, what it was like on the inside of the sex club run by my husband and his brothers. But just like Mito, everything is tasteful, elegant, and sophisticated. It's not some back-alley sex joint where everything smells like cum, and the filth of others clings to your skin while dirty sheets creep up your ass, and the clang of chains accentuates women's screams of pain.

We stop at a black door with a gold knob, and Alexius doesn't even hesitate before opening it and walking inside like he owns the place. Oh, right...he does.

The first thing I notice is the smell. It's a subtle fusion of vanilla and rose, the air warm and clean. But I can feel and smell the sex in the air. It's seeping through my pores and infecting me.

There's a four-poster bed with white chiffon curtains draped down the sides placed in the middle of the room, and tied to it is the masked girl who left with her Dom earlier. He's there, too, his shirt gone and only wearing his black pants, the zipper pulled down halfway, teasing a glimpse of a defined V and the outline of his straining cock pressing hard against the fabric.

I suck in a breath when I spot the pink vibrator in his

hands, slowly dragging it against her skin and up the inside of her thigh. Her ankles are fastened to a spreader bar, her legs wide. From this angle, I can see every part of her sex, and how she's squirming on the sheets tells me her body is in agony and in desperate need of release.

"What do you see, stray?" Alexius slips in behind me and wraps an arm around my waist, grinding his cock against my ass.

"I see a woman who wants to come."

"Remind you of anything?"

The man gently eases the vibrator against her pussy lips, brushing it up and down with delicate strokes. The woman's moan is loud, desperate, and a fucking aphrodisiac, sending my pulse racing.

"Mito," I whisper, my eyes transfixed on the couple in front of me. He's teasing her with the vibrator, dragging it upward across her pelvis, circling the tip around her hardened nipple. Her entire body is quivering, her pussy glistening with a need to come.

"Remember what you asked of me that night?"

I nod, an image of his hand between that woman's legs flashing in my head.

"Tonight," he rasps against my ear, "it's your turn."

"What?" I cut my gaze over my shoulder. "You want me to—"

"Make her come. Yes." Abruptly, his fingers dig into the flesh of my waist, and I can hear the hard tenor of his voice laced with lust and desire. "You are going to take that vibrator and fuck her with it until she comes while I sit in that chair and watch, stroking my own cock."

The idea is dirty, hot, filthy, and erotic as fuck. "And you don't mind me playing with her? Touching her?"

"As long as you don't come without my cock in your cunt, I'm more than okay with it. Just remember our rule. No talking." He lets go of me and retreats to the back, taking a seat on the single chair across from the bed. "Now, go on. Make her scream just like you scream for me, stray."

He nods in the man's direction, and the man drops the vibrator on the bed, stepping away. I look at Alexius, his eyes hooded with lust and raking down my body. I'm not the shy, naive woman he married. I'm confident in my own skin, confident in what I want and what I'll do to get it. Alexius taught me to accept who I am and not feel shame or uncertainty when it comes to my desires and needs. My fantasies. This is who I am, part predator, part prey.

Licking my lips, I pick up the vibrator and switch it on. The buzzing toy sends shivers down my spine, and I trail it up her thigh, watching her writhe. I already know what she needs. She needs it between her legs. She needs it inside her. She needs to be fucked by the pink toy in my hand.

I sit down on the side of the bed, glancing at Alexius. He's watching me intently, pulling out his cock and folding his fingers around his shaft, gently stroking it. The sight of him is enough to push me over the edge. He already had me teetering there earlier, ready to erupt. My body is still high and sensitive. Even the way my thighs rub together threatens to let me erupt.

"Make her come, stray," Alexius demands, his voice low and tone stern.

Her hips buck in search of the toy, but I slip my finger through her slit instead, air rushing my lungs as I feel her hot, swollen flesh beneath my fingertips.

"That's it, baby girl. Play with her pussy," Alexius growls, and I gently ease along the edges of her pussy lips, spreading her arousal, watching it coat my fingers.

"Hmm," she moans, and I continue to stroke her, appreciating the way her hips move, her cunt growing wetter because of the way I'm touching her. My finger prods her entrance, and I glance at her face, her eyes rolled closed, her pert nipples hard and tits gorgeously round.

I push my finger into her hole, and a whimper breezes past my lips. It's warm, soft, and so fucking wet I easily add another finger, slipping in two and working her pussy slowly and gently. Touching her, feeling her, working her cunt is far more arousing than I thought it would be.

"Please," she pleads. "I need to come."

I ease my fingers out of her; she's fucking drenched. I guide the tip of the vibrator through her slit, leaning my head to the side, staring at her swollen lips, drenched and glistening. Is this what I look like every time Alexius insists on staring at my pussy while he finger fucks me? Is this what he sees, a woman desperately searching for pleasure, her body willing to break to find it?

Her sensitive flesh is blush pink, wet, and so fucking enticing. I nudge the tip at her entrance, the vibrations buzzing against her sensitive flesh, and she squirms some more, moaning, pleading for me to put it inside her.

Holy fuck. It's exhilarating to have this kind of power, knowing I can drag this out for as long as I want, watch her for as long as I want. I decide when and how she comes. She has no control here and is completely at my mercy. Her pleasure is mine to give.

Gently, I ease the toy in, little by little. I watch the length of it disappear inside her greedy cunt, and it's one of the most erotic things I've ever seen, witnessing her body suck it in, taking it all.

My nipples are hard, and the fabric of my dress feels like sandpaper against the tight buds. It's like someone lit a match inside me, and I can combust at any second.

My lips part as I pull the vibrator out of her, the length coated in her arousal.

"Please, I need it inside me," she begs, the flush on her cheeks spreading down her neck, kissing the skin across her chest.

Oh, I could do this all fucking night. Tease her and deny her an orgasm until she sobs, her tears the payment I demand in exchange for her body's release.

Pushing the vibrator back in, I press one of the buttons and the vibrations pick up speed. Her back arches off the bed, and I can't stop staring at her beautiful pussy taking every last inch, her clit unhooded and swollen. Pulling it out again, I drag the tip over her center, and I swear she fucking convulses, screaming out.

I'm looking at Alexius still pumping his cock with slow, rhythmic strokes, my own sex throbbing, aching, and it's so damn sensitive. If Alexius had to touch me with a single finger, I won't have time to ask for permission before I come.

"More," the woman pleads, and I start pumping the vibrator in and out of her. Soon I don't even have to move it anymore, her hips slamming down, riding it as she chases her release. The sight of her getting off is wild and driving me insane with a lust consuming me, my control hanging by a goddamn thread.

I sink the toy all the way inside her, and she cries out. "Fuck me," she whimpers. "Please fuck me."

I pick up the pace, thrusting the vibrator harder and faster into her, the vibration on its highest setting, the buzzing sound filling the room.

I'm turned on, and high on power, slipping the toy out of her, leaving her empty and needy, her body writhing and agonizing, desperate for any sort of touch so she can just find relief from the ache that has her every muscle tied and twisted. "Please. Fuck. What are you doing? I can't take it anymore."

Tracing my fingers along her inner thigh, her skin smooth and milky white, I rake my gaze down her naked and tense body. It's torture, I know. Alexius loves to watch me squirm under his touch, and now I know why. The control sends a buzz through your veins that turns every second in pure fucking bliss.

Leaning down, I brush my cheek against hers—her skin fiery hot—and rasp against her ear in a whisper no one else can hear, "Come for me."

Plunging the vibrator back inside her, she throws her

head back on the pillow, arching her neck. "God, yes. I'm coming. I'm coming." Her legs pull taut, her hands jerking at their restraints as she comes with the toy inside her, and the second I pull it out of her, fluid expels from her pussy, soaking the sheets.

"Jesus, look at that, stray. You made her fucking squirt," Alexius growls, his voice strained and tone dark.

I'm on my feet and rush toward him, my dress already bunched up around my thighs as I get on top of him, grabbing his length in my palm, and the second the tip is at my entrance, I sink down, impaling myself on his cock, both of us groaning out loud.

My arms are tight around his neck, grinding myself hard and fast on his lap, the euphoria taking complete control. Reality doesn't exist here. It's just us and the fantasies we share. It's in these moments of ecstasy that I wish we could stay in our secret little world forever. Here, we're untouchable. Here, our desires are in control.

His palms are on my ass, and I'm riding him as hard and as fast as I can, bouncing up and down on his lap, taking his cock inside me over and over again.

"Jesus Christ, woman. You feel so good, stray. So fucking good."

"Alexius," I whimper, the tip of his dick hitting my core, and I'm sure I'm seconds away from burning into ash.

"Come, baby girl. Come on my cock." I arch my back, and my pussy clenches around him, sucking him in deeper as my mind shatters and my core explodes with the kind of intense pleasure I haven't felt in so long. He's hitting all the right spots, moving his hips and meeting my thrusts, sending me hurtling toward an orgasm that ripples through my bones, from my neck down my spine, crashing against my heated clit.

His arms snake up my back, hands clamping on my shoulders, forcing me down as he moves upward, and his low growl vibrates next to my ear as he comes, his cock pulsing hard and jerking, shooting his seed inside me. Sheer rapture singes my veins, my chest rapidly rising and falling as I struggle to catch my breath.

We both collapse against each other, gasping and shaking, the intensity of such profound pleasure still washing through us.

I weave my fingers through his hair, clutching him close, inhaling deep and loving his familiar scent. "We need to do this more often."

"Oh, we will." He looks at me, brushing my hair away from the side of my face, his eyes filled with promise. "You and I are only getting started."

EPILOGUE
ALEXIUS

I saunter into the Dark Sovereign room and feel an intense sense of relief when I see Nicoli sitting in his seat next to mine. After almost losing him the same night I blew Roberto's face off, there's always this soul-soothing relief that floods me whenever I see him. Even if we just pass each other in the hallway, I feel it.

Some days I find myself trapped in that moment when I thought I had lost him. I can still see the image of him closing his eyes, the fear in my bones telling me he's gone. For weeks, while he was recovering, I walked around completely on edge, as if the adrenaline surge I experienced that day didn't want to dissipate. It took me a long time to shake it, and a lot of sleepless nights trying to regain control over my own thoughts. I think almost losing my brother was one of those divine moments that changes you. It gave me renewed appreciation for all my brothers.

Rome left that night and took his uncle Ricardo with

311

him. We haven't heard from him since, and I doubt we will any time soon. He was never meant for our world, and for years I thought him a coward. But now I know he's not. He's just not like us, and something tells me his dead father scarred him far worse than we can imagine.

I take my seat, and Isaia sits across from me. He's officially claimed his seat at the Dark Sovereign table, and there's been a visible change in him. He's no longer this broody, miserable guy haunting the halls of this house with his doom and gloom expression. Leandra was right. All Isaia needed was to be a part of the family legacy, to share something as significant as this with his older brothers. It all worked out, and I finally feel a peace that's settled in my soul. A peace I never knew I yearned for.

"Are we all in agreement?" I glance from Nicoli to Caelian to Isaia, and they all nod. It's a unanimous decision, and I knew it would be. We all feel the same, and I am one hundred percent convinced if my father were here, he would have agreed, too. This is how it was always meant to be, and today we're setting it in stone.

Maximo appears at the door, his black T and jeans more in line with Isaia's choice in attire than the suits Nicoli, Caelian, and I choose to wear. "You wanted to see me?"

"Yeah, come on in."

He saunters in and stills a few feet away, his hands behind his back.

I clear my throat. "The day we ended the civil war with Roberto, I told you that your loyalty has not gone unnoticed."

He nods.

"I also told you that you were like a brother to me. To all of us. And that you and Mirabella are as much a part of this family as the rest of us."

Maximo's eyes flash with a humility that makes one aware that beneath all those layers of hard-ass, there's a heart beating inside there somewhere.

"We've come to a unanimous decision that we want you to officially be one of us."

His brow knits together with confusion. "What do you mean?"

I stand and walk to the one empty chair at the table, placing my hands on the back edge. "We want you to be one of us, Maximo. We're offering you a place at the Dark Sovereign table because God knows you've earned it."

He's stunned into silence, his eyes wide with surprise. "I... um... I can't accept this," he says, his voice strained. "I'm not a Del Rossa."

"Yes, you are. Our brotherhood goes far deeper than blood and in name. It's soul deep, and you are as much a Del Rossa as the rest of us." I turn to face him and place my hands on his shoulders. "There is no one in this entire goddamn world I want around this table with us more than you, Maximo. This is your family, too, and your loyalty has proven invaluable to us. Your children, Mirabella's children, your grandchildren will all be part of this legacy. I swear it. Please, brother," I say, my affection for him laced around every word, "do us the honor of joining the Dark Sovereign."

There's a long, silent pause as Maximo considers my

offer. It's been on my mind for weeks to include him, but I took my time to make the final decision and thought about it long and hard. But in the end, he's our brother, he's family, and there was really no choice to be made.

Maximo licks his lips and smiles subtly. "Thank you, Alexius. I'd be honored."

I pull him in for a hug, slapping my palms on his back. "It's good to have you on board, brother."

Nicoli steps up and hands Maximo a drink. "We wouldn't want any other fucker filling that open chair."

Maximo nods, and both Caelian and Isaia shake his hand. I'm about to make some big fucking welcoming speech when Mira comes rushing in and hugs her brother so tight his cheeks turn red. "Oh, my God, this is the best news!"

Nicoli, Isaia, Caelian, and I stare at her, dumbfounded. "Seriously, Mira?" I say. "You were eavesdropping?"

She leans into her brother, her arm wound around his waist. "It's not eavesdropping when you leave the door open."

"It's like high school all over again," Isaia groans.

"Do you know how many times she blackmailed me?" Caelian asks. "About the same amount of times I had sex in high school."

"So, that's what?" Nicoli feigns a look of thought. "Three times? Maybe four?"

"Fuck you."

We're all laughing when Leandra walks in with Aria

and Alessio in the twin pram. With two giant strides, I'm at her side. "Everything okay?"

"Yeah. I'm just trying to get these two down for a nap, so I decided to go for a walk with them outside. Alessio is down for the count, but as always, Aria is being stubborn." She smiles and glances at everyone in the room. "Seems like I arrived just in time. What's going on?"

"Your husband just made my brother here a member of the Dark Sovereign."

"Oh, wow, that's so great. Congratulations, Maximo," she says, her eyes filled with sincerity. "I can't think of anyone better suited."

"Thank you." Maximo smiles, and it's a rare fucking occurrence. Maximo isn't known for mustering up a lot of fucking smiles. He's more into the brooding, dark-soul look that intimidates the shit out of people who don't know him.

"I think this is a cause for some champagne out on the back porch," Mira says excitedly. "I'll ask the chef to whip up some snacks."

"Someone grab the whiskey bottle," Caelian calls out. "Champagne makes me want to fuck something. And since the only two women in this house are off-limits, I'd rather not walk around with a raging hard-on, because I choose life."

Everyone bursts out laughing as they walk out, leaving Leandra and me behind. Their loud, excited voices and laughter disappear as they make their way down the hall.

"That's a good thing you did," Leandra says, staring at me with so much affection I'm sure my heart's about to explode.

"As you said, no one is better suited."

Aria waves her arm around, and of course, I can't resist picking her up and cuddling her against my chest.

Leandra slants a brow. "She's supposed to nap. You're spoiling her."

"She doesn't look like she's napping to me...are you, little princess?" I place a gentle kiss on her forehead. "And a father spoiling his daughter is the natural way of life." Aria smiles up at me, and it's one of the few things in this world that can disarm me. "Our daughter looks like you. She has your eyes, your nose, your lips."

"And she has your stubbornness."

"Um, excuse me. If anyone is stubborn here, it's you."

"Let's agree to disagree." She pouts her lips, and I lean in, kissing her on the cheek.

I look down at Alessio sleeping in the pram. My son. All my life I wanted nothing more than to live up to my father's expectations, be the son he wanted me to be. Now, everything's changed. Now, all I want is to be the kind of father my son will look up to. Build our family's legacy and watch my son grow into the role he's been born to fill. Heir of the Dark Sovereign.

Aria isn't sleeping, but she's peaceful in my arms. I've already made peace with the fact that my gun will be flaunted freely whenever boys come knocking. This little princess is never leaving her father's side to cling to some boy who will never, ever be enough for her.

And Leandra, she's just...perfect, as she's always been. She's my lifeline. My conscience. She's the rhythm my heart beats in, and without her I'd be lifeless.

That day in my father's office, when he pulled the rug right from under my feet by demanding that I marry, I thought my life would turn out a miserable puddle of bitterness. I never thought a few years down the line, I'd be here with a loving wife and two perfect children. Not once did it cross my mind that my father's request would end up bringing out the best of me.

Being a husband and a father changed me for the better. For a long time, I thought I needed power, wealth, and influence to be a successful and respected man. But I was wrong. So fucking wrong.

I needed her. My wife. My stray. My filthy little slut.

And most importantly, the love of my life.

I catch her lips with mine, slipping my tongue through the crease of her mouth. It's a tender kiss—unrushed and gentle. She tastes of sunshine and perfection, and if I could bottle it, I'd sleep with it on my bedside table.

"Thank you," I murmur.

"For what?"

Clutching Aria tight, I place my other palm on Leandra's cheek. "For unraveling with me."

THE END.

Thank you for reading Alexius and Leandra's story.

NICOLI starts a new chapter in the Dark Sovereign world with a story that's loaded with secrets, lies, **some off-the-charts hot encounters**, and a fifteen-year-old promise that is finally fulfilled.

AVAILABLE NOW!

ROMANCE NOVELIST

Bella J. is an International and Amazon top 100 bestselling author,

Writing DARK ROMANCE with twists, Bella has an affinity for the ruthless men of the MAFIA world and weaves tales that will leave you breathless and questioning your own moral compass.

A firm believer that laughter is the best medicine, Bella infuses her fictional dark worlds with some wit and humor that peppers her novels.

So buckle up for a thrilling ride through the shadows of romance where happily ever afters have a dark side.

Printed in Great Britain
by Amazon

42127728R10189